The Step Dare

RILEY HART
DEVON McCORMACK

PEACH STATE STEPBROS, BOOK 3

OTHER WORKS BY RILEY HART & DEVON MCCORMACK

The Peach State Stepbros
The Step Bet (Book 1)
The Step Don't (Book 2)

The Metropolis Series
Faking It (Book 1)
Working It (Book 2)
Owning It (Book 3)
Finding It (Book 3.5)
Trying It (Book 4)
Hitching It (Book 4.5)

The Fever Falls Series
Fired Up (Book 1)
#Burn (Book 2)
Whiskey Throttle (Book 3)
#Royal (Book 4)
Game On (Book 5)
Boyfriend Goals (Book 6)

Stand-alone Novels
Weight of the World
Up for the Challenge
Beautiful Chaos
No Good Mitchell

PROLOGUE

Brenner

Late spring

fUcKboi4lifE: Show me your dick.

The message came through a little while ago. It's from this guy I've been talking to on a hookup app. We haven't met up yet because every time we try, something goes wrong. All we want is to have sex, yet the universe keeps cock-blocking us.

Me: Can't. I'm at work for another hour. Meet afterward?

fUcKboi4lifE: Will be busy. Maybe next time.

Well, shit. That sucks. Not that I care too much about meeting up with him specifically, but I would, in fact, like to get laid. It happens to be one of my favorite pastimes—that along with video games and drinking too much coffee when I already have more energy than should belong in one body. I'm basically a storm of chaos, but most of the time I feel like I do a good enough job hiding it.

I shove my phone into my pocket just as a customer

comes to the counter. "Hello. What can I get you today?" I ask the woman. She's gorgeous, with thick, black curls and pretty brown skin. She's probably about my age—early twenties—and considering the Feral Fox Café is close to Peach State University, I wonder if she's a student too. I haven't seen her around campus.

"A twenty-ounce iced caramel latte with an extra shot." She gives me a smile that shoots right to my balls. I'm not real religious, but sometimes the Lord taketh away my first hookup opportunity, only to giveth something else. Or wait. Maybe it's the other way around and he gives and takes away. Whatever. It doesn't matter anyway.

"My favorite," I tell her, and I'm not even making that up. It's what I always order. "I wonder what else we have in common," I flirt while ringing her up.

"You're good," she confirms.

"I've been practicing a while."

"The thing is…I only like girls. I give you an A for effort, though."

I laugh because, of course, that's just my luck to-day—a beautiful woman and she happens to be a lesbian. "One of those days."

"Eh, you're cute. I'm sure you'll meet someone else." Her eyes shoot to my name tag. "Brenner. I'm Mila, by the way."

"Nice to meet you." And really, it is. It's not all

about sex with me, and I'm the type of person who's never met a stranger. Scratch that. I like to talk to any and everyone, but I let in very few people, if at all, so I'm not sure the analogy works.

I finish making her coffee and hand it over.

"Maybe I'll see you again sometime, Brenner. I'm transferring to Peach State next year."

There's only a couple of weeks left in this school year, so I say, "I won't be working during the summer, but I'm down if you wanna share your snap." I always head back home to stay with Dad over the summer.

We exchange info, and then Mila heads out. I'm sure she wants to get to know a friend or two on campus, which I totally understand.

Since we're slow, I make myself a caramel latte too. Frank, the owner, doesn't mind if we have free drinks while on shift. I suck it down quickly and start wiping off machines, counters, checking inventory—anything to keep myself busy until it's time to clock out.

Just when my shift is about to end, the door opens, and I look up, expecting to see another customer, but it's my best friend, Taylor. We went to the same high school, and then we both ended up choosing Peach State. We spent our teenage years bonding over video games and…well, honestly, Tay and I don't have a whole lot in common. He's straight, I'm bi. He's quieter than me—most of the time, I can't shut up. But we work.

"Hey, Tay. What's up?" I take off my apron and hang it up.

"You out of here?" Jess, one of the other employees, asks.

"Yep. See you later." I tell her goodbye, then clock out on my phone and meet Taylor on the other side of the counter.

Taylor's in one of his signature tank tops, showing off his lean but naturally defined arms. He runs his fingers through his dirty-blond bangs, a vacant look in his eyes as he reads something on his phone. I'm not even sure he's noticed me or realizes I spoke to him until he says, "I'm bored. I messaged Atlas to see what he's up to, but he's busy with Troy." Atlas is our other good friend. He started dating his stepbrother a while back and spends most of his spare time with him now. "Then I thought I would see what Ash and Colin are up to, but they're doing one of their semi-public sex things. Their bedroom door was open, and they weren't exactly quiet."

Colin and Ash are yet another set of stepbrothers who have recently started dating. Clearly, there's something in the water. The only reason I feel safe from accidentally catching a relationship is the fact that I have zero stepsiblings. Dad hasn't even dated since my mom passed away ten years ago. Losing her was hard on both of us, and I don't think either of us knows how to put our heart out there.

"Nice that I'm your last resort, and do you think there's still time to watch Colin and Ash if we head right over?" I tease Taylor.

He doesn't so much as flinch, just shakes his head, as if he doesn't expect anything different from me.

"What? They have an exhibitionism kink. Really, we're helping them out." I nudge his arm as we head into the humid weather. "And we both know you've been…curious lately."

As more of our friends paired off or realized they're queer, Taylor's occasional questions and comments have made me wonder if he's interested in exploring.

"Just because your brain is made up of sex, video games, and coffee doesn't mean the rest of ours are," he says playfully. Tay and I always rib each other good-naturedly. There's not a sex-negative bone in his body, but what kind of best friends would we be if we didn't tease each other?

"That sounds like a dream brain. Everyone should want it," I reply, then add, "We can go back to your dorm and play some COD. My place is a mess."

"Your place is bigger though."

We'd applied to be roommates in a suite-style dorm, but we'd been rejected. I'd ended up in a suite with another guy and Taylor got stuck in a standard. "Yeah, but do you want to deal with stuff everywhere?"

"Good point. We're going to have to figure out how

to deal with that when we get an apartment together next year."

We're in the dorms now, but we're planning to get a place in Atlas's apartment complex. It'll be nice to be close to a friend and have more freedom than the dorms allow.

"I'm too scatterbrained to stay organized." It's not a flex; it's true.

Taylor must hear something in my voice because he adds, "You do fine, Bren. You do good in school."

But I work hard on having some kind of schedule when it comes to classes or homework. It doesn't come naturally to me, and it's a struggle. Plus, "Yeah, but I like architecture, so it's easier to keep on track. I hate cleaning."

We chuckle as we walk to campus, heading straight for Taylor's room. Our dorms are adjacent—two boring redbrick structures. The campus has gorgeous architecture, but they clearly went with dreary for the dorms.

Taylor is on the third floor. He unlocks the door, and I immediately plop down on the love seat. The space is small, with the love seat, a bed, a desk, and a TV on the wall, with a shelf beneath it.

"Thirsty?"

"Sure." I turn his system on while Taylor grabs us each a Coke from his mini fridge, then sits down beside me. My leg bounces, but when Taylor pushes his knee against mine, it slows.

We put on headsets and load the game. We play online with other people and like to talk shit. I'm basically the world's best *Call of Duty* player, but Taylor is a close second—okay, maybe he *is* a whole lot better than me, but we don't talk about that.

Partway through our second match, one of the guys playing elsewhere says to another, "What? Did you take a break for a circle jerk with your buddies?"

"That's what we're doing over here," I lie. It's really a thing that happens sometimes—not between me and Taylor, obviously, but guys jerking off together on games is for sure a reality.

"And you're still not a match for us," Taylor adds, playing along. "I can make Bren come and still have time to kick all your asses."

His choice of words sends a shock through me. I turn off my mic and say, "*Make* me come? You do realize the point is that everyone jerks themselves off at the same time, not people jerking each other off." I mean, I'm sure that happens sometimes, but that's not what we're talking about here.

Taylor's head twists in my direction, pupils blown wide as if he didn't realize what he said. He recovers quickly, flipping his mic off too and saying, "Whatever. I could get you off and still win the game."

Okay, two things: First, I love that Taylor will say

shit like this to me when he wouldn't with others. And second, these are the types of comments from him that have my head spinning. I've known him a long time, and before the past year he wouldn't have been joking about jacking me off. Him saying this stuff is coming from somewhere.

"Feel free to try," I play along to see what happens.

He swallows noticeably and says, "Shut up," trying to shake it off like I'm joking. Maybe I kinda am, but I'm also not. If Taylor is curious, who better to experiment with than me?

"Fine. Whatever," I say, then turn the mic back on. We continue playing, but I can feel Taylor's gaze on me, feel him watching me in this way he doesn't typically. I must admit my dick is feeling more interested than it probably should when this is simply a joke between two friends. But it's been a while since I've hooked up, and Taylor *is* hot, so it makes sense.

A little while later, I lean back on the couch and say, "I'm done," before tossing the remote to the table. Once the headset is off, I adjust my cock, which still isn't playing nice with me—I guess it's mad I'm not playing with it.

"You ever done that?" Taylor puts his equipment aside too.

"Done what?"

"Jerked off with guys while playing."

I shrug. "Yeah. It's not a big deal. It's what helped me come to terms with being bi. Remember Ricky from high school? We used to get together and game. It went from watching each other jerk off, to jerking each other off, and then I'd always end up blowing him." I've never shared that with him before. It simply never came up. "Hey, you should give it a try. Everyone around you is queer, so why not join in on the fun?"

"Let you…blow me?" he asks, a surprised lilt to his voice.

Not what I meant, but now the idea's playing on repeat in my head. I'm horny. I have been all fucking day, and since my other hookup didn't work out, if Taylor's interested, I am too. It would just be a little fun, and we're too close to let something like this affect our friendship. "It'd be the best head you've ever had," I tell him. I'm fucking excellent at sucking dick.

Taylor shifts, and when I look at his lap, I see the bulge growing there. It's a fight not to lick my lips. I've always thought Taylor is hot, and this conversation and how I've been jonesing to get off with someone…the perfect storm takes flight in my gut. And again, if Taylor does want to explore with a guy, at least he knows I'm a safe place to do that.

"I dunno, man. I've had some pretty good mouths around my cock."

My dick swells, little pings of electricity sparking

inside me. I have no idea what's going on between us right now. This is totally new, but I'm not complaining.

"That's because you've never had mine." I silently challenge him, my gaze traveling up and down his body, taunting him, daring him. We've issued a lot of dares back and forth between us in the time we've known each other, but mostly for stupid shit—*I dare you to streak around the block,* or *I dare you to try and peel that banana with your toes.* Okay, so it's mostly me with the stupid dares, but Taylor always plays along, and I think he gets something out of them too.

"Prove it." Taylor throws down the gauntlet, as I hoped he would.

Still, I don't want to push him, want to give him time to change his mind, so I pretend nonchalance. "Hmm?"

"Suck my dick, Bren."

The spark of courage, of desire and curiosity in his eyes, goes straight to my dick, making my mouth water at the thought of having Taylor's cock between my lips.

"Prepare to be amazed," I say playfully, then kneel on the floor.

I reach for the band of his shorts. Our gazes meet, his pupils blown wide, and I pause, again giving him time to change his mind. It's just sex, but this will be the first time Taylor gets head from a guy, and it happens to be with his best friend, so I'm sure it's a lot to take in.

"Dare you," he gives the consent we both need, and damned if it doesn't make my dick throb even harder. I pull Taylor's shorts off, taking his briefs with them, and watch his cock spring free.

It's a great dick—I'd be lying if I didn't admit that—his balls big and full, shaft flushed and swollen, his head redder than mine. Taylor is long and veiny, just how I like. It's a pretty cock, and just looking at it makes the buzz beneath my skin grow, makes my heart beat faster.

"This what you want?" I ask Taylor, not breaking eye contact as I lean forward, pressing my tongue against the base of his shaft, then letting it take a slow journey up to his leaking tip.

"Fuck," he grits out. "Suck me."

"Bossy, bossy, aren't you? I haven't even done anything yet, and you're already dying for it." I don't give Taylor time to respond, holding his dick at the root and swallowing him down. I have zero gag reflex, which comes in handy when you're claiming the prize as world's best cock sucker.

I pull back, then lower my head again, over and over and over. Each time his dick hits the back of my throat, I swallow around it, open for him so he can fit all the way inside. I smell the musk and sweat on his skin, feel his cum-filled balls against my chin as little gasps and pants and a string of curses fall from Taylor's lips, urging me on. When I feel his thighs trembling, I pull back.

"That all you got?" Taylor asks breathlessly.

"Aw, come on, Tay. Don't pretend you weren't going to shoot your load. Quick trigger." He wasn't going to come yet, but I can't help teasing him.

In response, he threads his fingers through my hair, gripping it tightly and pulling me back down toward his shaft. I tug him so he scoots down farther off the couch, then bury my face in his nuts first, licking and sucking them, breathing in the scent of him.

"Eh…" he pants. "Not…bad so far."

"Yeah, because you're not struggling to even speak right now."

I suck his dick to the back of my throat again, bob my head on his shaft, tasting the salt of his skin that makes me dizzy with lust. I use my hand to play with his balls, wetting his cock, treating it like it's my favorite damn thing as Taylor drops his head back against the couch.

I pull off him, stroke him a few times as he gazes down at me pleasure-drunk, and honestly, looking a bit loopy.

"Fuck. Want your mouth again," he says as my hand slides up and down his hot, hard length.

"When I let you back inside, I want you to show me what you can do, Tay. I love having my face fucked, love the feel of choking on a dick."

"Jesus," he groans, and as soon as my mouth is close

enough, Taylor thrusts up into it, lets loose on me the way I asked, and I can't help wondering if he would have been this comfortable with anyone but me. Taylor knows he doesn't have to hide any part of himself from me, though; that's not how our friendship works.

He makes my eyes water as I let him use my face the way I crave, feel the tight muscles of his thighs beneath my hands. Taylor isn't a big guy—he's skinny and doesn't have a lot of bulging muscles, but I feel them tense and constrict as he moves.

The sound of my sucking is loud, saliva running down my chin and his shaft, wetting his balls that I'm dying to taste again.

I shove my left hand under his shirt, plucking at his nipples while sucking his dick, and trying to ignore my neglected, aching cock.

"That's so good. Shit, Bren. I can't. I'm gonna…"

I rip my mouth off his dick and say, "Give it to me," then take him deep again. His hips flex upward, body trembling as he tries to hold off on his orgasm as long as he can before he tenses, body bowing slightly as he's filling my mouth with his thick, salty load. I keep swallowing around him, sucking his balls dry, wanting more even though I must admit, Taylor has a huge fucking load.

"I love cum," I tell him, licking some that dripped down his shaft and collected on his balls.

His chest rises and lowers with deep breaths. "That's it. Lick it all up."

Who the hell is this Taylor? I never expected to hear orders like that fall from his mouth, but still, I do what he says, wanting every drop of jizz I can find. Then I'm shoving to my feet, tugging my shorts down, kneeling on the couch, spitting in my hand and jerking myself off until the bliss pulls me under and I'm shooting all over Taylor's chest. "Aw, look at you. You look pretty all painted with my load," I tease, then fall to the couch beside him.

Taylor keeps breathing heavily, and I wait for him to come down, ready to hear what he'll say next.

"Sooo?" I ask.

His gaze wanders slightly. "Six out of ten."

"Liar," I reply, and we both laugh. I say a silent thank-you that we're okay, that this wasn't a mistake and nothing will change between us, because I don't know what I would do without my best friend.

1

Taylor

Late summer

BREN RESTS HIS elbows on the pool deck, his abs naturally flexing as he glances up, the sun reflecting off his sunglasses and glistening on the sunscreen across his tanned flesh. The bronze of his skin is the perfect backdrop for the tats on his chest and arms—each with a meaning.

Each with a story of when he finally decided to get it.

The face of the tiger on his right pec, for strength.

The poetic scene on his forearm, displaying his creativity.

And a few others just because he was in the mood, his impulsivity.

We're a few feet from each other, waist-deep in the swimming pool of the cruise ship. Brenner takes a sip of his giant-ass rum punch, then says, "This is the fucking life. I can't believe how long we've known each other, and you've never invited me on one of these cruises before."

Mom and I have always taken our little trips together. A sort of ritual we made since she divorced my dad. Little vacations to get away from it all, but apparently this past year, I made them sound fun enough that my buddy asked if he could tag along on our seven-day Caribbean getaway. I must admit, it's been even more fun than usual since now we can hit up the bars. I'm also not the outgoing, charismatic person Bren is, so I meet a hell of a lot more people whenever he's around, which is always nice. I've never been much of a talker. Maybe that's why I like being around him so much—he can do the talking for the both of us.

"I've been telling you for years that cruises are great. You should have trusted me."

"Yeah, well, I was telling you something else was great, and how long was it before you let me try that on you?"

Kinda glad my cheeks are a little sun-kissed because he might give me hell if he noticed I'm blushing about the fun we shared a few months ago.

Dare you.

I knew what I was doing when I said that. I was already curious, but something about that night made me want it. Not just because I wanted my dick sucked, but because Brenner gets a little edgy when he doesn't get any action, and I figured, two birds, one stone-hard cock.

I imagined it would feel good—a mouth around my dick. I knew he would be amazing at it, which is an understatement. What I wasn't expecting was to not be able to look at Bren's face without taking an extra minute to admire those sexy lips.

"Speaking of which"—he glances at my crotch—"I'm getting a little hungry."

Since that time at the dorms, he's blown me a few other times. And I've let him come on my chest or abs. All in good fun. Bren doesn't make things complicated. He knows me and gets that I just want to vibe it out and see where it leads.

I'm queer…based on my attraction to my best friend. Probably bi. Which wasn't something I was expecting to discover last spring. I've noticed hot guys in my life. Hell, I knew Bren was hot, but not I-want-to-get-sucked-off-by-him hot. Until then, I'd only messed around with girls, and always had fun, so I assumed I was straight. I'm still figuring this shit out, though. Whatever it is, doesn't really matter. Bren's bi, and I've never cared about anything other than he's my friend. He's like that with me too. Doesn't give a shit about whatever this means. Never pushes or asks me to explain what I'm starting to realize about myself. He's a good friend like that.

"So you wanna stop by the burger bar?" I ask, which makes him cringe.

"Burgers?" He wades through the water toward me. "I know you were still identifying as straight at the beginning of last year, but you have to know that's not slang for anything."

I snicker.

"I'd rather hit up the milkshake stand," he says.

I don't even want to say this. Fuck, I try to bite my tongue because I know what he's suggesting, but I can't help pointing out the obvious. "There's no milkshake stand on the boat."

"But we can make one real quick, if you're interested."

"Quick? Is that what I am?"

"You sure as hell were that first time." Even with his sunglasses on, I know the expression he's making—narrowed eyes as he revels in the playful dig. It's one of the things I like about us—we can roast each other, but we know where the lines are.

"Is that why you keep coming back for more?" I ask.

Bren shrugs. "Someone has to do the hard work of training the noobs."

"You're a real saint, aren't you?"

"I am. And I think you're almost ready."

Once again, I know better, but I can't resist seeing where this leads. "Almost ready for what?"

He holds out his giant-ass cup so the straw's just inches from my lips. "Come on. I've tried yours. Don't you wanna try mine?"

A smile tugs at my lips, but his words tug at something else within me.

That familiar burst of curiosity.

It's something I've definitely thought about…especially when he gets his cock out. Wondering what he would taste like…wanting him to feel that same pleasure he's helped me feel.

"I don't know that I'm ready for that," I confess. "But I'd be curious to play around with it some."

"Really?" he asks, and I nod. "Do I need to dare you?" he teases, but his expression is deadly serious before I hear, "Tay!"

I love my mom, but right now, it's the most annoying voice in the world. We both turn to the deck, where Mom and Keith—Brenner's dad—stand together, sipping their drinks.

Initially, the trip was supposed to be Mom, Brenner, our friend Lance, and me. But Lance caught COVID right before, and fortunately, Brenner's dad was able to step in and cover the other half of Brenner's room. Also, kind of worked out. Bren and I went to the same high school, where Mom and Keith worked on the PTA together. They've always gotten along pretty well.

"We're heading over to the singles meet and greet on Deck 9," Mom says. "You guys think you'll be here a while?"

"Probably," I say.

"Have fun," Brenner adds.

I watch as they head through the automatic doors leading back into the ship before Brenner and I turn to each other. I'm still thinking about Brenner's suggestion. His drink isn't far, so I take the straw between my fingers and bob it up and down.

"You think that's how you get the rum punch to come out?" he teases.

"I guess there's only one way to find out."

I can't fucking believe the words coming out of my mouth, but as Brenner grins, it's hard to think about much other than getting back to one of our rooms.

"You're gonna have to get out and grab our towels," he says.

"Huh?"

"I'm hard and wearing a Speedo. You're hard in board shorts. Got it?"

"Got it."

I make a quick adjustment before crawling onto the deck and getting our towels from our nearby lounge chairs. I dry off and wrap mine around my waist before helping Bren discreetly get out of the pool. Then we head back to our lounge chairs. I throw my shirt on as Brenner picks up his phone and checks his texts. He takes a minute, responding to someone—someone who caught his attention.

"Your boyfriend text you?" I ask.

"I don't have a boyfriend, and you know it."

Even though I meant it as a joke, I probably wouldn't be bringing it up if there wasn't this flare of jealousy burning in my chest.

Brenner doesn't have a boyfriend. Over the summer, we became friends with this frat guy Lance whom we have mutual friends with. Brenner and Lance got pretty tight—tight enough that they were gonna share a room on this trip.

"So is it Lance?" I press, surprised by my interest.

"Yeah, it was him. He's feeling a lot better."

"That's cool," I say, reminding me of what a fucking asshole I am.

"So…" he says, slipping his phone into his pull-string bag, "your room is closer."

As his attention returns to me, the tension Lance's texts stirred eases. We head to the cabins, taking our usual walk back to the room. Since the cruise started four days ago, he's only blown me once in a restroom, and for obvious reasons, we had to make it quick, so it'll be nice to have a moment to take our time and fully enjoy the experience.

When we get to the room, Brenner heads in first and practically drags me in behind him. The guy's so fucking fast, it's hard to keep up with how he even got both our towels on the floor. He pushes his abs up against mine so that our cocks are sliding up against each other. His body radiates heat, his warm breath pushing against my lips.

"Jealous of the little Alpha Theta Mu prez, are you?" he asks as he removes his sunglasses and tucks them into the waistband of his Speedo. "You think I invited him along to give him some of these BJs?"

"Whatever. You know I'd be fine with that." I haven't hooked up since that first time we messed around. Knowing him, he must have at some point, which, as I said, is fine by me. "But after we move into the new place, if I find out you're playing *Call of Duty* with him behind my back, I'm gonna lose it."

"You worried I'm gonna be inviting other buddies over while you're out making food deliveries?"

A.k.a. my part-time gig while studying finance at Peach State. Perfect for a guy who doesn't love chatting and wants to work his own hours.

"I wouldn't do that to you," Bren assures me. "You're my number one guy."

It probably shouldn't feel as good as it does, but I like him calling me that. "Well, your number one guy needs to get off right now."

He leans back and reaches into my board shorts, his hand sliding over my stiff cock. A smirk plays across his lips as he offers a few pumps.

I fall back against the wall, moaning. "Fuck."

He pulls his hand away and licks his palm before

gripping my cock again and getting to work.

"Fucking hell, how do you do that so good?"

"Lotta practice," he says, which makes me burst into laughter.

It's not how I laugh when I'm around other people. With Bren it's free, uninhibited, because he's one of the few people I let see me. Really see me.

As my laughter subsides, I notice he's staring at me—don't really get why.

"Take these fucking things off," he says, removing my sunglasses. He slips them into the pocket of my board shorts, continuing to jerk my dick, then leans close, whispering into my ear, "I can feel a future finance bro precoming already," his hot breath hitting my flesh, making it prick with sensation. He offers another big pump that hits my nerves just right, and my body vibrates before he pulls back and watches my expression again.

"What?" I ask.

His brown eyes light up. "Kind of wanna see your *come face*."

"Huh?"

"The face you make when you come."

"I understood. I meant, I don't get why you want to see me…"

His thumb slips just under the head of my dick in a way that really gets me going, makes me forget what the fuck we were even talking about.

While I recover from the sensations sweeping through me, he takes his hand off, and I wonder why the hell he'd do that, before I feel a tug at my waistband, and soon, he's on his knees, sliding my cock into his mouth.

My hand rests on the back of his head as I encourage him along, that warm mouth demonstrating its expertise once again. "Fucking hell, Brenner," I mutter as he gets me worked up quickly. Too quickly. "Brenner, stop," I demand.

It's funny how fast he freezes, my cock pushed to the back of his throat. He raises his hands out to his sides and pulls off. As he pushes to his feet, I notice some precum on his lip, which he licks right up before his gaze meets mine. "Not good?"

I glance at his Speedo. His cock is peeking out of the waistband. I pull the Speedo back to see my buddy's dick twitching.

"Maybe I want to see *your* face when you come," I say.

"Do it, Tay. Jerk me off. Fuck, you're killing me here."

"Dare me?" I tease, and his expression turns serious as he says, "Dare you."

2

Brenner

IT'S NOT EVERY day a guy gets a handjob from his best friend. This whole thing with Taylor happened so suddenly, but also in a way that makes sense. We don't even have to talk a lot about it, don't have to have tons of discussions about what this is because we both know it's just two buddies having fun together. It won't affect our friendship and doesn't have to be a big deal.

But yeah, it's one thing when I'm the one blowing said bestie, and something else altogether when he's got his hand on my cock. It's something I've been hoping for, but, teasing aside, would never push him to do.

"Spit in your hand," I tell him after he gives me a long, slow stroke. He does as I say, licking, then spitting before wrapping it around my shaft again. It's just a simple touch, but it makes my eyes roll back, makes my nerve endings feel on fire in the best possible way.

"Like this?" he asks, with the sort of honesty Taylor reserves for me. I might be obnoxious, that guy everyone thinks is a little too much, but for whatever reason, that's always worked to my benefit in our friendship. Somehow it seems to be exactly what Taylor needs.

"Fuck yes," I reply. He moves his hand faster, squeezes with just the right amount of pressure. "Get on your knees, Tay. Take your shirt off. I want to come on your chest."

"Ask nicely."

I flutter my lashes playfully. "Please let me come on your chest, asshole."

Taylor laughs but gets into position. He works my cock, which is so damn close to his mouth that just thinking about pushing inside it almost makes me bust my nut.

Patience, Bren.

I'm known to jump first and ask questions later, and that's not something I want to risk with Taylor. Us experimenting together is perfect because I know Taylor is comfortable enough with me to let his inhibitions go, but that doesn't mean I need to jump out of the plane without a parachute.

"Use your other hand to play with my balls," I tell him, and he does, stroking with one and fondling my nuts just right with the other. I might be the only guy he's ever hooked up with, but Taylor knows his way around a cock. Pleasure shoots through my groin with each jerk of his hand. He rubs his palm over the head, using my precum to slick me up so the glide is smoother.

"Christ," I grit out. "You look good down there. Who knew my best friend would look so good on his knees?"

"I always look good," he counters, that simple cocky line from him making my dick twitch in his hold.

"Fuck. This is gonna be quick," I tell him, needing to bust a nut more than I need to show off my stamina. I spit in my palm, nudging his hand out of the way so I can wrap it around my shaft. "Tell me I can come on your chest."

"Only if you finish blowing me after."

"Like I'm not fucking dying for it," I reply, jerking my dick in fast, tight strokes. Taylor plays with his, jacking himself, mouth open on a gasp, which is entirely hotter than my best friend has a right to be.

A full-body shudder rocks through me, pleasure popping off like a damn firework inside me as I aim my dick at him, the first spurt of my load landing in the hollow spot between his collarbones. I keep tugging, watching another ribbon of my release on his pec, sliding down over his nipple as I continue painting Taylor with cum.

The second my balls are drained, he's pushing to his feet and I'm wrestling him down to the bed.

"Suck me," he says.

"Don't mind if I do." I take his cock to the back of

my throat, Taylor arching toward me as I work my way up and down his thick erection. He tastes like pool water and salt, his dick hot, veins pulsing against my tongue.

I bob on him, Taylor mumbling a string of curses, his hand tangled in my hair as he says, "Fuck yes. Suck it," in this commanding way I've learned he does during sex, when that's not typically his MO.

When he's buried deep in my throat, I flick my tongue against his balls just before I get a mouthful of cum. I pull back enough to swallow it down, sucking and taking all he has to give me, too busy draining his load to get to watch his expression the way I'd hoped. A moment later he goes limp against the mattress.

"Holy fuck, that was good."

"A whole lot better than a six," I joke, lying down beside him, Speedo still around my thighs.

"We should have started doing this earlier."

"Let's not focus on the past and just be glad we're doing it now."

"We should get up before our parents get back." He sits up, swinging his legs over the side of the mattress.

"You don't want them to see my cum all over you?"

"Small load," he teases.

"Fuck you." I tug off my Speedo, then go to the bathroom and grab a washcloth. I wipe myself off, pull my Speedo back up, then bring a second rag to him. Once we're all cleaned up and dressed, I say, "Another drink on the deck?"

"Perfect."

I PUSH MY hair back as it falls into my eyes. Dad's got the bathroom door open as he shaves before dinner with Taylor and his mom, Nicole. It's so good to see Dad out and enjoying himself. I don't want to make it sound like he's spent the last ten years hiding away, but he sure as shit never did something like randomly going on a cruise with me and my friend's parent.

It was hard on both of us when we lost Mom. One minute she was sick with what we thought was a bad cold, and the next she was in the ICU with lung failure. It had nearly broken him when she died, and me too, but I'd been really worried about Dad for a while. He loved her so damn much, and we didn't know what to do without her. There were weeks when he couldn't even leave the house. Eventually, we started to heal, but we were never the same, and I've always wondered how happy he truly is. He would do anything for me, including hiding how he feels so as not to upset or worry me, but I'm hoping this trip is a sign that he's going to start doing things for himself too.

"How was the singles thing? You meet anyone?"

He turns his back to me, grabbing a towel. "Nope,

didn't meet anyone. What did you and Taylor do?"

I don't think he'd want to know what we did, and I'd rather not share that with him either. "Just hung out." I pull on a different T-shirt. Dad's wearing a fucking polo, so I'll probably be underdressed, but that's my style. "Did you at least talk to any new women? Or men. Sexuality can be a little more fluid these days."

Dad laughs. He's known I'm bisexual since my senior year in high school. I never had to worry about him not accepting my sexuality. We're not that kind of family. It had been the same when Mom was around.

I rub a hand over my chest. Damn, I miss her.

"We should go. We don't want to be late for dinner," Dad says, changing the subject, clearly not ready to talk about moving on. Unless he's done it on the down-low, my dad hasn't gone on even one date since Mom died. I hate the idea of him being alone, especially now that I'm in college.

I run my fingers through my hair. "I'm ready." Now probably isn't the time to talk about it anyway.

We meet Taylor and Nicole outside the restaurant, Nicole welcoming us with a wide smile.

"Aw, did you miss your son's much more charming best friend?" I tease her.

"You wish," Taylor replies.

"I think you're both charming." Nicole hugs me. I met Taylor not long after losing Mom, so I've known

Nicole for a long time too.

"Yeah, but you like me better." I hook my arm through hers. Dad laughs while Taylor fake-coughs the words *suck-up*. "How was your day?" I ask her.

"Taylor…what are we going to do with this guy?" Dad says to my best friend.

"Your guess is as good as mine."

The hostess leads us to our table. When we arrive, Dad and I reach for a chair to pull out for Nicole at the same time. I chuckle and let him do the honors. I've been kissing ass enough, so I reach for another chair and signal for Taylor to sit down—from kissing ass to being a smart-ass. That tracks.

When he cocks a brow at me, I ask, "What? Just being a gentleman."

"Gentleman my ass." Still, Taylor sits down, and I take the chair beside him, our parents sitting across from us, just as a waiter approaches.

"I'll give you a few minutes with the menu, but can I get you all anything to drink?"

Dad orders a bottle of wine.

"That's Mom's favorite," Taylor says.

I've had enough drinks for the day, so I settle on water, Taylor asking for the same. While we've been here together for a few days now, this is the first time we've all gone to dinner together, most of the time Tay and I doing our thing and being assholes by ditching our parents.

"Are you enjoying your first cruise?" Nicole asks me.

"For sure. Dad and I should have done this a long time ago. We might have to crash your vacations every summer," I tease, and Dad clears his throat.

"So what's everyone going to get? I'm starving," he says, just as my stomach growls.

Our parents look at the menu, pointing out items to each other, Taylor leaning close to me. "Didn't eat enough protein earlier?"

"Oh, Tay. Come on. That was only an appetizer."

His pupils flare in this fiery, hungry way that goes straight to my cock. I'd venture a guess it went straight to his too. I wink, knowing Taylor will be thinking about me sucking his cock all through dinner.

My work here is done.

3

Taylor

"YOU DIDN'T HAVE to come with me," Mom says as we settle into the stadium seats in the main theater of the ship. "You probably would have had more fun on the bar crawl with Brenner and Keith."

I would have enjoyed that too, but Mom wanted to hit up a midday acrobatics show, and I didn't want her to go on her own. Not when we only have two days left on our cruise to spend time together.

"Eh, I've been hungover one too many times already the past week, so a show would be nice. Also, wanted to give the guys their space. Brenner needs to see his dad as much as he can over the summer, and same for you and me."

"We've had plenty of quality time together," she says with a chuckle. "But it's nice you still want to spend time with your mom, even when she's going on shopping sprees, which I know drives you wild."

"Guess this is why you work in HR and not finance."

"But happy to have my financial planner with me to keep me on my budget. Reminds me of when you were a kid and helped me come up with and stick to the budget so I could pay the mortgage."

Mom wasn't the best with money, but fortunately, I enjoyed managing the budget, and it led to my interest in a career in finance.

"I appreciate your coming with me," she adds. "I'm sure you'd rather spend time with your friend."

As people continue filing into seats around us, a few rows ahead, a couple walks through with a girl who's maybe two or three. Mom's gaze zeroes in on her, and I feel her pain to my core.

It's happened a few times since we've been on the ship. Hell, it can happen anywhere—when we go to a restaurant, the grocery store, a movie.

When I was ten, we lost my little sister, Aria, who was only a few months old.

Heart defect.

NICU.

She seemed to be getting better…until she didn't.

Even after all these years, we can't shake it.

"Mom," I say, drawing her attention.

Her eyes glisten as she forces a smile. "Isn't it nice that Keith came along for the trip?" she says, clearly trying to avoid the uncomfortable subject.

"Yeah. He's cool. And it's nice seeing what an actual

dad looks like for a change."

It's not an accident that the words spit right out like that after seeing that little girl.

It's more than that, though. I've been around Brenner and his dad plenty, but something about all these days together, seeing what a great relationship they have—how kind Keith is to Brenner and how respectful he is to Mom—it's poked at a sore spot within me, a fire intensifying for reasons I've tried to push out of my mind so I don't spoil everyone's fun.

"I mean…" I try to think of a way to reverse course, to draw attention away from my comment, but when I glance at Mom, the fine lines in her forehead reveal her concern. I wish I could have kept my shit together for just a couple more days.

"Taylor—"

"It's nothing."

"It's not nothing. It's great that Brenner has an amazing father, and I've noticed some moments where you look at them like you wish—"

"We don't have to talk about this," I insist, since I just want to shut it down.

We don't need to get into details about my asshole dad. About how nasty he was to my mom when I was a kid. How it got worse after the greatest tragedy in our lives. How, when Mom finally decided to leave his deadbeat ass, he made our lives hell by dragging us through custody battles. Turning eighteen was the best thing that ever happened to me because I never have to see that sick fuck again.

She starts to say my name again, and I barely move my lips as I spit out, "I'm *fine*."

I know Mom can sense my tension, and she knows perfectly well what we went through, so it's not like I can pretend I'm not bothered. I take a breath to calm myself.

Doesn't work.

"Mom, he took up too much of our lives already. I don't want to give him another second to ruin any more moments. Let's just enjoy the show."

She nods, but I can't just wish away the awkward moment, like I can't wish away the painful memories.

A couple sits close enough that I'm not worried about any other personal shit coming up, but when the show starts, I can't really enjoy myself, my mind tormenting me.

Dad's cruel comments that made Mom feel like shit.

The chaotic aftermath of losing Aria.

Watching Dad become crueler and crueler as Mom steadily became less and less of herself.

Throughout the show, I'm on edge. Mom seems a little off too. Which sucks because we've had such a good time this week.

And is it terrible how much I wish I could have Brenner's lips around my dick, helping me forget all this bullshit?

After the show, when we leave the theater, we find Brenner and Keith standing in the hallway outside, chatting. They're grinning ear to ear, their amazing relationship picking at the tender, reopened wound, but really, it's never healed.

Their gazes shift to us, and Keith's eyes light up, like he's genuinely excited to see us. "How were the acrobats?"

I force a smile. "Great. They had a bunch of different things. Tumbling, contortions, aerial stuff with silks and hoops—whatever the hell those things are called."

As Brenner's forehead creases, I realize I've given myself away by saying so much, when normally I would've just said *great*.

Brenner continues inspecting my expression, like he's trying to read my damn mind.

Not fucking now, Bren.

"Hopefully you can tell us more about it over some Thai food," Keith says. "There's that restaurant we still haven't made it to, and I figured we could have lunch there."

"I'm gonna swing by the burger joint," I say. "Maybe head back to the room and take a nap."

Bren's still eyeing me. If anyone can tell something's up with me, it's him.

"I'll join you," he says.

"No, no. I'm good. You love Thai."

He shrugs. "We have another night."

I grit my teeth, avoiding eye contact because it's like some part of me fears if he looks into my eyes, he'll know exactly what I'm thinking—which is ridiculous because no one ever knows exactly what I'm thinking, not even him.

"Keith and I can just stop by the buffet, then," Mom says.

"Yeah, I'm good with that, Nic. Maybe we can try that Thai place tonight or tomorrow."

It's settled, so we go our separate ways.

As I walk alongside Brenner, I'm kind of wishing we'd all gone to Thai. Although, I really want to get back to the room for a bit, on my own, and get it together.

Bren checks behind us, like he's making sure our parents are out of earshot, before he takes me by the arm and stops me in the hall. "What's up, man?"

Brenner is my best friend. He knows more than anyone else in my life about the shit my dad put us through, but I feel bad bringing it up.

"Nothing," I say.

He angles his head, his brow rising. "You expect me to believe that?"

"I don't want to talk about it."

"That's cool. You know I'd never push you."

I do know that. Sometimes when people run their

mouth as much as Bren does, they can be pretty insensitive, but not him. From the moment we met, the guy picked up on my vulnerabilities right away, and never presses where he knows it will hurt.

"Let's go to the burger place," I say, starting down the hall.

I've never known Brenner to be at a loss for words, and since I'm so used to the guy just going off about one thing or another, like silence might kill him, the fact that he's not saying anything starts to get to me. We head through the automatic doors of the main pool deck when he finally says, "This isn't about anything we've done, is it?"

"What?"

"Like…" He glances around, as if to make sure no one's close enough to hear our conversation. "You aren't regretting messing around, are you? Because we can drop it. It's not a big deal."

When I turn to him, he's smiling, since he knows damn well that's not why I'm upset, and his pretense sets me at ease.

"I mean," he goes on, "I can find some other guy's dick to suck and who'll let me come all over their chest." He shrugs, his smile expanding.

"You do that, Bren. Seems like a waste when I'm gonna have to find someone else to suck my dick and come on my chest, but whatever."

I can't believe I'm chuckling again. I guess I shouldn't be surprised. Cheering me up is Brenner's superpower.

He drapes his arm over my shoulders, pulling me in close. "Look, I don't know what's bugging you, but I sure as fuck know what would fix it, and it's not gonna be a damn cheeseburger."

Once again, I'm reminded how well this guy knows me because if anything can take my mind off this crap from my past, it's an epic blowjob from my best friend.

"Besides," he adds. "I was so greedy for your cum last time, I didn't get to see your come face."

"I feel pretty greedy because I keep seeing yours." I imitate his sex face, the way his eyes narrow and his lips twist up, making it a little more dramatic for comedic effect.

He rolls his head back for a laugh, effortlessly redirecting our path as he whirls back around to head toward the next hall.

On our way back to my room, which is the closest from this part of the ship, he tells me about the bar crawl, and the closer we get to the room, the stiffer I'm becoming…and the more that bullshit that came up is fading to the background.

When we round the corner into the hall where my room is, Brenner pulls me over to the wall and pushes me up against it, stroking my crotch, this mischievous expression on his face. "Feel kind of bad Ash and Colin aren't here. All the places they could mess around and nearly get caught."

And with Brenner rubbing me in the middle of this hall, where someone could walk out and see, I can kind of get why. Maybe more than kind of.

"It's the Piece of Shit," I confess, which is the nickname Brenner and I have for my asshole dad.

His expression softens. "Figured that's what it might be."

"Mom says I've been looking at you guys strangely this week. I'm sorry. It's not about you. Keith is just a reminder of how shitty the Piece of Shit was, you know?"

Brenner's lips twist into his dimple. I'm waiting for him to say something to cheer me up or crack a joke, but he moves close and wraps his arms around me, offering a hug.

Fuck, he gives the best hugs.

I embrace it, appreciating that even though a lot of people wouldn't get it, he does.

As I pull away, he says, "Now I'm gonna have to really work to cheer you up, aren't I?"

I'm laughing again. "I don't think you'll have an issue in that department. Although, no way you're gonna be able to watch my come face."

His brows tug together. "And why is that?"

"Because you can't watch my expression when you're

busy making sure you've swallowed every drop."

He winces. "Gonna have to give it a try this time."

He hooks his arm around me again, and we continue to the room. I scan the key card, and as I push the door open, I hear Keith's voice. "Fuck, Nic." It barely registers before I see Mom's back as she—Holy hell, is she straddling Keith?

"Shit," Bren says as we both bolt from the room, closing the door behind us.

I only wish it were as easy to close the door on the image that will surely be burned into my mind for the rest of my damn life.

4

Brenner

"**B**RAIN BLEACH. I'M pretty sure I need brain bleach," I say, pacing the hallway. My thoughts are spinning fast, the way they do sometimes, my heart running the fifty-yard dash.

My dad and Taylor's mom…

I look up to see Taylor staring at the door in a trance, as if his brain is short-circuiting.

"Dude…*dude*," I say. "Our parents are *banging*." And then *"Fuck, Nic,"* plays in my head, and I'm back to wishing I could remove the last couple of minutes from my brain.

I can hear noise behind the door, which is probably, grossly, our parents getting dressed because they realized we walked in and saw Nicole riding my dad. I gag. I mean, maybe it's a little dramatic, but that's me, and no one ever wants to see their parents screwing someone.

"Are you okay?" I ask when I realize Taylor hasn't said a word, which is unlike him. He must be processing what we just saw.

I don't really care that our parents are…doing whatever it is they're doing. Still, it's weird, and not something I ever want to see again, and… "Holy shit. Have they been sneaking around like us this whole trip?" I walk over to my best friend and put my hands on his shoulders. Is he upset? Or just confused like me? "Tay?"

"I never want to see that again," he finally replies, and I can't help smiling. Taylor is better at making me do that than he realizes.

The door opens behind me. I have my back to it, facing Taylor, and whisper, "Should we make a run for it?"

"Don't even think about it," Dad says, and I'm not sure if it's because he heard me or just knows me that well.

I turn and stand beside Taylor. Dad's salt-and-pepper hair is messy. He's tugged on shorts, and his T-shirt is inside out. I have no idea where Nicole is. "I hope you're using protection. We haven't had the talk yet," falls out of my mouth because I blurt out uncomfortable shit when I'm not sure what to say.

"Jesus, Bren. Come in. Both of you."

"Do we have to talk in there?" I ask, but I'm looking at Taylor, seeing him studying my dad. I know Taylor better than anyone else, but in this moment, I'm having a hard time reading him. I don't think he's pissed. Again,

I figure he's trying to understand what's happening, how long it's been happening, and what it means. But then I think back on what we were just talking about: his dad and how much anger Taylor has over how the Piece of Shit treated them; Nicole telling Taylor she's seen him watching me and Dad. And all I know is that if what Dad and Nicole are doing hurts him in any way, I'll lose my shit.

Nicole comes out of the bathroom, peeking around Dad, gaze landing on her son. "Taylor, I'm so sorry. We didn't want you to find out this way. Either of you."

Hearing his mom seems to snap him out of his trance. "How long?" he asks simply.

"Come in, you guys. We should talk." Dad steps aside.

Waiting for Taylor to react, I'm caught in this place where I want to support my dad because he deserves this, but Taylor is my boy and I want to have his back too. When he steps toward the room, I walk with him. Dad closes the door behind us, Taylor sits on the couch, and I go down beside him, pressing my thigh against his for support.

Dad and Nic sit on the edge of the bed, which thankfully someone took the time to straighten. "We spent time together earlier this year," she starts.

"Before Atlas's party?" Taylor asks, and she nods.

"We've run into each other off and on since you boys

started college but hadn't really spent time together, until…January? February? We both ended up out to lunch alone at the same restaurant and decided to eat together." Nicole's hands shake slightly, and I watch as my father reaches over and places one of his on top of hers. It's so odd to see. My dad has never touched another woman in front of me like that except my mom, and it twists me up a little.

"We didn't plan for anything to happen, but lunch turned into a couple of hours," Dad adds. "I hadn't enjoyed talking to someone like that in a long time. It felt…good. I felt normal for the first time in years."

A sharp pang lands in my chest. I hate that Dad has been so lonely for so many years, that he hasn't felt normal.

"One lunch led to two, and three, then dinners and hikes or movie nights." Nicole watches Taylor as she speaks. "We didn't say anything because at first it was just as friends, but then one day, we realized it was more."

"*Why* didn't you tell us?" Taylor asks.

"I think because we were afraid. I feel terrible having kept this secret from you, Tay, but I was so happy, and I was scared of losing it…and I was scared of hurting you. What happened with your dad, I know how difficult that was on you. This is the first time I've dated since then, and it's your best friend's father. I was scared that if something went wrong with Keith and me, it could hurt you and Brenner."

I can understand that thinking, and really, it's not like I want my dad to have told me he's boning Taylor's mom, but the way they're talking, I don't think this is just two friends having some fun together like me and Taylor.

"We messed up," Dad says. "We didn't do this the right way. I apologize about that, but Nic…she means a lot to me." Dad focuses on me, and I know what he's going to say before the words come out. "I'm in love with her…we're in love with each other."

I let that sink in a moment, and I know Taylor must be doing the same.

"I know this feels like a lot," Nicole says. "I'm sure it seems fast, but we've been serious about each other for months, and now that it's out there, we don't want to keep anything from you."

I look over at Taylor, who nods. "I trust you," he tells his mom. They've been through a lot together, and he believes in her. As awkward as this is, we both just want the truth.

"So you're in love?" I confirm.

Dad looks at me. "We are, and if it's okay with the two of you, we would like to get married."

If it's okay with the two of you… Those words spin through my head like a washing-machine cycle. There's not a doubt in my mind that they love each other. Casually dating isn't Dad's or Nicole's thing. All I want is Dad to be happy, and in some ways, it's really fucking cool that he could find that with Taylor's mom, but still, as much as I want this for him, there's an ache deep in my chest. He's spent my whole life loving Mom, and now he loves someone else. It's a strange thing to get used to. A strange thing to hear.

"Okay," is all I can say as *if it's okay with the two of you* plays on a loop. That's the thing about our parents. There's no doubting their love for us. Dad has been alone for so damn long, but despite the fact that I'm a grown-ass adult, if this was going to hurt me, he wouldn't do it. Nicole hasn't been able to trust anyone after what the Piece of Shit did, yet she trusts my dad, but if this was going to hurt Taylor, she too would do right by him first. "I've always wanted a brother."

I turn to Taylor, who looks at me. I wink, which in some ways is absolutely ridiculous, but I'm hoping it conveys *are you okay* and also *hey look, now we're stepbrothers who hook up too.*

Taylor grins, offering a small shake of his head that's just for me. "I've always wanted a brother too."

"Really?" Nicole's eyes fill with tears, and I swear, I see both their bodies relax, see how much they want this and need us to be okay with it.

"Yeah, Mom. I just want you to be happy."

"Eh, you're all right, I guess," I chime in. "Though I don't see a ring. Am I going to have to give you pointers on how to treat a lady?" Dad and Nicole laugh, and then he pushes to his feet. Nicole does the same, and I nudge Taylor with my arm.

When we stand too, Dad pulls me into a hug. I look over to see Nicole doing the same with Tay. "I'm sorry for not telling you," Dad says softly. "But I'm happy, Bren. I didn't know I could feel this way again."

My eyes tear up, but I try to fight them back. I don't want Dad to feel like I don't want this for him, because I do. I've been telling him for years, and apparently every time I've said it recently, he must have been afraid to tell me about him and Nicole. "I'm glad you have her. Just…I don't know, put a sign on the door next time. I'm literally scarred for life." I swipe at my eyes with the back of my hand as he pulls away.

"We thought you guys were getting burgers. Why did you come back here?"

Well, that's definitely not a conversation for to-day…or like, ever. There's absolutely no reason our parents need to know Taylor and I are hooking up. What we're doing is just for fun, and the last thing I want is to make things even more awkward than they already are. *So, Dad…I know you're marrying Nicole, but I'm blowing her son so he has some experience with what it's like to be with a guy.* No thanks on that convo.

"Stomach was a little upset," I lie. "Thank God we didn't get Thai."

"Can I have a hug too?" Nicole says to me when she and Taylor part.

I shoot a quick glance at Taylor to make sure he's okay. "Yeah, of course."

Just as Nicole's arms wrap around me, I see Dad do the same to Taylor. "I love your mom. I promise I'll be good to her."

Taylor nods, and Nicole thanks me for being supportive. My brain is still spinning, but I know Dad will treat Nicole the way she deserves to be treated. He was so fucking good to Mom. Dad is probably the best person there is at loving someone.

"Do we know when the wedding is?" I ask.

She chuckles. "We're thinking February but wanted to speak to you first."

"You know me. I have no patience. Ooh, maybe Tay and I could be wedding planners."

Nicole's eyes widen like she's not sure how to respond to that, and Dad just laughs. "A beer-pong-themed wedding isn't happening."

"Come on! It would be fun!" I joke, then wrap an arm around Taylor. "My new stepbro and I got this."

"I'll leave the wedding planning up to you," Taylor says.

"You'd miss out on the fun?"

After another round of laughter, things get awkward and quiet for a moment, maybe all of us remembering what was happening when Taylor and I walked in.

"So…I think Tay and I will go now. Let you two kids get back to your…date."

Dad smiles. "Only you, Bren."

"Or if you'd rather, the four of us can spend some time together," Nicole adds. "Or just you and me, Taylor, if you want to talk."

"No. I'm good. I think Bren and I will really go get that burger now."

I don't know if he truly wants food, or if we're gonna find somewhere else to do what we originally planned, or if he just wants to talk. Whatever it is, I have his back. And honestly, I wouldn't mind talking this through with him.

5

Taylor

I DIDN'T THINK I was actually hungry, but now here I am, scarfing down my burger and chasing it with some fries.

After discovering my mom riding Brenner's dad like a mechanical bull, we hit up the burger joint, maybe just because neither of us really knew what the fuck we were supposed to do next. Not really a handbook on how to deal with everything they just dumped on us.

Dates.

Messing around.

And now getting married?

As I swallow my food, Brenner says, "Apparently, catching your mom in bed with your best friend's dad really works up an appetite."

I tap my finger near his untouched tots.

"Or maybe not," he amends.

He's using humor to crack through the tension, but he must know a joke isn't gonna make it any easier to process all this.

"So how you feeling?" he asks for what must be the tenth time.

"How are *you* feeling?"

His gaze wanders. "I thought they were gonna say it started on the trip. Not…"

"That it's been going on since the beginning of the year."

"And they're getting married."

"And we're gonna be stepbrothers."

Our recap is enough to make my anxiety flare up again, though not nearly as bad as right after we walked in on our parents fucking.

As I chase away the image in my head, my thoughts return to our discussion, how open and honest they were. And those things they didn't have to say that we both picked up on.

"It's…a lot," I say, which sounds like an extreme understatement. "I know my mom, and when she was talking about your dad, I could tell she loves him. Looking back, there are moments where she seemed awfully excited to see you guys. Not that you're not great and all, but I was completely oblivious to it."

"Same here. I know my dad as well as you know Nicole, and I'm kinda hating myself for not catching on sooner."

"Right? They're shit at even keeping surprise birthday parties secret."

"Yeah," Brenner says with a slight smile. "Guess that shows how much they didn't want what they were doing to wind up hurting us if things didn't work out."

He's right about that. That's so them, it's almost annoying.

I say, "I feel like sometimes they might put our needs a little too far ahead of their own, and the way they handled this one really blew up in their faces."

"I don't think that's where Dad was going to blow up."

I cringe. "Bren, you're making a joke about… I can't even finish that."

"Only fair since we didn't let them finish." Even he cringes at that one. "I'm never gonna have enough therapy to recover from that."

I take another bite of a fry, chuckling as I swallow. "I can't believe this is really our lives right now."

"Does this mean you're gonna be a bridesmaid?" Brenner asks. "Or the bride's groomsman?"

"I know you're trying to be silly, but please let's not start making plans for the wedding we found out about less than twenty minutes ago."

Brenner raises his hands in surrender. "Sure, but we're definitely too old to be ring bearers or flower girls."

I glare at him.

"That was the last one, I promise."

Although, he's got me grinning, which I'm sure was his real goal.

But there's more to it than that. Something else has to be on Brenner's mind, and I feel like a selfish prick for being so shocked, I didn't even consider how hard this must be for him. "You know, it's weird for me, but considering the Piece of Shit, if it makes Mom happy, then I'm happy. But I can't imagine it's that simple for you."

He's unusually quiet, staring off. "For sure. I love Dad. I want him to be happy, and obviously I love Nicole, but there's a part of me that never wanted to see my dad with anyone else. Like just pretend that his love for Mom was enough for the rest of his life."

I reach over and rest my hand on his shoulder, and his gaze meets mine as he goes on, "That's a selfish thing to say, isn't it? Of course I want more for him. Hell, I've even told him to date—and now I can see why he was so against it—but...I guess I never thought it would happen. Which is ridiculous. He can't be alone forever, and I don't want him to be, but...fuck. I don't even know what I'm saying. It's just weird to think of my dad with someone else."

"I think it just says how much you love your mom. And how painful it was to lose her."

He's quiet again, looks out over the deck, to the ocean.

It's hard watching Bren going through this. To most people, he's the laughy, fun-loving guy, like he's never had to deal with real shit. But I know him better than that. I know that behind the friendly banter and that charming-ass smile is a hell of a lot of pain too.

"How about we head back to your room for a bit?" I say. "Just to chill out. I'll get us a box."

"Yeah, I'm sure I'll want these tots later."

We grab boxes and head back across the ship. As we near the room, I ask, "You think they started boning again after we left?"

"It's probably worse than that. Probably got really emotional and started cuddling and whispering how great they think the other is." He scratches at his skin. "I'm getting hives just thinking about it."

I laugh as he uses his key card to get us into their room, and I'm relieved his dad hasn't returned. Not that I don't think he's great, but Bren and I need some space.

I set my box on the desk and fall back onto Brenner's bed.

"So we're gonna be stepbros, huh?" I say as Bren lies beside me.

"Looks like it."

"I hope you haven't given Troy or Atlas or Ash or Colin any shit about messing around because if you have, they're gonna make hay if they ever find out we've done stuff together."

"Well, I'm not gonna tell them," Brenner assures me. "I mean, you might. I'm surprised you haven't run around telling the whole school about these amazing blowjobs."

"Even knowing it's true, I'd take that shit to the grave because I know it'd make your ego even bigger than it already is."

Bren rolls toward me, repositioning on his elbow so he can gaze down at me, his dark bangs a wave over his forehead, his earrings sparkling in the room light. "Or maybe because you don't want to offer free advertising. Want to keep me all to yourself."

I wince, reaching up and placing my forefinger against his bottom lip. "Maybe just that mouth."

"You tease that this mouth gets me into trouble, but sometimes you like the kind of trouble it gets me into." He bites at my finger, then gently nibbles.

"Maybe I like the trouble it gets *me* into."

Releasing my finger, he grins that life-giving smile, the sort of smile that reminds me that no matter what we're dealing with, everything will be all right.

"Speaking of," he says, his expression more serious, "now that we're gonna be stepbrothers, this stuff we've been doing…"

"Yeah…"

It would definitely make things messy.

Well, messi*er*.

"It's been fun," I say, and quickly realize it's a fucking understatement. "Like, a lot of fun."

"What can I say? I'm a lot of fun."

"Now is not the time to be cocky, Brenner."

"What? I know what I'm good at."

I roll my eyes.

"I love my mom more than anything. She's been through hell…from losing Aria to finally leaving Dad. She's spent years in therapy after that, getting a good friend group, working on herself. Your dad's a good guy, and she deserves to be happy."

"Despite that stuff I have in my fucked-up head—"

"It's not fucked up." The words come out harsher than intended, but not like I'm mad at him for saying them. "Sorry, Bren. I just think anyone who lost their mom like you did would feel that way."

"I got what you meant. It's just gonna take some time. And I do know Dad deserves to be happy too, and I mean, he's maybe just nearly as awesome as Nicole, but someone as amazing as her has to settle a little, right?"

We laugh because he knows damn well he has a great dad.

"I brought that up," I go on, "because even though what we've done has been hot as fuck, now that the dynamic's changed, I don't want anything we're doing to make them self-conscious about their relationship."

Brenner's expression turns serious again. Playful as he

can be, he knows when it's time to have the hard conversations too. And this is definitely one of those times.

"It would mess with Dad's head if he knew what we'd done," Bren says.

"Same with Mom. I can just see her worrying that if something went wrong between us, then there might be tension. Hell, that's clearly why they kept it from us to begin with."

We're quiet, and I wonder if he's thinking what I'm thinking before he says, "So…maybe blowjobs every other Thursday?"

I glare at him. "I think we need to stop altogether."

His eyes bulge. "Like cold turkey? Fuck, Tay. Don't say that."

"We went for years without doing anything. We'll just go back to that, right? Be friends and play video games, hang out at parties."

His jaw tenses as he eyes my crotch, and just the way he's looking at it makes my dick shift.

"I'm being serious," I say.

"It looks serious as hell in your pants right now."

"Bren, our parents want to get married. That's way more important than getting our rocks off with each other, right?" Even the way that last word escapes my lips, it's a genuine question, as though I want him to say, *Fuck no.*

But he nods. "Yeah, we shouldn't do anything to fuck that up."

I take his hand and rest it on my torso. "Hey, we're still Bren and Tay. Just without the horny stuff."

He strokes his fingers against the threads of my tank top, making his way lower to where it's hiked up, exposing my abs.

"If we're not messing around," he says, "you gonna find some other guy to play with your dick? So you can work out whatever you're feeling?"

I shrug. "I haven't thought that far ahead."

Because the thought of him messing around with anyone else is like a pin driving into my chest.

His gaze drifts, and he takes a breath. "You're right. There's no reason to risk what they're doing over some fun."

He trails his fingers through my happy trail, then tenses them and pulls back, as though he knows he's gonna have to learn some self-restraint if we're gonna pull this off.

And his fingers leaving my body is fucking killing me.

"It would be stupid to keep doing," he says.

"The stupidest."

He rests his hand back on my abs, and my body viscerally responds to his touch, excitement coursing through me, relief that wasn't the last time he touched me like that.

Not yet.

"We just go back to being Bren and Tay," he says. "And we'll be best friends forever anyway. And now stepbrothers, and that's enough for me."

"Same here." I'm certain the guy who knows me best can tell that's a lie.

He runs his fingers down to the waistband of my pants, tugging against it. "Guess I won't be seeing your come face after all," he says, frowning.

A knot bunches up in my gut because all I want is to give Bren what he wants. Who am I kidding? What we both want, and being all stressed about this parent shit only makes me want to release with him that much more. Probably like he wanted to do for me when that stuff came up about the Piece of Shit.

He starts to pull his hand off again, and I snatch it.

His gaze locks with mine, his eyes wide like he's shocked by this superspeed I've just discovered.

Something feral controls me, this desire I have, stronger than I've ever felt with him. As though my body knows what he can do for me, and I don't want to miss out on it.

"We shouldn't do anything else," I say, even as my hand guides him down to my pants.

"You're right." As I position his hand under the waistband, he grips on to my cock before stroking.

"We just said not a minute ago how stupid this would be," I remind him.

"We've never been the smartest guys, though." He offers a few more strokes, firming my cock up.

As he massages me just right, a web of nerves shoots sparks right through me. "One more time might not be such a bad idea."

"Just get it out of our systems."

As I unfasten my fly, Bren releases my cock. This time, though, I know it won't be gone for long. He licks his palm. I pull my pants down before he continues stroking me, then crawling down, his lips wrapping around my cock once again.

"Oh fuck, Bren."

I thread my fingers through his hair for what I know has to be the last time as he deep throats me. I wonder if he's doing what I'm doing—trying to etch this moment into my memory so that even when I deprive myself of this, I'll remember what it was like to feel his tongue swirling around the head of my dick just before he creates a little pressure with his grip as his hand comes up to the head.

He keeps on until I say, "I'm getting so fucking close."

His mouth releases me, and he keeps his grip tight, still stroking as he glances up at me, studying my face. A subtle smirk creeps across his face. "Yeah, let me see your come face. Show me, Tay."

As he speeds up, heat swells in my face before I wind up right at the edge, gripping the sheets as the cum bursts free, shooting across my happy trail, but Bren's still watching my expression, his eyes wide, like it turns him on seeing how out of control I am—teeth gritted, the muscles in my face contorting.

"Fucking hell," he mutters as he finishes milking me.

While I recover, he undoes his pants, crawling on his knees close to me. He's hard as a fucking rock, and it doesn't take him long before he shoots, his cum joining mine, pooling into my navel.

And this time, I get to watch his face as he comes, licking my lips as he grunts and a last drop falls onto me.

Once he's drained and gets a few breaths in, he collapses beside me, resting his hand in the cummy mess.

"Yeah…" he says as he catches his breath. "That's…a good…note to end on."

But as good as it felt, the rush he gave me quickly fades at the thought that this will be the last time I ever have this kind of fun with my best friend.

6

Brenner

THE SCHOOL YEAR starts in a couple of days, and Taylor and I are finally moving into our off-campus apartment together. It's cool getting to be Atlas's neighbors. Although his stepbrother-boyfriend, Troy, still officially lives in the Alpha Theta Mu house, they spend a lot of time at Atlas's apartment. I figure they like the space away from everyone else. And the good thing is now I'll be close enough to bug him all the time. It's good for him.

"Pivot!" I shout to Atlas and Colin, who are carrying the couch up to our second-floor apartment.

"You say that again, and I'm gonna drop this couch and make you carry it up," Atlas shouts back, offering his best grumpy scowl, which is mostly just for show.

"Can you not drop it with my boyfriend carrying the bottom end?" Ash asks from beside me.

"I'm basically carrying the whole thing by myself already. I didn't realize he was actually doing something," Colin teases, making Atlas scowl again. See? Good for him.

"Okay, I'll be taking over for Colin before my boyfriend kills him." Troy jogs for the stairs and takes Colin's place.

We continue to wait with our boxes while they make their way up the stairs. I must admit, it's nice to be back in Peachtree Springs. The end of summer has been interesting, to say the least. Now that the cat's out of the bag, our parents aren't holding anything back when it comes to their relationship. Dad even asked me to go ring shopping with him, which I did. We had another good talk, and he made sure I'm okay with everything, and I am…mostly. I mean, I am, but I can't help the fact that it's a huge change too. I'm still trying to find that perfect spot where my happiness for Dad and my sadness about him officially moving on from Mom meet, and all I can do is hope everything is okay when I reach it.

"You good?" Taylor wraps his arm around me as Ash and Colin follow Atlas and Troy up the stairs.

"Fuck yes." Softly, just for him, I add, "Just thinking about the fact that we're a group of stepbrothers who all know what their counterpart's cum tastes like." Or at least, I know what his tastes like.

"That's true, but also not what you were thinking about."

No, it wasn't, but I'm not in the mood to worry

about something I shouldn't even be worried about, so I bend down, pick up my box, and say, "Race you upstairs."

I always have a lot of energy to burn, but I've had even more lately. I still haven't hooked up with anyone since Tay and I stopped messing around. I'm not sure why and definitely need to make a plan for that to change, and soon, but I just haven't done it for some reason. Maybe it's because we were back home, wedding planning and watching our parents shoot heart eyes at each other all day, so I've been too distracted to go looking for sex.

While I understand the reasoning behind Taylor and me stopping getting each other off, I can't pretend I don't miss it. He's got a great cock, and there's something comfortable about hooking up with a person I'm so close with. Has Taylor found another guy to experiment with yet? I don't think he has. I'm pretty sure he would have told me. Plus, it's kinda hard for the two of us to do much the other doesn't know about because we've spent all summer together.

Taylor grabs a box and follows me.

"I don't like the couch in that spot," I tell Atlas and Troy as soon as I get into the apartment.

Atlas flips me off, and Taylor asks, "Are you causing trouble again?"

I mock gasp. "I would never do such a thing! I can't

believe you would blame me. We're supposed to be stepbrothers. That means we have each other's backs."

"Actually, I'm pretty sure it means you'll start boning any day now," Colin jokes, and Taylor becomes real interested in the box he's setting down.

"I still can't believe your parents have been secretly dating. That's wild, huh?" Ash asks.

"Yeah, I can say I don't recommend walking in on your parents going at it. I still have nightmares."

"It seems to me the two of you are doing something wrong. It's supposed to be you getting caught fucking, not them," Ash continues, making the guys laugh. Little do they know that we are—well, *were*—doing exactly that. And just the thought makes me bone up slightly. Fuck, I really need to get laid. I've been jerking it like crazy, and nothing is taking the edge off.

I plop down onto the couch, wishing we hadn't gotten into this conversation. Taylor walks into the kitchen and comes back a moment later with a Cherry Coke for me. Thank fuck. I needed this, and of course, he realized it. I also didn't know he'd bought some. Cherry Coke is my favorite, and Taylor doesn't even drink it. "Thanks, stepbro." I wink at him.

Thankfully, the subject changes, and we shoot the shit for a while before going back downstairs to finish unloading our things. Then they help us set up our beds, and when we're finished, the guys leave, so it's just me and Tay in our new place. It's a small apartment but perfect for us. The front door opens into the living room, a small dining room and kitchen on the other side. There's a sliding glass door in the living room for the balcony, then the hallway that leads to the two small bedrooms, Taylor's with a small bathroom.

"So I'm assuming we hook up the TV first." Taylor grins, reading my mind.

I pump my brows. "Obviously."

It doesn't take us long to get it all plugged in and our video game systems up and running. It doesn't matter that we have a shit ton of things to do—boxes everywhere and probably no food unless Tay got that with my Coke. We have games to play.

We sit close enough on the couch that our legs are touching. That's not new, but every time one of us moves, the feel of his warm skin against mine shoots straight for my balls. I've spent years being close to Taylor, and it never made me feel like I'm crawling out of my skin to bust a nut.

"Fuck," I curse when I get my ass shot in the game. Taylor almost always beats me, but that doesn't mean I don't try everything in my power to win.

"What's up with you? You always suck balls compared to me, but you're particularly bad today." He snickers, and I laugh.

"Asshole." I nudge him with my leg, and as dumb as

it sounds, I swear I feel a zing shoot through me. Taylor's pupils blow wide as if he felt it too, and I must admit, I'm glad it's not just me who's dying from pent-up sexual tension. "Let's play again."

Taylor nods, and we restart the game. His thigh pushes against mine, but he doesn't move it away this time. It's not just a casual brush here and there now, it's a constant press that makes my skin heat and my dick throb.

"You're doing that on purpose," I tell him.

"Doing what?"

"Getting me hard."

Taylor turns his head in my direction, his gaze finding my swelling bulge. "Jesus, Bren. You're dying for it, aren't you?"

"Don't pretend you're not," I grumble, and he adjusts himself behind his shorts too. "But I agree. It's not a good idea."

"Can you remind me why?"

I snicker, nudging him with my elbow. "You're supposed to be the responsible one between the two of us...stepbro."

"Ah, yes. Our parents."

"They totally ruined our lives."

"Right?" He chuckles, and the sexual tension eases off, doesn't feel as suffocating. "I didn't think it would be this hard to stop."

"Same, man. I swear it doesn't matter how much I jerk it, I'm horny all the fucking time."

Taylor groans, and I figure my words went straight to his balls, and yeah, that makes me smile.

"It's the right thing to do for our parents," he reminds me.

I scratch the back of my neck, wishing it wasn't true. "I agree. Not gonna lie, the whole stepbrother thing is hot, but again, I know my dad, and he'll be concerned. I don't want to ruin this for him."

"I don't want to ruin it for Mom either. And like we said, it was just a little fun for us. Not worth fucking stuff up for them so we can drain our dicks."

Maybe if we tell ourselves that enough times…

"I'm sure it'll get easier soon," I reply, just as my phone buzzes with a text.

Mila: Hey, you're back in town today, right? Want to get a coffee or something?

We've been texting off and on all summer. She's cool. I like her and definitely want to hang with her now that I'm back. She's met a few people here this summer, but she's still getting used to a new town.

Me: Bet. In about thirty minutes? Does that work?

"Who's that?" Taylor asks.

"Mila from the coffeehouse. I think we're gonna chill for a bit."

"Oh…right now?"

"Yeah. I'm gonna clean up real quick and go. Is that

cool?"

I have no idea why it wouldn't be cool, but then Taylor nods and I realize my question was silly. "Of course. Why wouldn't it be?" He stands up, so I do the same.

"Do you want to come?" He'd like her, and there's no doubt in my mind she'd like him too. If we hadn't been gone for the summer, I would have already introduced them, but I haven't seen her since we met in the spring. All our communication has been on the phone.

"No, I think I'm gonna see what Lance or the guys from Alpha Theta Mu are doing."

I get a strange twitch in my chest. Lance is hot as fuck, but from what I know, totally straight. Not that it matters. Lance can be queer, and Taylor can bang the whole frat house if he wants…and if he was going to experiment with any of them, it would probably be Marty, who I think is bi-curious.

I shake those thoughts from my head, not even sure why I'm thinking about Taylor having sex with any of them.

"What?" he asks.

"Nothing."

"So…what's the deal with Mila?" he asks as I follow him to his room.

"Nothing." Why the hell is he asking me about Mila?

"You know what I heard? Dax, the guy I told you I banged last year, he's Sigma Alpha now. And there are some wild rumors about him." He's apparently a pretty kinky motherfucker, and…why am I bringing this up to Tay?

"What? Didn't you learn all his kinky secrets when you hooked up?"

I grin. "That too, but I've heard other stuff."

"You're such a gossip," he teases.

I just shrug because it's kinda true.

Dax would totally be the type to experiment with Taylor. The thought makes my skin prickle with annoyance, but I figure that's just because I don't know the guy well enough to trust him with my best friend.

"Are you going to go get cleaned up to hang with Mila?" he asks.

Oh yeah. Shit. I forgot. "For sure. Have fun with the guys."

"Have fun with Mila," he replies, and I walk out of the room, grumpy for a reason I don't understand.

7

Taylor

"**L**ANCE, GET IT! Get it!" Payton shouts as Lance bounces the basketball past another frat, sprinting across the Alpha Theta Mu driveway, and when he reaches the basket, he jumps, hitting the ball against the backboard before it sinks in the net.

I know that's called a thing—a layup?

Whatever the hell it was, my fellow skins are going wild as they high-five, fist-bump, chest-bump.

This really isn't my vibe.

I'm not sporty or fratty, but since Atlas started dating jocky Alpha Theta Mu's Troy Locklear, we've become closer to a lot of the frats, like Lance. They're actually pretty cool, so I don't mind getting out of my comfort zone and hanging with them occasionally. Especially because it sort of forces me to let go and enjoy the moment.

After all, that was the whole point of coming over here—to get my mind off my stepbro. Not really my stepbro, *yet*, but considering our parents are engaged, we basically are.

He's probably gonna fuck her.

It's a thought I've had one too many times since I arrived at Alpha Theta Mu.

Who is this Mila person anyway? I mean, I know what Brenner's told me about her. She's an art major, rock-climbs with friends, plays *Fortnite* and *Witcher 3*, and enjoys jogging.

But now I'm actually gonna meet this girl he's told me so much about, more than he tells me about most of the people he wants to screw.

Not that it should matter. Not like I meet up with every guy or girl Brenner hooks up with. Still, now that I know what that mouth is capable of on a dick, I can't stop thinking about what he must do to a pussy.

Fuck you, Bren. You show me how good it can feel, how hot it can be to have you swallowing me, and now leave me fucking stranded.

We agreed not to mess around—for a damn good reason—but it doesn't change how it feels in my gut.

Whatever. Enjoying Brenner swallowing my load isn't enough to fuck with what our parents have.

"Nice shorts," one of my fellow skins tells me, and I notice the bulge I'm sporting.

This is all Bren's fault. Of course, I can't fucking say that to anyone.

I release a nervous chuckle, and the guy fixates on me, his brow creasing. Is he expecting an explanation?

"Just, uh, been a minute since I've…"

The hell? I was gonna say *jerked off*, but I stop myself because it's not true. It's really just been a minute since Brenner has milked the cum out, and I don't know that I've ever had so many boners just walking around as I do now.

Also Brenner's fault.

For whatever reason, my comment catches the guy's attention, and he won't stop looking at me. But as the game starts again, fortunately, I go back down before anyone else comments.

After our game, I chill with the frats around the front yard. We still got that good Georgia heat, so even the shirts have become skins, and some of the girls from the nearby sorority are heading this way, their timing almost too convenient.

I settle on the front porch steps, grab my vape from my bag, and take a drag.

Before I started hanging around Atlas's frat friends, I wouldn't have felt comfortable around a bunch of bros and jocks, but they're not bad, and I realize that maybe I had some bullshit stereotypes in my head. That frats aren't different from oddballs like Bren and me.

That guy who commented on my erection steps away from a group of guys he's chatting with and comes over.

"Pot?" he asks.

"The legal shit."

"Eh, I'll take what I can get." He settles on the porch beside me. "Unless you don't want to catch my cooties."

"More concerned about viruses, actually," I joke, passing it to him, and he takes a hit.

"They say vaping's bad for you."

"And alcohol's what? Best friend to the liver?"

He laughs, showing off a gorgeous smile. "Guess not."

In the past, I wouldn't have given his pretty smile that much thought. I've noticed attractive guys before Brenner and I started doing stuff, but now, it brings to mind this thing we were exploring. The questions that linger.

"I quit vaping for a bit," I confess, "but started again after a cruise over the summer. And I figured I'd treat myself to it today, you know?"

Because apparently not having Brenner's mouth on my cock means I need something in mine.

Gorgeous Smile Guy winces.

It reminds me of the way Brenner was when we first started talking. I'm not chatty and definitely don't wear my heart on my sleeve, but Brenner picked up on it, asked questions, probed where most people would have accepted my curt, basic responses.

It's weird having this guy look at me like this, as

though he's picking up something from my awkward shifts and twitches.

"You seem like a lot of fun," he finally says.

My expression twists up.

"What?" he asks. "You don't hear that a lot?"

I shake my head.

I know I'm not a big talker, but this is ridiculous, even for me.

"I have a kind of superpower," he goes on. "Like a sixth sense about people."

"Think you've had a little too much of that," I tease, taking my vape from him.

He chuckles. "See, I knew right away you'd be funny."

His gaze shifts to my crotch, then meets mine, and suddenly I'm not looking into his eyes, but at his mouth, like my body's curious if that mouth could do for me what Bren's did. I lick my lips, and he grins.

"What?" I ask.

"That was it." He spins on his ass and lies back, resting his head in my lap.

That's bold.

Who the hell is this guy?

"What are we talking about?" I ask.

"My superpower," he says, flashing those pearly whites.

My cheeks warm because it's clear he gets what's

going on with me in a way only Bren has picked up on.

"Sorry, I didn't mean to make you uncomfortable," he says.

I glance around, wondering if anyone's overheard us, but he didn't really say anything, and no one seems to give a fuck about the guy with his head in my lap.

"I'm not uncomfortable," I tell him, which seems to please him.

As I take another hit, I notice this intense look in his eyes—determined, even—and it picks at something in me. Not just how horny Brenner's made me, but that he's hanging out with this Mila fucker. If he's running around hooking up, then I'm free to do whatever I want too.

And no, this isn't about petty vengeance. But if Gorgeous Smile Guy wants to do some of the things Brenner did with me, maybe that would help me get my mind off my future stepbro, which would be great for both of us. And really, this guy too.

Besides, he's hot. And I've been chatting with him for less than five minutes, and he seems fun too.

"Your name is Taylor, right?"

"Christ, you seem to know a lot about me for a guy whose name I don't even know."

"Well, that's something I can help you with. I'm Dax."

Holy fucking hell.

I burst into a laugh. "No fucking way."

Wild to think Brenner mentioned the guy before I came here. Too much of a coincidence.

His head shifts against my crotch. "What is it?"

"I know who you are."

"We've definitely never met, so I'm assuming my reputation precedes me."

"You know Brenner Dean?"

It takes him a moment, which tells me the guy's likely got a list as long as Bren's. I see the wheels spinning and the aha moment before he says, "Yeah, I know the guy. We hooked up last spring after chatting on Grindr. He leave me a glowing review?"

Now he's got me smiling. "Oh yeah. You made the top five, for sure."

"Top five? That mean I gotta kill four other fuckers?"

"It means I'm not telling you where you fall on the list, but you're up there. He had fun. I thought you went to another school."

"I was at Georgia State, but my brother goes here, and every time I'd come to visit, I'd get so fucking jealous, and the guys are so good to me, so I applied here. Then I was at a party—that Task Frat Challenge thing—and at an after-party, and oh my fuck, I had the best time. It was like the universe was telling me this is where I belong."

"A lot of great sex?"

"It was more than that." His eyes are all lit up, practically sparkling. "Let's just say I had a ton of fun and learned this is where my kind of people are at." I wait for him to explain, but he says, "So you and Brenner are good friends?"

"That's an understatement. He's my best friend."

"Oh, wait, wait," he says, readjusting his position, rolling toward me and resting his elbow next to my hip as he props himself up. "You the guy he had to text to tell you he wasn't coming over to play…?"

"*Remnant*. Yes, that was me. I'm his best friend, and now his roommate too."

"So how's that work? Like when you bring people back to the apartment?"

I tense up. It's something we talked about, but that was before we couldn't stop getting each other off. "It hasn't come up yet, but we figured we'd give each other a heads-up and a chance to beat it."

"Like, you listen to each other and jerk off?"

"Not that kind of beat it!" I say, laughing again, and I can tell by his pleased expression he enjoyed making the pun. "It's all good, though. I found someone else to play *Remnant* with, and he told me all about you guys afterward. Well, not *all* about it."

I'm trying to backtrack, since maybe Bren shouldn't share as much as he does about his sex life, but Dax says, "It's cool. I don't mind, and I'm sure I even said something to that effect to Brenner afterward. We're similar. Chill about stuff like that."

They are. And I'm noticing, with him hovering around my crotch, they're similar in other ways too. Like the way he's keeping me stiff.

If we did anything together, it wouldn't mean much to Dax either. He would be the perfect guy to explore with, now that Bren's off-limits.

But even considering fucking around with this guy feels like a betrayal.

Like I'd be fucking cheating on Brenner?

Fuck, my best friend would give me such hell if he knew that.

I shake it off.

"Why did you just do that?" he asks.

"Huh?"

"You just shook your head."

"Oh, you noticed?"

"You're real interesting, Taylor. And like I said, fun." He leans closer, and I feel the heat he's giving off.

The guy's hot as hell, and there's definitely a vibe here. It's not like Brenner-and-Taylor vibes, but maybe it could become something like that. Well, maybe not that, but something better than the relationship I have with my hand at the moment.

"I hear a bunch of guys are heading down to Crave tonight," Dax says. "You're gonna meet me there."

"You mean, will I meet you there?"

He smirks. "Sorry, didn't mean for it to sound like a question."

As I laugh, that smile returns. "Fuck, never met a stranger, have you?"

"Or a dick I didn't like."

Again, his gaze is right on mine, in a way that makes me a little nervous, but also excited at the possibility that I might get some action tonight. And with a guy Bren's already vetted, so I know it'll be good shit.

Maybe just what I need right now so I don't lose my mind when Brenner tells me he wants to be tongue-deep inside Mila tonight. When I wind up having to leave our apartment, just to be thinking about how loudly he's making her call out…fucking scream his name.

Shouldn't piss me off, but I should be the one calling out his fucking name.

Wait, what? No. What the hell has he done to me?

Still, if he's gonna have fun, why shouldn't I?

"Sure," I say. "I'll be at Crave."

8

Brenner

"**I** GET THE last piece." Mila grabs the small bite of cinnamon roll and pops it into her mouth.

"Not fair," I tease, but really, I don't mind. We've been here for hours, and the conversation hasn't stopped the whole time. She's chatty like me, which might be kinda dangerous for anyone else if they're spending time with the two of us together, but it's fun. Taylor would like her. Maybe not the talkative part as much, but she loves video games, and from what I've learned about her today, she had an asshole dad similar to Tay's, so they have a few things in common. "You wanna come chill at our apartment a bit?" I ask her. I try to pretend it's not just because I'm wondering what Taylor is doing, like if we spend too much time away from each other, I'll die.

"Oh God. She's gorgeous. Look at her," she says, and I turn to see a curvy woman with black hair and freckles walk in.

"Holy fuck."

"I know, right? Anyway. Sorry. I get distracted by pretty girls with nice curves. We can go back to your place."

"Are you sure you don't want to stay and shoot your shot?" The last thing I want is to cock-block…pussy-block? Is that a saying? Whatever. I don't want to stop her from hooking up or meeting someone if that's what she wants.

"Nah. I'm good. I want to see your apartment and meet the bestie you've been talking about all day."

"I haven't been talking about him all day." I stand up and grab our plate to put it away. I'll be back working here next week, and I know how it feels when people don't pick up after themselves.

"Yeah. Okay. Sure you haven't."

As we walk to my truck, I'm trying to figure out what she's talking about. Taylor is my boy…my future stepbrother. Of course he's going to be mentioned some, but she makes it sound like he's basically all I've talked about.

"I don't even know if he'll be home."

"Ooh, why did you have a voice when you said that?"

"I have a voice when I say anything. That's part of talking." I didn't have a *voice*. There would be absolutely no reason for me to have a voice.

Mila laughs. "You know what I mean."

"I do not," I say as we get in the truck. "But I think

he went to chill at the Alpha Theta Mu house."

"Wow. You don't strike me as the frat type."

It's my turn to chuckle. "Oh, I'm not. I wouldn't mind boning frat guys, but that's the extent of it. We've been hanging out with them ever since Atlas got together with Troy."

"They're the stepbrothers, right?"

"One of the couples. There's also Colin and Ash. They're both frat members."

"And stepbrothers who are dating? Wow. Who knew so much kinky shit was going on at Peach State? You know that means you and Taylor are next."

The last time we were together flashes through my head—the feel of his cock against my tongue, the way he grabbed my hair and lost control in the way that Taylor doesn't often let himself do. Jesus, he's hot. Why did our parents decide to get married again? But then I remind myself that Taylor and I are just friends.

"What was that?" Mila asks.

"What was what?"

"You made a weird sound. Like a whimper or a sigh."

I frown. "No I didn't."

"Well, I'm not hearing things. Something was going through your head that had you feeling some kind of something."

I shake off her words, then get back to wondering if Tay will be at the apartment when we get there. I hadn't meant to stay out with Mila so long. Hopefully he's not wondering where I am or working on the apartment on his own because I ditched him.

"Nice complex," Mila says as I park next to our building.

"Yeah, we like it. The price is good, and our friends are close."

The door is locked, but that doesn't mean Taylor isn't there. As soon as I open the door, I feel the emptiness of the space and know he's still out. Jesus, what the hell is he doing at the frat house for so long?

I pull out my phone to text, but then put it away. I don't think it's weird that I want to message him, but I'm suddenly not sure.

"Want a drink?" I ask Mila.

She says yes, and I grab us each a soda before we sit on the couch and play video games. It's fun that she's as into them as Taylor and me, but annoyingly, I can't stop myself from looking at the time every five minutes. I guess it's just that Taylor and I are almost always together. He doesn't really hang out with the guys all that much unless it's the both of us.

"Fuck yes!" Mila says, and I realize she's carrying me and get back into the game.

"To the left. Watch right there," I tell her. "Fuck. I got him! Holy shit. I just saved your ass," I tease, then hear a throat clearing behind me. Shit. Taylor got home, and I didn't even notice. "Oh. Hey. You're back. We were wondering where you were."

Okay, well, I'm sure she wasn't, but I was.

He looks at Mila, then at me. "I was at the frat. Dax was there. Everyone is meeting at Crave tonight, so I came home to get ready to go."

Something's off about his voice, but I can't place what it is. Is it because he's into Dax? I push off the couch. "The Dax-I-fucked Dax?"

His gaze shoots to her again, then back to me. "Is there another Dax?"

"Bet. I'm down. Mila, you wanna go to Crave tonight?" It's the local gay bar we all hang out at.

She stands and walks over to us. "Hi. I'm Mila. I've heard a lot about you. It's nice to finally meet you." She holds out her hand for Taylor.

"Oops. My bad. Tay, this is Mila. Mila, Taylor."

He shakes her hand and offers a quiet, "Nice to meet you."

"Now that we have that out of the way," Mila says, looking at me, "you just invited us to Taylor's night out. Maybe he wants to be alone with this Dax guy."

Um…huh? I frown. "Why would he want to do that?" As soon as I ask, I realize she's right. This very well could be a sex thing, and I could be the biggest idiot on the planet. I turn to Taylor. "Do you want to be alone with Dax?"

"I don't want to be alone with Dax. Do you want to be alone with Mila?"

"No. Why would I want to be alone with Mila?" I scratch my head.

"Oh my God," she says.

"What?" we ask in unison.

"Nothing. You two are just…you know what? Never mind. Sure, I'll go with you guys to Crave."

"Hell yes." I give her a one-armed hug.

"I'll go change." Taylor walks down the hall to his bedroom.

As soon as the door closes, I pump my brows at her. "You missed your curvy girl at the coffeehouse, but we just might get you laid tonight after all."

"Taylor's cute."

"No shit. He's hot. And keep your hands off. You only like women, remember?" Not that it matters if Taylor hooks up with her or anyone else, so really, I have no idea why I said that.

"I remember."

"Why are you smiling?"

"No reason."

Girls are so weird. I'll never understand them. "I'm gonna go change too. Do we need to stop by your place, or are you good?"

"I'm good."

She takes a seat again and gets on her phone while I

head to my room. My clothes are all thrown into bags instead of neatly folded like Taylor's, so hopefully I can find something that's not too wrinkled. Luckily, at least my bed is in the proper place and my nightstand placed beside it. Taylor is more orderly than me, so I don't want to leave things too messy for him.

I find a pair of black jeans and a black button-up shirt, grab some underwear, and head into the bathroom. I do a quick job of cleaning up, get dressed, wet my hair, and run my fingers through it a few times before I go back into the living room. Mila is waiting for me, but Taylor isn't out yet.

"Tay?"

"Coming."

A second later he comes out in a tank and pair of jeans I always thought look really great on his ass. He runs his hand through his lengthy bangs, and they fall right into place, as though they only needed that extra stroke to curl just right. "You look hot." I peek at Mila, but she's busy with her phone, so I grab his shoulders and lower my voice. "Think you're gonna…" I let the words hang, figuring he knows what I'm trying to say.

"I might. What about you?"

"I might." I wink, and he rolls his eyes.

"She's pretty." He motions to Mila, who has changed her hair since the last time we saw each other. Now it's in braids.

"Yeah. She's cool. I like her." I pull back, then give my attention to Mila. "You ready?"

"Actually…something came up. I called a car. I'm gonna head home."

"What? Is something wrong? I can take you back to your place."

Mila waves off my concern. "Everything is fine. Plus, I'm a big girl. I can get home on my own."

"Are you sure?" She nods in response. "We'll wait for your car with you."

The three of us walk out together. Taylor is being even quieter than usual, and I figure it's because he doesn't know Mila or maybe because he's planning on hooking up with someone tonight. As far as I know, that will be the first guy other than me.

Which is fine. No reason he can't, but…is it bad that I'm kinda wishing I could drain another load out of my best friend's balls?

Mila's ride pulls up, and as I open the door for her, she whispers, "You're welcome."

"Huh?"

"Bye, Taylor! Again, nice to meet you," she says, and he tells her the same before she's pulling the door closed on her ride.

Okay…that was weird, but whatever. I put my arm around Tay and pull him close. "You ready to do this? It feels like so fucking long since we've been out."

"Yeah, it's been a minute. Are you mad Mila's not going?"

I feel my forehead wrinkle. "No. I mean, she's cool, and I like hanging with her, but if she doesn't feel like going out, that's fine too."

"Just wanted to be sure you didn't want to hang with her."

"Nah, we can meet up again."

"I called us a rideshare too. Figured it would be easier. They're almost here."

I nod, appreciating that Taylor is always one step ahead, then ramble on about my day while we wait for the car.

Once we're seated in the back, Taylor's phone buzzes.

"Who's that?"

"Dax. He just got there."

"What do you think of him?" We haven't really talked about other specific guys Taylor's attracted to.

"He's...hot."

"No shit, right?" Dax is a great fuck. I nudge Taylor's arm. "But not as hot as us."

"Well, at least me."

"Oh, check you out. You've been awfully cocky lately," I tease, and Taylor laughs.

It doesn't take us long to get to Crave. There's a line outside, everyone wanting to get some partying in before school starts. Dax is waiting for us, and I see the look of surprise on his face when he notices me.

"Where is everyone else?" Taylor asks.

"They're already inside. I was waiting for you," he flirts, and I freeze, unsure if I'm interrupting something, and honestly, not sure how I feel about it. Then he flicks his gaze my direction. "And it looks like you too. I think tonight could be a whole lotta fun."

9

Taylor

WHAT IS GOING on?

When Dax invited me to Crave tonight, it seemed like he was into me, but as soon as he saw Brenner, his eyes lit up like he was thinking about what a good time they'd shared the night they hooked up.

A flare of jealousy pulsed through me at first, but then his gaze returned to me, and it was clear his interest in me hadn't magically disappeared the moment he saw my friend.

We get some drinks in before hitting the dance floor.

Dax is fun. Just lets loose like Bren and finds friends to dance with, and while he's off with a group, showing off his moves, I guide us over to a corner on the dance floor where I can actually hear Brenner talk. It's darker over here, not as many people either, so not nearly as loud, allowing me to get to something that's been on my mind since Brenner and I headed out.

"Are you sure you're not upset that Mila didn't come

with us?" It's something I've struggled with since I saw them playing together at our place. On the one hand, he didn't seem interested the way he usually would. On the other, she's hot as fuck and totally his type.

Brenner eyes me curiously. "It would have been fun if she'd come, but no, I'm not upset. Why would I be?"

I figure I might as well get to the point, so I press, "Did you guys fuck around before I walked in?"

"Huh? No."

"Because I'd be cool if you did."

Yeah, fucking right.

"Are *you* cool? Because that officially sounded not cool at all."

"Oh, officially? Was there a committee that agreed?"

"Someone has attitude. Maybe they're just pissed they can't have my mouth around their dick anymore."

"Well, it definitely would be easier if it could take a load for me."

"Maybe that's not such a bad idea."

"We established it would be a bad idea." And I fucking hate myself for it. As much as I kept telling myself what we were doing wasn't a big deal, it was so much fun. And a perfect way to let off steam.

"Yeah, true," Brenner says. "Which is why you already found my replacement."

I roll my eyes.

"Hey, he's a good lay. I approve. I can find someone

to mess around with while you guys bone."

I'm curious about Dax.

Hot guy.

Fun personality.

Doesn't hide that he's into me.

But that interest isn't as intense as the good thing I know I can get from Brenner.

"You really should," he goes on. "You and I only did some stuff, and there's so much more to explore with a guy."

I glance at his lips again, regretting that we didn't even kiss before calling it quits.

"And," Brenner adds, "I do want you to explore all the things you can do with guys."

On cue, Dax dances over to join us in the corner, slipping between us. "Quiet Taylor and Chatterbox Brenner, what are you doing hiding over here?"

I chuckle at his apt descriptors.

"Talking about me?" He raises a brow.

Brenner starts in with, "As a matter of fact—" before I tell him to shut it.

Dax dances closer to me, rubbing his pelvis against mine. It's hard not to notice how excited he is, which makes my dick shift.

"Mmm…" Dax says. "I like that."

Brenner moves behind him and starts grinding against his ass to the beat.

"Ooh, I do love being in the middle like this," Dax says, staring me down.

"Uh…uh…"

He smiles. "You're so cute when you get all flustered." He rests his hand against my crotch. "Told you I'm good at reading guys, and I have a feeling once we get you started, you won't be flustered at all."

Brenner leans close to Dax's ear, saying, "There's definitely something waiting to be unleashed with this one."

As Dax smirks, I confess, "I'm not experienced with this kind of stuff."

"I find that hard to believe," Dax says before glancing back at Brenner. Their lips are just inches away from each other's—why is that turning me on?

When Dax turns back to me, I say, "I don't have *much* experience."

"Guess we'll have to change that." He moves in close, his lips pushing against mine, his tongue sliding right in. The guy's smooth, too fucking smooth as we lock lips, and the heat he works up, the electric charge he ignites assures me I'm definitely into him.

I feel another set of lips moving in from the side, and we open up, allowing Bren to get in on the action. Even with just part of his mouth against my lips, there's a spark to it—that spark that reminds me of the times we've experimented together.

We said no messing around, but in this moment, the only thing I want is to make up for my mistake of not tasting him sooner, so I give Bren my attention as we lock lips. Dax is a great kisser, but something about having Brenner's mouth on mine, his tongue sliding in, it's not just a charge, it's a surge pulsing right through my nerves.

"That's fucking hot," Dax says, shaking me out of this blissed state, and as our lips part, Brenner and I gaze into each other's eyes. I can tell, know this guy well enough to know he liked it too.

And fuck, am I catching my breath?

Dax sports that gorgeous-ass smile. "I think this could be a lot of fun. Why don't I slip away and let you guys decide how much fun you want to have tonight."

He drifts to another group near us, leaving me stunned.

Maybe because of his kiss…or the threesome kiss…or Bren's kiss. Or that, for the first time in my life, I'm seriously considering a three-way.

And I'm wondering if it's not just an excuse to get back into bed with my future stepbro.

"Well," Brenner says, "he wasn't wrong. That was hot." He studies my expression. "What are you thinking?"

"That you're an asshole for not kissing me before we made our rule." I must admit I'm even more pissed now that I know what a good kisser he is.

He smirks, but I'm not amused.

"Guess we went against our rule," he says.

"I mean, it was a slipup. No big deal, right?" I gulp because I don't believe that for a second.

"Wasn't it, though?" He has this glint in his eyes as he says it, and then his gaze shifts to my lips, as if he's considering going in for another. I'm tempted myself, but he says, "It seems like we have more important things to talk about right now."

"About messing around with a hot guy together?"

He glares at me. "No, the other thing that came up a few seconds ago."

He means our kiss.

I smile. "I'm still curious about this stuff, but despite this one fuckup, we shouldn't mess around."

He squints. "We can make an exception, right? We'd technically be messing around with him."

"Seems like cheating."

"It's our agreement, so if we decide this doesn't count as cheating, then it doesn't."

I consider his logic. "I'm not sure if you're making sense or if I just want to try this so much that I don't care."

I do know, though. I want Dax, and I want Brenner, and I have no doubt that if I'm ever gonna experiment with something like this, these are the guys to do it with.

Brenner's lips twist into that adorable-as-fuck Brenner grin that takes the edge off, but there is one thing that worries me. And I know I have to say it to keep anything from building up in me. "With Mila…I'm kind of weird. Like jealous-weird."

"Jealous? I knew you'd fall for me the moment I showed you how good my blowjobs are."

I roll my eyes. "That's not what I meant. I just…don't even know why I feel it. Maybe because it was so much fun, and I miss it a little."

I didn't think his grin could get much bigger, but it does.

"I'm seriously done stroking your ego now, Bren."

"Clearly not what you want to be stroking."

"Stop."

He gets serious. "Just so you know, I'm not Mila's type."

"Meaning?"

"Women who are only into other women."

"Oh," I say with a chuckle. Guess I hadn't considered she might be a lesbian, which immediately makes me feel better about her. But it doesn't change the fact that I was jealous. "You never mentioned that," I note.

"Didn't I?" He shrugs. "Guess I haven't, but not like I used to go around introducing you as my straight bestie back when…"

"We thought I was straight," I tease.

He snickers. "Exactly. But hey, back to the horny guy who's got a boner for us right now, it's fine if you don't want us to do anything with him. He's cool, though. And I think it'd be hot."

"That's the thing. I think it'd be hot too."

Fuck, am I blushing over that?

Brenner, of course, notices. "If we do this, let's have a safe word."

"A safe word?"

"Like people have for BDSM. If either of us feels uncomfortable, we use the word, and bail immediately. Full stop."

His suggestion sets me at ease.

"How about…pterodactyl?" he asks.

"Pterodactyl?" I can't help laughing.

"I mean, T-Rex will obviously be said when you're talking about my cock, and we're about to go to town on Dax's ass like raptors, so pterodactyl seems like something from the Jurassic period that won't get a mention."

"Why does it have to be a prehistoric flying reptile?"

He shrugs. "Not a subject that will randomly come up while we're messing around."

And now I'm in stitches as Dax returns, glancing between us. "So…where did you guys say you lived?"

I roll my head back for a laugh. Dax really does have superpowers, and one of them is finding a way to get me to let my guard down.

I can feel the excitement pulsing through me when Brenner says, "Not far."

We slip out of the bar and grab an Uber. The whole ride over, Dax makes himself comfortable, draping his arms across our shoulders as he glances between us like he hit the jackpot. When we get to our place, before we're even in the door, Dax pulls both of us close for another kiss like we shared at the bar, the taste a mix of the tequila from Brenner's drink and…gin from Dax's?

We go wild with our lips, teeth, and tongues in this messy cocktail I'm totally into, each kiss assuring me just how into guys I really am. Why haven't I ever experimented before?

Once we manage to break away, we scramble for Brenner's room.

Dax is like some kind of sex robot. He unfastens our flies, and before I know it, he's got both our pants dropped, and he's on his knees, jerking Brenner's cock and sliding mine into his mouth.

"Oh, fuck," I mutter as Brenner's eyes roll back, both of us enjoying Dax's talents.

Brenner shifts to face me, and I can't pull my gaze away from his lips, thinking about how good they felt, from the first taste with Dax and then when I had them all to myself. Bet they'd feel even better while I'm getting blown.

He leans close. "This okay?"

"T-Rex," I whisper, and he grins before his lips mash against mine once again.

I savor it, reveling in his taste and how good it feels to have his tongue sliding into my mouth and Dax taking my dick to the back of his throat, before there's a sucking sound as Dax pulls off my cock.

"Time to switch up," he says. "Don't worry, I'm good at making sure everyone gets attention. And I'm not leaving this room until you're both satisfied customers."

I smile as he wraps his hand around my dick and starts to work his mouth on Bren's dick. Fuck, Dax knows his way around a dick too. Not that I should be surprised.

Even though there are still some nerves around all this, Brenner soothes them with each kiss.

Dax takes his time with Brenner, same as he did with me, before pulling off and saying, "Damn, these are two fat cocks." He pushes to his feet. "Wouldn't mind the two of you running a train on me."

"Like fuck you?" I ask.

"Only if you're comfortable with that," Dax says. "But I do love having cocks in me."

"I remember," Brenner says, which makes me laugh.

Should I even be laughing at that?

But just as soon, there are the nerves again.

"It'd be my first time topping a guy," I admit.

"Mmmmm," Dax says. "That makes it hotter. Maybe, Bren, we could show him what he needs to do."

It's like he plucked a wish right from my head. After all, what better way to learn how to fuck around with a guy than with two experts?

We all strip down, and Brenner heads into the bathroom to get condoms and lube from the duffel bag where he's keeping a bunch of shit until he gets unpacked. I pull back the sheets, and Dax spins me back to him, taking another kiss. Heat flares in my cheeks, adrenaline coursing through me.

He starts to pull away, then offers another gentle peck. "You ever sucked a dick before?"

I shake my head and open my mouth to say no, but nothing comes out.

"If you think he's sucking your dick before mine," Brenner says, "you're out of your damn mind."

My heart races, not just from the thought of sucking a dick, but how much it sounds like Bren wants me to suck his.

Dax chuckles. "I was actually gonna ask him to suck yours so I could watch. Is that what you want, Taylor?"

I turn to Brenner, whose brows are hopped up on his forehead, clearly full of interest.

"You don't have to, Tay."

This is one of the reasons I feel comfortable doing this with him. I know he'll look out for me. Make sure this is a good time. But I'm still uneasy. I'm definitely not gonna do as good a job with it as either of them, not on my first go.

"I could try," I say. "After all, I'd be lying if I said I wasn't curious as hell."

Bren throws the condoms and lube on the bed.

I kneel in front of him, and his cock bobs up and down like just the thought of me putting him in my mouth excites him. I take it in my grip, squeezing to get a feel of it, thinking about how if we hadn't found out about our parents, this would've already happened. A little voice in me tells me we shouldn't be doing this, but one fun night won't change anything. We can still have our rule and have a little fun too.

I give Brenner a little lick, then another, testing him out.

"Yes," Dax mutters, and when I glance over, he's stroking himself. "God, that's hot. Take Bren's cock."

Dax's encouragement eggs me on as I slip it into my mouth, my lips gliding along Bren's flesh. I'm curious to find out what Bren's experienced each time he's taken me like this. I notice the more of him I get in, the more I want. Who knew cock tasted this good? Well, for starters, Bren and Dax.

"He's doing good for a noob, isn't he?" Dax says, and I can tell he means it.

Brenner moans, and as the sound hits my ear, goose

bumps prick the back of my neck. I suddenly feel like I want to show them both just how good I can be—or at least see me giving it my best shot. I really throw myself into it, exploring his cock with my tongue as I stroke back and forth, moving in a frenzy.

"Christ, Tay," Brenner says, his hands resting on either side of my head. "You need to stop going like that, or you're gonna make me shoot in your mouth."

"Oh, hell no," Dax says, and I slide off Bren's cock, gazing up at him.

Brenner smiles down at me, runs his knuckles over my cheek. "Guess I've taught you pretty good."

I laugh. "Maybe you did."

"Okay, boys," Dax says. "Brenner, why don't you get in this bed and show Taylor how I want to be fucked."

As I push to my feet, Brenner turns to me, and I see some apprehension in his expression. "Sure you're up for this?"

I move close and take his mouth again, hooking my arm around his waist and tugging him flush against me as I push my tongue into his mouth. As I pull away, he chuckles.

"Consider it a dare," I tease, winking, feeling so fucking playful, and eager about whatever the fuck is about to happen with these guys.

10

Brenner

I CAN'T BELIEVE this is happening. It's hands down one of the hottest moments of my life, mostly because I'm sharing it with Taylor. Definitely never thought a threesome would be on the list of things we do, but I'm not complaining. Still, the most important thing for me is that he's as into it as I am, that he's having fun and feels comfortable and wants to be doing this.

The look in his blue eyes tells me that despite the nerves, Taylor is exactly where he wants to be, and I know I am. I didn't think we'd get to do this again. It's been weighing on me. Sex has always been great, but sex with Tay is next level, which is wild to think about, considering we haven't even done much. I guess it's because he's my best friend, so of course, it feels different to be exploring these things with him.

I press a quick kiss to his mouth before climbing onto the mattress with Dax, who wasn't lying earlier when he said he loved to take dick. The guy is insatiable in his quest for cock. It's hot as hell to see someone shed their inhibitions so completely.

"Hands and knees. Ass up," I tell him.

"You're lucky I want to be fucked so badly that I'm letting you get away with bossing me around," he replies, quickly scrambling into position.

"Ah, come on. You know you love it." I pick up the bottle of lube and pump some onto my fingers. "Look at his hole, Tay. Isn't it fucking sexy?" I circle Dax's tight rim. "Come on. Get up here with us." I want Taylor to be as involved as possible, even when I'm the one dicking Dax down. I snicker.

"What?" Taylor asks as he kneels on the bed beside me.

"If this was a porno, it could be called *Dicking Dax Down.*"

"That's what you're thinking about?" Taylor asks.

"I'm game." Dax looks at us over his shoulder, pupils wide and clearly dying for it.

"We're getting there," I tell him, then ask Taylor, "What do you think?" as I push a finger into Dax's ass.

"So hot." Taylor gets a little closer, and I breathe out a sigh of relief.

"I'll get him worked open for you, fuck him real good, and then you're gonna take over, okay? You're gonna pound him, and I'm gonna watch…then, after you make Dax nut, we're going to come together."

I have no idea if we can make that happen, but the thought is hot and I'm down to try. The way Taylor's face flushes darker and his cock jerks, it's obvious he loves the idea.

"Fuck yes."

I grin, then give my attention to a hungry Dax. "You gonna give up your hole to both of us?"

"Yes. Fuck yes. Been wanting it all night."

I push a second finger into him, twist them, fuck him with them, opening his ass. His hands fist into the blankets on the unmade bed as he pushes back against me.

"He's our needy little bottom tonight, isn't he, Tay?"

"Yeah. Fuck him, Bren. I'm dying to see you fuck him."

God, this was the perfect idea for one last time with him, but…what would it be like for Taylor to take me? What would it feel like to have him pound me the way we're going to do with Dax?

I shake that thought out of my head. We can't do that. It will only make things weird between us, and that's the last thing I'd ever want.

I grab the condom and rip it open, then roll it down my shaft. Once I've slicked up with lube, I nod toward the mattress beside Dax. "Lie down, Tay. Watch me and jack that pretty cock of yours."

"And wish it was your mouth around me again,"

Taylor admits before doing as I asked.

Dax reaches out with one hand and strokes him. "It is fucking pretty. You tasted it?"

"Yeah. I've worked a few loads out of his balls." I wink at Taylor, then tell Dax, "Now let's get your tight little hole all open for him."

"Hell yes." He pushes his ass back toward me, hungry for more.

I press the head of my cock against him, watch him let me inside, feel the tight grip of his body while Dax takes me in.

"What does it feel like?" Taylor asks, hand stroking his dick, eyes firmly on me and Dax.

"So fucking good. He's so damn tight, so hot around my cock. Jesus, there's nothing like feeling the grip of an ass around your cock. You're gonna love it, Tay. Gonna always want to find a hole to stick your dick."

"Oh fuck." He arches up, fucking into his fist. "Hurry."

"Yes. That. Hurry," Dax adds. "You know how much I loved it last time."

My whole body burns with want. I grab his hips and thrust into him. I take him hard and fast, gaze going back and forth between Dax's ass swallowing my dick and Taylor's stare firmly on me, watching me fuck Dax while working his own cock.

My balls are ready to unleash. I'm not normally this

quick, but something about fucking Dax while Taylor watches goes straight to my head.

"Fuck yes. Harder," Dax says breathlessly.

"I want your mouth," Taylor tells me, voice husky with need. "Give it to me."

My best friend and future stepbro gets up on his knees, leans in close, and takes my mouth while I slam into Dax's body. The position is slightly awkward but still hot, one of my hands at Taylor's nape, holding him close while I tongue-fuck his mouth.

I'm teetering on the edge, my whole body over-whelmed with sensation, the feel of Dax's hole and the taste of Taylor's tongue. It's too damn much, and I have to pull back from the kiss, from Dax before I shoot. I don't know why I want to come so badly with Taylor.

"Fuck, Tay. Take him. It's your turn. Show us what you can do."

We're quick and frenzied while we change places, Dax staying in position with his ass up in one hell of a sexy offering.

Taylor's fingers are shaking slightly as he tries to roll the condom down, so I put my hand on his, meet his gaze, and ask softly, "We good?"

"Yeah. Do it for me," he orders, and those four words are hotter than they should be. Taylor taking control like that sends heat zipping up my spine, partly because it's sexy as hell but also because I know it's something he feels comfortable doing because of me.

I roll the condom down Taylor's thick shaft, then grab the lube and slick him up. "Gotta admit…I'm a little jealous," I say. "He gets to have all this."

A sexy shudder rips through Taylor.

Why did our parents have to go and fall in love?

"I want to give it to you," Taylor admits. "But right now, Dax deserves some more dick."

"Damn right I do," Dax says.

"Help me put it in him," Taylor says with a mischievous expression.

It's something he could easily do himself, but I love the idea of helping him into his first guy. I grab his stiff cock and line him up, watching every inch push in until his dick disappears into Dax's hole.

"He feels good. You opened him up good for me, Bren." Taylor slides in and out, watching himself sink into Dax before pulling out again.

"You like that? Like taking Dax's ass after me?" I run my fingers down his spine, touch him in a way I maybe shouldn't be. We said that this worked, that this was okay because we were just messing around with Dax, so it doesn't have as much to do with us. But Taylor knows the safe word. He's not using it. Everything in his expression, the way he moves, the sounds he makes, the way he looks at me, all of it says he's enjoying this as much as I am.

"Yes. God yes." His fingers are digging into Dax's slim hips as he fucks into him. Taylor concentrates on what he's doing, the muscles in his neck corded. He's good at everything he does, so it's no surprise that fucking is the same. Something about Taylor just makes people feel good no matter what he's doing.

I rip the condom off and toss it to the floor. Just as I take myself in hand, Dax says, "Fuck that. You're not wasting a load when I'm around. I want you both."

I have to admit, that's a good fucking idea.

"Why don't you fuck his mouth while I take his ass," Taylor says.

My dick twitches—something about that is insanely hot. And I love seeing Taylor more confident about sharing what he wants now that he's balls-deep in his first guy.

"Yeah," I say. "But we still have to come together. I won't have it any other way."

"Me neither," he says with a playful smirk, licking his lips like the thought of us coming in Dax at the same time is getting him as worked up as it's getting me.

And now it's like my only mission is to make his dirty fantasy come true.

We move around the bed so I can kneel in front of Dax. He swallows me down immediately, the hot, wet suction of his mouth making me see stars. When my vision clears, I meet Taylor's gaze over him, both of us fucking into Dax together, almost like our movements are synchronized, some kind of dance we've never practiced but know the moves to.

Dax is as good at taking dick as I remember. I move my hands up and down his back, then feel my fingers brush against Taylor's. An electric shock sparks where our skin meets, then shoots up my body.

I do it again…and again, simple touches while we enjoy the man between us.

Dax's movements become more urgent, and I can tell by how he swallows my cock that he's getting close. No one has even touched his dick, but evidently, he doesn't need it, at least not tonight.

"Oh fuck. His ass is tightening," Taylor says, and Dax jerks slightly, no doubt shooting all over the blanket beneath him.

He keeps going, though, keeps taking us, keeps sucking me through his orgasm, and then I'm falling. "Fuck, Taylor. I'm gonna fill him up. Come with me."

Our fingers touch again, and then his jaw tightens, body stiffening as I spill down Dax's throat and he fucks his way through an orgasm of his own.

That was. So hot.

The three of us collapse onto the bed, Taylor getting rid of his condom. Dax is between us, clearly dick-drunk, his eyes glazed and blissed out.

"Holy shit. That was so damn good," he says.

I nod, feeling oddly speechless, which might be a first.

"I should go," Dax says.

"You don't have to," I tell him. The last thing I want is for the guy to feel like he's been used and kicked out.

"I know." He grins, pushes up and kisses me, then does the same to Taylor. I can't help watching their tongues move together, and a moment later, Dax is climbing off the bed. "It's still pretty early. I'm gonna head back to the bar."

I laugh, totally not surprised.

"You only live once." Dax shrugs while picking up his clothes. "I'm gonna clean up in the bathroom, then see myself out. Thanks for a good time."

I watch as he leaves, closing the door behind him.

"Is he going to hook up again?" Taylor asks.

"Yep." I roll to my side, sitting up on my elbow. "Are we good? That was…"

A smile stretches across his face. "Fun."

I chuckle. "Yeah, it was."

"And technically, we didn't really break the rules."

"I'm pretty sure we did."

"They're our rules, Bren, so only we get to decide that."

I nod, then for some reason, I touch his hair, letting the strands fall through my fingers. "But it wasn't very stepbrotherly."

"I'm sure Ash, Colin, Troy, and Atlas would beg to differ."

"So remind me again why we can't keep having fun together?" But really, I know the answer.

"Because our parents are getting married, and if they somehow found out, it might be weird for them. We love them and don't want to do anything to hurt their chances at happiness just because we have fun getting off."

He's right. Of course he's right, and I agree with him, but… "It's only sex. What are the chances they would find out we're hooking up? It's not like we're in love."

"Exactly. It's not like we're in love, but they are. If we had feelings or something like Atlas and Troy or Colin and Ash, that'd be another thing. But my mom's been through too much already with the Piece of Shit, and if Keith makes her happy, I want her spending her time planning the wedding, not being more concerned with my feelings because of what we're doing."

And there he goes making another good point. Why can't we just be dumb twentysomethings and not consider the consequences? But really, just like Taylor wouldn't want to take that chance with Nicole, I don't with Dad. "I know what you mean. I feel the same about my dad. He loves your mom, and I'd say there's no way they could find out, but I'm sure they thought the same thing with what they were doing."

And they both care about us so much, I can imagine them going out of their way to ensure we're cool when they should be focused on what they have with each other.

"Plus, think how strangely they behaved keeping their relationship from us. We just don't know how they would react if they knew what we've been up to."

I sigh, hating his logic. "You were always smarter than me."

"Yeah, you're right, I guess."

"Fuck you, Tay. You're not supposed to agree with me."

"You know I'm kidding. You just like to pretend you're not as great as you are. You forget I know you." He moves to sit on the edge of the bed, which is probably safer since we're not going to do this again. "I should probably go to my room."

"Yeah, you're a bed hog."

He cocks a brow at me. "Do you know you? The way you can hardly stay still while awake? It's the same thing when you're sleeping."

We laugh together before Taylor stands.

"Are you sure we're good? That that's what you wanted and you felt comfortable the whole time?"

"We're always good, Bren. I'm glad you were there with me...my first time with a guy. That made it even better."

"Of course. I make everything better," I say, but really, my chest feels a little funny. I watch as Taylor grabs his things and heads for my bedroom door.

"Night, Bren."

"Night," I reply, and then Taylor slips out of my bedroom. "You could have at least taken the used condoms with you!" I call out and hear him laugh.

11

Taylor

"I DON'T GET it," Lance says. "I thought we had a great night, and then she tells me she's not vibing with me."

After my last class of the day, I bumped into Lance and Ash, and they invited me to hang with them at the student center. I was planning to do some deliveries before heading home, but it's been a minute, and it'd be nice to catch up with the guys. And I'm glad I did, since apparently, Lance isn't having the best day.

"I'm just glad you're dating again," Ash says. "You took so long to recover after Shannon."

"I know, right? I don't know that I would have been able to push myself if it hadn't been for you and the guys, but now I'm starting to think, 'Why even bother?'"

Ash winces. "You get very attached very quickly. I think because you and Shannon fell hard within a couple of dates, you expect it to be like that again, and that's not how it works. Taylor, back me up here."

"I don't think I can have much of an opinion on this. I haven't been on a date since…it would have been last spring."

"Really?" Ash says. "Like you haven't even had some fun?"

"Uh…"

That's not what I was saying, but I should've known that if anyone would probe, it'd be Alpha Theta Mu's resident whiz.

He and Lance perk right up.

"Oh, do tell," Lance says. "Who's the mystery girl?"

I chuckle nervously because I sure as hell can't tell them about what my life looks like right now.

About what Bren and I did at the start of the summer and continued through the cruise.

And then the other week when Bren and I were going at Dax's ass, which was an unbelievably good time. Fun, frisky, and both were great at making me feel comfortable and then like some kind of sex god. And the way Brenner's eyes were fixed on me throughout, like he was so impressed with how I topped… I still get a semi just thinking about that night.

"There's no mystery girl," I say with a laugh.

I'm sure I could trust Lance and Ash with this, but it's not really anyone else's business, and I've enjoyed this being my thing and Brenner's—assuming Brenner's big mouth can keep any of this quiet, that is.

And now I'm thinking about that mouth again…and all the things it can do to me.

"We'll ask nicely once more," Ash says, "and then we'll just ask Brenner and he'll tell us more than you'd ever want us to know."

Ash winks. I know he's just playing. He'd never go behind my back, any more than Brenner would say something I genuinely didn't want anyone to know.

"There's no girl," I insist, since I can be honest about that.

Ash's expression turns suspicious. "So someone's been playing the field. Learning Brenner's tricks?"

He's more on the nose than he could possibly know. "You could say that. I've just been having fun."

Lance's jaw drops. "Seriously? You like, don't even talk and girls are throwing themselves at you? I have to get like seven rejections before one finally says yes."

"Seven?" I ask. "That seems like a lot."

"I get nervous," he says, somewhat defensively.

"Yeah," Ash says, "because you're already thinking about heading down the aisle with them, and they're just wanting what's in your pants."

"I'm not that bad," Lance says. "I just don't get the whole hooking up. I'm more of a relationship guy. I like sex when you know the person. When you get them and they get you, so it's not just the mechanics, like you're trying to simulate something hot from porn. You can make a cheesy-ass joke during or be a little goofy, and it's fun. There's an intimacy to it. And look who I'm telling this to. The guy who gets to fuck around with his stepbrother-boyfriend every night."

"Every night? Seriously?" Ash says, his expression twisting up. "Sometimes we have to wait until the morning."

His lips tug into a mischievous smirk as Lance glares at him. It's clear that Lance is jealous of Ash's setup with his stepbro, and I must admit, I feel a twinge of envy too. It's much worse having to go home to your future stepbro you can't fuck no matter how much you may want to.

"I get it," I tell Lance. "There's something nice about knowing a person who really gets you in a way other people don't. It's definitely not the same as a one-night stand, which can be fun. But it's not the same."

That's how it is with Brenner. We've been friends for so long, I can't imagine anyone getting me more than he does. And it doesn't hurt that he has plenty of experience pleasuring guys.

Yeah...I definitely haven't minded benefiting from that either.

Lance and Ash exchange a look.

"What'd I say?" I ask.

"For a guy who doesn't talk much," Ash says, "I feel like you're saying a lot today."

"Huh?"

"It sounded like you were playing the field," Lance says, "but now it sounds like she's someone you either dated in the past or maybe a friend."

Fuck, I really have said too much.

"It's just—"

"You don't have to share anything," Ash says. "Trust me, I'm the last to judge, since Col and I kept our relationship a secret from even our best friends in the house before we said anything. Just be glad it's not something like you and Brenner hooking up."

They share a glance, enjoying a laugh, which buys me time to gulp and stiffen my expression to not give anything away.

Fortunately, the conversation shifts to school and then my mom's Pinterest boards with her plans for her wedding, and I get their opinions before heading out to do some deliveries.

After I've made my daily goal in tips, I return to the apartment, where I find Mila, Atlas, and Brenner on the sofa, shouting to each other as they battle a boss. The place stresses me out less since we've had a chance to get most everything set up. Although, we're still waiting on some new furniture and artwork to make the place look more like a home and less like Dorms 2.0.

Mila mashes her thumbs on the buttons of her controller as she directs Brenner to, "Strike! The head! The head!"

"Where the hell do you think I'm trying to hit him?" Brenner asks.

Despite feeling a hint of jealousy when Bren first introduced me to Mila, it's worse now that they're buddies. It was one thing if he just wanted to hook up with her, another if he wants her to replace his best friend.

"Hey, man," Brenner says. "That new artwork came earlier if you want to help me put it up in a bit."

"Sure."

"What the fuck?" Atlas says. "We could have helped you with that."

"Focus, Atlas," Mila tells him, and he continues working his controller like he's trying to break it.

"You only have until seven before your date with your stepbro," Brenner tells Atlas. "And we are getting this boss before you leave."

I chill with them, and after they finish with their boss, they switch games so I can slip in. I sit next to Brenner, our legs touching. In the past, this wouldn't have felt like much, but since we started messing around, it feels like everything.

Maybe because even the subtlest touch promises my body that we might mess around again.

That Bren might let me get a go on his ass like I got a ride on Dax's.

That he would bend over and tell me how he likes it.

That he'd teach me to be a good top for him.

And like what Lance suggested earlier, it'd be so much more fun because it's him. Because he gets me and tells me what he likes. And even if I fucked something up or made shit awkward, it'd just be a funny thing that happened. And we'd still have fun. I always have fun with him.

"Taylor, where the fuck are you?" Atlas asks as I make my way through the tunnels.

Fuck. I probably shouldn't be thinking about dicking down my future stepbro's ass, but here we are.

I refocus on the game.

An hour later Atlas and Mila head out, and I help Brenner with the artwork we bought for the living room—a cool black-and-white piece of a dying welded figurine, about the length of the sofa.

"This is definitely gonna be a conversation piece," I tell him.

We place the nails into the wall, then grab either side, stepping on the sofa to put the frame onto the nails. Don't think Brenner even means it, but he keeps sticking that ass out like he's begging me to get in there.

"Stop checking out my ass," he says, and I glare at him.

"This coming from the guy who's been wearing his briefs lower than normal the past few weeks?"

It's been driving me wild. Brenner loves walking around in his underwear, and it seems like it creeps a little lower each time, revealing just enough of his crack to make me about lose what self-control I have around him.

It's not like the guy doesn't know what he's doing. Every time he catches me staring, he'll give me a look and say some shit like, *Oh, sorry. Did I accidentally give you another boner?* As frustrated as it makes me, I'd be lying if I said I didn't fucking love it.

Brenner can tease me all he wants.

"Is it sturdy?" Brenner asks, and when I check my crotch, he laughs. "The frame, you horny fuck."

My cheeks flush with heat. "Right," I say, giving a shake and a tug.

He does the same and the frame pops out, making him stumble. "Fuckin' hell," he says as the frame pivots and he catches it.

"You good?"

Brenner braces himself on the sofa. "Fuck, that was close."

"Is the wall okay?"

He glares at me. "You concerned about my safety or our security deposit?"

"Both, but you're obviously fine."

He checks the spot on the wall. "The nail must've fallen out. Your side still in good?"

I check it. "Yeah. You know once I'm in, I don't have any issues."

He laughs. "Just grab the nail and hand it to me. I'll get it back in."

While he keeps the frame up, I hop down and do a quick search, but I can't find where it fell. The box is on the sofa, so I grab one, and as I do, I notice my face is just inches from that ass.

The one that's taunted me since we moved in together.

The one he's teased me with.

The one that my cock desperately wants to spend some time with.

I lick my lips.

"Well, well," Brenner says, glancing over his shoulder. "What have we here?"

"Shut up."

"Maybe you should put the nail back in for me."

"You were able to do it before, so I think you can do it again."

"Really? I suddenly forgot how I did that. Maybe if you stand up and get right behind me, you can get your hips real close to my ass and put the nail back in the hole."

He wears a wicked smirk, and though this is total bullshit, it's also kind of hot.

I step onto the sofa and slide in behind him. He pulls

down the frame so I can see the hole, and as I push the nail in, he says, "Yeah, just like that. I got my nail in first, and then you stuck yours in. Remind you of anything?"

I chuckle. "Can't imagine what you could be referring to."

He pushes his ass back against me. "Just right in the hole. You know how it goes. You're a pro now. I made you a pro."

Funny as his comment is, it doesn't keep me from getting hard as fuck against that tight ass. He rolls his hips subtly, and I close my eyes, reveling in the sensation, allowing my fantasies to break free. Thinking of how much I just want to yank his pants down and have my way with him—

"The nail in the hole," he reminds me.

"Stop distracting me."

"It's called dickstracting, and it happens to be something I'm good at."

I shake my head and insert the nail. Then Brenner positions the frame, sliding it back into place.

I've finished my part, so I should step off the sofa, but I keep my crotch tight against him, and he keeps moving his hips, massaging my stiff erection.

He glances over his shoulder at me, and I recognize that hungry look in his eyes. He's not his jokey, playful self. There's a determination to it, and I move quickly, taking his lips again. As soon as they meet, there's that burst of charge, like that first kiss we shared, though so much more explosive since we'd deprived ourselves of this for too long. I wrap my arm around him, tugging him closer, thrusting against that ass as I moan into his mouth.

"Fuck, Taylor," he manages to say after a kiss.

I lean back, then thrust against him again. "You've been teasing me with this ass for weeks. It's so fucking mean."

"How do you expect me not to show it off when you look at it the way you do?"

"We said we wouldn't do anything. For our parents. We can't think with our dicks on this."

"You're right," he says before kissing me again.

I push him toward the wall, and he places a hand beside the frame to brace himself as my hands get to work, pulling down his athletic shorts, exposing that gorgeous ass.

"I just want to see it," I say.

Just another lie I tell myself.

"You'd like the view better if you pulled down your pants too."

He's not wrong, so I undo my fly, pull down my pants and underwear. My cock springs free, and I run it between his ass cheeks, telling myself this is totally fine.

Not breaking our rule.

Not at all.

"God, you're so fucking hard," he whispers.

Even the way he's talking right now is getting me going, and I thrust. "You want it inside you? Is that why you've been fucking torturing me?"

"You know I do."

There's a release in my chest, the freedom that comes from being reminded how much he wants me too.

He licks into my mouth, and I say, "We have to stop."

"Yeah, we do," he says before offering another kiss.

I grab hold of his ass, gripping firmly.

"You know you want to, Tay. You also know I'm great, and it's been a while since I've bottomed, so it'd be nice and tight for you."

"Dammit," I say, grunting as I struggle against the intense, feral desire overtaking me.

I have to have him.

He's mine to fuck.

Knock. Knock.

Brenner and I turn at the same time toward the door.

"I'm killing whoever that is," Brenner says before kissing me again.

I refasten my fly, he pulls up his shorts, and we answer the door. It's Atlas, who forgot he'd brought his own controller over. He takes it and leaves.

Brenner and I stand by the door, cooled down a bit,

but still sporting intense erections.

"Glad we stopped before anything happened," I lie.

"Yeah." I know Bren well enough to know he's lying too.

"I should probably do some homework."

"Same."

"Feels like I'm the one doing all the talking now. That's your thing, isn't it?"

"Uh-huh," he says, cracking a smile, and we share a laugh.

In the moment, when we were fixing the frame, our cocks took control, but now that I can think straight again, I remember what a shit idea it would be to selfishly cave.

"Our parents," I remind him.

He nods. "Yeah. That was a dumb slipup."

"I agree."

"Bound to happen. Just…I'm gonna go to my room now."

"That's a good idea."

I kind of wish he hadn't said that. I would have loved to get him back on the sofa and finish what we started.

I head to my room, knowing we did the right thing, but really wishing Atlas hadn't interrupted so I could have dicked down my future stepbro.

12

Brenner

I T'S BEEN A long month…a long five weeks?…since the threesome that will go down in Brenner's Book of Sexual Escapades as one of the hottest experiences of my life. Strangely, quite a few of them involve Taylor, even though our experience together is pretty limited. Something about our hookups is always different, this mixture of fun, sexy, and just…next level? For whatever reason, touching him is better than when I hook up with someone else.

Something I haven't done since the last school year. It was one thing when I was having regular orgasms with him, but I haven't had one with anyone other than myself in too long. Hence why it feels like it's been a long five hundred years…

The incident with the picture nearly did me in. I'm not sure if Taylor knows just what he's doing to me. I swear I haven't walked around with a boner this often since I first started jerking off and discovered the joy of orgasms. I wanted him to fuck me so bad, still do. I'm vers and love both giving and receiving, but the thought of taking Taylor's cock makes my whole body come alive. Like, I swear, it alters my brain chemistry, turning everything up a notch, and for someone like me, who's typically already running on a higher frequency, it's a lot. I'm more than a little obsessed with the idea, so I have to constantly remind myself why we can't.

I should also be focusing on the lecture my professor is giving in my Regional Infrastructures class rather than thinking about Taylor's dick.

I force myself to pay attention to Prof. Rector, and eventually lose myself in what he's saying. I really do love this, both the theoretical and the practical aspects. I always have. My dad owns a construction company, one that does a lot of large contracts and big designs. While he's always been the builder, I've always been more interested in design, which is why I'm majoring in architecture. When I was a kid, Mom used to buy me every possible kind of Lego, robotics kits, and these little gear things where I could build just about anything. I was always creating something, then taking it apart to build something new. When I got older, I would draw out my plans and then construct them—houses, skyscrapers, whatever I could think of. It's always been a natural thing that keeps my brain engaged.

After class, my last of the day, I'm halfway through

the quad when my phone rings. *Dad* flashes across the screen, the photo of me, him, and Mom when I was a kid making me smile. It's one of my favorite photos of us. We're at the beach, and we look over the moon... Dad looks so happy, and I remind myself that Nicole makes him feel like that again.

"Hey, old man," I tease.

"You're only as young as you feel, kiddo."

I grin at the *kiddo*. "So that makes you eighty?"

"Hey now. Maybe a year ago, but not anymore. I'm living my life, remember? We went on a cruise, and Nic and I are already planning our European honeymoon."

Emotions fucking suck. It's so hard to feel a sting of pain while simultaneously being happy as hell for someone. I don't get how it's often so easy to feel more than one emotion. "Europe, huh?" He's always wanted to go. I tried to talk him into taking a trip when I left for college, but he never did.

"Yeah. She's never been either. It'll be an adventure. That's not why I called, though. I'm in town. I had a single-day conference. I expected it to go longer, but it's done, so I thought we could meet up for an early dinner before I head home. Do you have time?"

That's how my dad is. He's the type who wants to spend time with me every moment he can. I really did get lucky in the father department, unlike Tay. My dad is the kind of person who would always put me first, who has always put me first. That's why it's so important to me to put him first now.

"Eh, I can squeeze you into my busy schedule," I tease. "But only if we go to that Korean BBQ place I like."

"You say that like there's anywhere else I would take you to eat."

We both chuckle, say our goodbyes, and I hop into my truck and drive over to meet him at the restaurant.

Me: Hey…I'm having dinner with my dad…our dad? Too soon? Anyway, he's in town for the evening. Want me to bring you food?

Tay: Good stepbros always bring their brothers dinner.

Me: Do good stepbros also dick each other down? Because if so, I definitely want to be the best stepbrother there is.

Tay: Now I'm getting a semi at work.

Me: Good. I like you that way.

I add a winky-face emoji, then stuff my phone into my pocket. If I don't, I'll spend most of my dinner with my dad sexting with his fiancée's son.

Dad pulls up beside me as soon as I get out of my truck. It might sound cheesy, but it really feels like he has an extra pep in his step. If I'm honest, I'll admit it's something I noticed even before we walked in on him and Nicole. Dad had seemed different, but I just didn't stop to wonder what that meant.

"What?" he asks as we walk toward the building.

"You're looking at me funny."

"You just seem happy, is all."

He gives me an almost sad smile then, one that says he's happy but worries he should feel guilty for that.

"She would want you to move on," I tell him. "She'd probably kick your ass that you didn't do it sooner."

He chuckles, and we lean against the wall before going inside. "She definitely would. That's how we know ghosts aren't real. She would have haunted my ass until I started to live my life more."

The cool thing is that we're not exaggerating. That's the kind of woman she was. She would have hated the idea of Dad being alone all these years. "I miss her," I admit.

"I know. Me too."

I turn to look at him. His hair is dark like mine, except for that little bit of salt mixed into the strands. He has a few wrinkles around his eyes—which seem less deep now that he's with Nicole. A question sits on the tip of my tongue, but I'm not sure if I should ask it, if bringing it up makes me an asshole.

"What is it, Bren?"

"Even now that you're in love with Nicole? You still miss her?" I feel like a kid. It's so fucking dumb to act this way, but sometimes my emotions are so big, I can't keep them locked away like I normally do.

"Of course. That won't change, no matter how much

I love Nicole. And you know what's really cool? Nicole knows that. She understands it. She asks me about Mom. We talk about her—her and you. I hope you know she would never try to take Mom's place."

"It's stupid of me to ask that." I swipe at a stray tear. "I'm an adult. I shouldn't worry about someone trying to take Mom's place."

"You're allowed to feel what you feel. It's valid. Your mom will always hold a special place in my heart. Her memory and the love I had for her won't get erased by what I feel for Nic."

Sometimes you need to hear something you already know, and this is one of those moments for me. Hearing him say the words helps ease the weight I keep pretending I'm not carrying. "You're right. I know that. I'm sorry. I don't want you to think I'm not happy for you or that I don't love Nicole." I think about everything she's been through with her ex, how much she loves Tay, and how good she is to her son…and my dad. "I'm glad it's her."

"I love you, kiddo." He wraps an arm around me, pulling me close. "I'm glad it's her too. And look at what this means for you and Taylor. He's been your best friend for a long time, and now he's going to be your brother. There's always been a special bond between you two, and now you get to see how that transforms into something new."

If only he knew how deep the bond is between us and all the ways it's transformed into something new the past few months. "Stepbrother…yeah. That'll be fun." If a constant case of blue balls is fun.

"It's going to be great. I know it. We'll take more trips together, like the cruise. We're going to be one big happy family." Which is what Dad has always wanted.

Only I can't stop jonesing for my stepbro's cock, and I'm scared to death it will mess up everything.

"I GOT YOU fried rice, spicy chicken, with zucchini, broccoli, and onions," I tell Taylor when I get home. He's sitting on the couch, shirtless, with his laptop and schoolbooks around him.

He whips his head in my direction, and I have to bite my cheeks so I don't smile. "Onions?"

"Extra," I lie. I'm not an idiot. Well, at least not when it comes to Tay, who has a deep aversion to onions.

"Shut up. You asshole." He gives me the finger, and I laugh.

"I can't believe you almost fell for that. Do you even know me at all?" I place the container on the coffee table in front of him.

"I thought for a minute *you* didn't know *me*."

"But I do." I sit down beside him. "What do you want to do?"

His brows draw together. "Um…eat and do my homework. You just got home, and you're already trying to figure out something to do?"

"Ugh. Fine. You're so boring." It technically is homework time for me too, but luckily, I don't have anything that needs to be done today.

He cocks his head slightly, his eyes doing that thing they do when he's trying to read between the lines. Fucking best friends. They can be so annoying.

"Are you okay? Did something happen with your dad?"

I shake my head. "No. I mean, nothing happened with him, and I'm okay. We had a good talk. I feel even better than before about things, but you know how talking about Mom gets me."

"All up in that head of yours." I'm surprised when he reaches out and pushes the hair off my forehead. "It's busy in there."

"And I'm horny."

"You're changing the subject."

"Sex is a good distraction."

Taylor snickers and takes his laptop off his thighs, putting it on the table.

"Oh God. You're gonna do that thing where you try to get me to talk about my feelings, aren't you? You're the worst best friend and stepbro ever. I wish you didn't know me so well."

"No you don't."

No. I don't. He's right.

"Talk to me, Bren. Dare you." He reaches over, placing his hand on the tiger tattoo on my chest, maybe to remind me of the reason I got it.

"Oh, I see how you are. Gotta bring out the dares, huh?" I ask, instead of mentioning that I know what he's doing with his hand placement and how much it means to me.

"They haven't steered us wrong yet." His hand lowers to my thigh, and blood rushes toward my groin. Damn him and the effect he has on me.

"For someone who keeps reminding me how this is a bad idea, you end up touching me an awful lot."

"Want me to stop?" He draws circles on my thigh, getting higher and higher.

"No." I drop my head back.

"Tell me."

So I do. I share the conversation we had about Mom and Nicole and all that shit. What's the point in pretending that Taylor wouldn't get it out of me? That he doesn't always know when something is going on inside my head?

The good thing is, he keeps getting closer and closer to my dick, which probably means I shouldn't be as honest as I'm about to be. "Then he started talking about how great it'll be to be one big happy family. All these family vacations we'll go on, and how awesome it will be for me to have a brother."

"Oh." Taylor's hand stops moving, and damn it, why did I tell him?

"Yeah…*oh* is right. They really owe us. We're excellent fucking sons."

"Fucking sons?" Taylor asks, and we laugh together the way we're so good at doing.

I sigh, then drop my head on his shoulder. "Even though I'm dying for you to fuck me, and this sibling thing is both hot and a pain in my ass…I'm glad it's you, Tay." Because that makes moving on easier.

"I'm glad it's you too," he replies, with something in his voice I can't read. I lift my head, look at him, and he seems almost sad for a moment, but then shakes it off. "Movie marathon?"

"Yeah," I reply, giving him space to sort out what's in his head, before I try to get him to do the talking thing too.

<h1 style="text-align:center">13</h1>

<h2 style="text-align:center">Taylor</h2>

I FINISH DINNER with our first movie, and while Brenner makes popcorn, I list off different movies we could watch next, working through the usual game of "Seen it," "Seen it twice," "Don't want to see it." With all these streaming services we subscribe to, we sure as hell better be able to find something.

"What about *Misery*?" I ask.

"What is it?"

"Don't know. Has Kathy Bates in it. Older movie."

"Like thirties old?"

"What the fuck are you talking about? Don't you know who Kathy Bates is?"

"An actress from the thirties?"

I laugh. "You'll recognize her. It's nineties old."

He shrugs. "Put it on. Let's give it a shot."

I wait for Brenner to bring the bowl of popcorn and settle beside me on the couch before pressing Play. As the opening credits start, I lounge back, and he rests his head in my lap, tossing a piece of popcorn up and catching it in his mouth.

"Okay, open up," he says.

I obey, and he tosses a piece I catch in my mouth.

"Here comes another."

We go again, but I miss this time.

"Ooh, so close," he says before popping another into his mouth.

"I can do better than that," I press. "Hit me again."

"Determined thing tonight, aren't you? Ever since you got hole, you're ready to take on the world."

I chuckle. "It's not *not* true."

Bren grins, his eyes sparkling under the room light before he tosses another piece, and I'm ridiculously proud of myself when I get it in my mouth.

"So two out of three," I say. "Let's see how you do."

I grab a piece out of the bowl and toss it up. As it comes down, Brenner shifts and takes it right in the forehead.

"Oh fuck," he says. "No, that doesn't count."

"What do you mean?"

"I'm at a disadvantage in this position."

"Not my problem."

I throw him another, and he shifts and catches it in his mouth. Then I go for a third, and he does the same.

"Another," he insists.

"No, because then you're gonna feel like you won,

even though we've tied."

"Not a tie when that first one didn't count."

I roll my eyes. "I'm not letting you think you won."

"What are you talking about? You love when I win."

"And you know I don't like to make it easy on you."

He pouts. "Pretty please, Tay. All those times I sucked your dick, wasn't it good enough for me to deserve a second chance? Didn't I find you a good boyhole to fuck?"

"I think that boyhole found us," I say with a laugh before grabbing another piece and tossing it for him.

Of course he catches it, and he looks so fucking pleased with himself before he says, "So I won?"

"If you say so."

"Thank you. I do."

"Speaking of that boyhole, Dax is always really smiley when I see him around campus. Think he had a good time."

"No shit."

"I don't know," I say. "Figured he might have thought you were fun, and I was just some noob who didn't know what he was doing."

His brows tug closer together. "Trust me, Taylor, he was loving our cocks every way we gave them to him." My cheeks warm, and his expression turns serious. "Don't blush like that." It's like he's trying to command me to stop.

"What?"

"You're just trying to torture me since you know I can't kiss you again."

"You're just gonna make it redder if you keep talking like that."

"That works too," he says with a wink.

I've seen the guy work his charm on people countless times, but it's wild having him direct it at me.

"Shut it, Bren," I say, though I'm not exactly hating it.

The lighthearted moment is great, but playful as we are, something else lingers too, ever since Brenner brought up his conversation with his dad earlier.

He studies my expression, his smile fading. "Talk to me. What's wrong?"

Damn, this guy knows me.

He reaches up, rests his hand on my cheek, then slides it up, running his fingers through my bangs. "Come on, Tay. I told you my stuff. Your turn."

"Okay, there's something, but it doesn't have anything to do with popcorn or hole."

"It's okay if you don't want to talk about it."

That's the thing about Brenner—the way he's so careful with me. Knows not to push too hard.

"I hope you don't think it's anything you did, but when you talk about your parents, it reminds me of the Piece of Shit. Here you are, wishing you had more time with your mom, and I wish I could have so many years back from him."

I quiet again, and Brenner runs his knuckles down my cheek. "I remember when you told me about him. That night after we'd been drinking at that party senior year. But I knew about it before then. Not the specifics, but I would watch you when you brought up your dad or when I was talking about mine. There was something there, something off."

The memory stirs a warm sensation in my chest. The night I finally spoke to someone, in a way I couldn't even speak to my mom about that bastard.

"But you never pushed me to share," I say. "You just let me get it out in my own time."

I keep waiting for Brenner to say something, crack a joke or diss the Piece of Shit, but he's silent. Listening. It's a side of Bren not many get to see. Like it's just for me, which makes it that much more special.

"I still remember the night that changed everything," I say. "At the kitchen table, when he was getting onto Mom about how he would have rather had lasagna than stroganoff, and he wouldn't let up, which really was just another night in our house. I could see how uncomfortable it was making her. And it'd only been six months since we lost Aria. She finally got up because she couldn't take it anymore, and like he was punishing her for daring to get away from his bullshit, he comes out with those fucking words: 'if you can't handle that, I don't know how you thought you could handle having another kid.' Just so vindictive, so nasty, so impossible for me to understand why he would utter them when she was still in so much pain."

Bren's nostrils flare, his jaw tensing. He might be one of the few people who could hate the Piece of Shit as much as me or Mom.

"But you stood up to him," Brenner says, since this isn't the first time he's heard this.

And it feels good knowing he remembers the details. Not that it surprises me.

My eyes water. "As much as a ten-year-old can. Bottled it up for so long, and I guess all that pressure had to be released. All I did was tell him he was being mean and hurting her, and he didn't look so high and mighty then. I could see he was ashamed I'd called him out. Like he knew I fucking saw him for the monster he really was. Because that may have been the worst thing he said, but there were so many cruel comments, so many jabs wearing on Mom. For long enough, even before Aria, that I forgot how bright Mom could shine."

"But you see it now."

"Yeah, I do. And it wasn't easy. A lot of therapy and support from friends, steadily rebuilding her life."

"She's earned every bit of happiness she has."

"That's for sure." I shake my head, fighting my teary

eyes. "Anyway, just sounds so nice hearing you talk about your parents. And seeing how kind and compassionate your dad is with you and your feelings because the only kind of dad I know made my mom feel like shit about my sister's death, and then when she couldn't take it anymore, dragged her through court just so he could spend his half of custody ignoring me and resenting me for choosing her."

Brenner rests his hand against my cheek, stroking softly, like he knows I need his touch right now.

"I hope you know, Bren, that just like I know your feelings with your mom don't make you want my mom or your dad to be miserable, I'd never want you or him to be miserable because of my experience with the Piece of Shit. Even if sometimes a part of me feels a bit sad seeing how amazing your dad is."

A tear finally breaks free, and Brenner wipes at it with his thumb. "I know."

"Of course you do. I just wanted to tell you."

"I'm glad you did."

"Me too," I say, leaning into his palm as I gaze into his beautiful dark-brown eyes, appreciating the warmth of his touch. As much fun as we can have fucking around, I love moments like these just as much.

When it's just the two of us.

The real us.

The us that isn't just wanting to get each other off or

watch each other get off.

Or all jokes and laughs, like we don't have a care in the world.

The us we only show each other.

"I wish there were magic words I could say," I add. "Something that would take away the sting of what's happening, and what happened to your mom."

"I wish I could do that with your shit too. It'd be nice if we could just have a quick chat about all the dark shit in our minds and that could clear it all up, but things aren't ever that easy, right?"

I nod. "Right."

His cheeks puff before he exhales slowly. Then he shakes it off. "Let's restart the movie. And I'll cuddle the shit out of you to make me feel better. Come on, assume the position."

"Oh, do we cuddle now?" I ask.

"Shut up and be a good big spoon."

I laugh as we adjust. I slide down, resting my head on the pillow as he pushes his body against me. I hook my arm around him, tucking my hand under the hem of his shirt as his ass pushes close against my crotch.

"Let's see how long it takes me to get you hard like this," he teases.

I glide my hand across his abs. "You get me hard," I say, "and I swear, I'm gonna tickle the fuck out of you."

Being besties, we've had our share of tickle fights,

and as I get close to where I know he's sensitive on his abdomen, he grabs my hand. "Uh-uh." He glances over his shoulder. "Don't forget I know where you're sensitive too, and I'll go right for under your arms."

I grunt. "Guess you win this time."

"Second win of the night," he says.

"First win!"

"Uh-uh, you agreed to the first. And working on my third now." He jiggles his ass against my crotch, making me laugh, even as I find it's working pretty fast.

I can't help noting that even though the threat of a tickle is gone, he keeps his hand on mine, relaxing his hold. I grip gently to remind myself that, despite everything that happened in the past, I'm safe here with him.

I grab the remote and restart the movie, and as the credits start rolling, I keep waiting for him to let go of my hand.

He doesn't, though.

And I don't want to let go of his either.

14

Brenner

S O...APPARENTLY, CUDDLING IS something we do now. Not every day, but over the last week, since our first cuddle session, we've done it two other times. I don't know why it's suddenly a thing, but six months ago, I never expected blowing Taylor to be a thing either, and it was for a while.

I can't pinpoint what made our talk the other night feel so different. It's not like we haven't spent years sharing secrets and real parts of ourselves, but now it feels like...more? Maybe it's because of our parents getting married, and the emotions I felt after dinner with my dad combined with Taylor opening up to me, but...yeah. Cuddling. And just...more. For someone who talks as much as I do, I've never claimed to be the best with words.

I'm at work, and the Feral Fox Café is full of people from around campus. Caffeine and college go hand in hand. I had one of my longer days of school today, and

I'm tired as fuck, but again, that's what the coffee is for.

I'm making a twenty-ounce mocha with an extra shot, feeling a little jittery and bouncing on my toes, when the bell over the door jingles. I look up to greet the customer and see it's Mila. "There's my girl," I tease her.

"Are you guys dating?" Stephanie, one of my coworkers, asks. "I've never heard you call someone *my girl* before, and she's been here often over the last month."

"Ew. Boy cooties," Mila jokes as she approaches the counter. "I'm a lesbian. He's just my bestie."

Stephanie chuckles. "I was going to be shocked. I didn't know Brenner dated."

I mock gasp. "I date!"

"You hook up. You don't date."

I snicker. "Oh yeah. Good point." Except I don't even hook up anymore. No, I sit at home and cuddle with my stepbro. "I'll make your drink," I tell Mila while Stephanie meets her at the counter to pay. Mila always gets the same thing.

"You get a break soon?" Mila asks as I hand her the latte.

"Yeah, in like ten minutes."

Stephanie looks around and says, "It's slowed down. You can go ahead."

"Thanks." I make myself a drink and then meet Mila at her table. She got lucky and was able to grab one in the back corner. "Miss me?" I ask her.

"I had sex last night," she blurts, and I chuckle.

"Ooh. Nice. Who is she?"

"This girl I met on an app. It was supposed to be a hookup, but she ended up spending the night, and we like…talked and stuff. At first I was worried the talking would give me a case of hives, but she's cool."

Man, I love her. We're more alike than we have any right to be. "Aww. Do you have a crush? What's her name?"

"Alexis, and I don't have a crush…oh God, do I have a crush?" She covers her face with her hands, and I can't help but laugh.

"I don't know. I've never had one." I guess I must've at some point, but clearly, they weren't memorable. And just the thought of loving someone and risking a broken heart like Dad got when Mom died gives *me* hives.

"Shut up. Like you don't have one now." She snickers, then takes a drink of her coffee while I try to figure out what the fuck she's talking about. I wait for her to say *just kidding*, but she just looks at me with her brows drawn together before saying, "Wait. You realize you have a crush, don't you?"

"I'm not sure if you woke up in a different reality today, but please tell me who I would have a crush on."

"Taylor." She shrugs like she's making any sense at all.

I clutch my stomach as I give an exaggerated laugh. What is she on about? "I think you've totally misjudged my relationship with Taylor. Sure, we've hooked up, but he's just my best friend." I figure Taylor won't mind me telling Mila. It's similar to Dax knowing and feels different from telling our friend group. That would be harder to control.

"You really don't know? I thought you were pretending you didn't. The way you follow that boy around with your eyes…"

I shrug. "He's hot. I like the taste of his cum. Of course I look at him." See? She has no idea what she's saying. "There's a difference between attraction and a crush."

"You talk about him *all the time*."

"Again, best friend. We're always together, so of course I would talk about him a lot."

"You smile dopily when you do it."

"I'm a dope. That's nothing new." I chuckle but shift a little uncomfortably before taking a drink. "You just don't get us. We connected at a really important time in our lives. Tay trusted me with pieces of himself, and…I guess he was the first person to do that, to see beyond the annoying, obnoxious Brenner, and it connected us." Whoa. I didn't even know I felt that way, didn't realize how much Taylor accepting me and seeing more in me was something I really needed. Or need, I guess.

"Okay." Mila shrugs. "Back to Alexis…she was really, really good, and I needed it. She did this thing with her fingers where—"

"You don't believe me," I interrupt.

"I said *okay*."

"Yeah, but it was one of those placating okays. I don't have a crush on Taylor." I can't have a crush on Taylor. What if it ruined everything? Plus, I don't do crushes.

"I believe you that you don't think you have a crush on Taylor."

"You said *think* because you believe I do."

"Well, I'm allowed to have my own feelings, aren't I?"

She might have a point there.

But…what if I do have a crush on him? How could I not know that? Sure, I'm not always in touch with my emotions, but I would have to be an idiot to miss a crush on my bestbro…hey, that's cute. Best friend and stepbro.

I'm different with Taylor, though…and I like cuddling with him, talking to him, having sex with him. Isn't a crush more than that?

Mila reaches over and puts her hand on top of mine. "I feel like you're spiraling. I didn't mean to give you a hard time. Maybe you have a crush on him and maybe you don't. I'm sure you know your feelings best."

"I would have thought so five minutes ago, but I'm

not so sure now. Thanks for that."

Mila laughs, and I can't help doing the same.

"Are you feeling better now?" she asks.

"I don't know. I kinda feel like my whole life has been a lie," I tease, and we dissolve into laughter again. When I settle down, I say, "I need to get back to work. Tell me about the fingers later?"

She grins. "Absolutely."

I pinch her cheeks, and she curses me out.

As I get back to work behind the counter, I keep thinking…she's so wrong about me and Taylor.

She has to be.

BY THE TIME I get home that evening, I'm convinced Mila's clueless. She simply doesn't understand my relationship with Taylor. We get us, though, and that's all that matters. And even if I did have a crush on him, which I don't, it would be a small one. It's practically impossible to be as close as we are and not have some kind of small something. It's completely normal.

I'm surprised to find Dax sitting on our couch, playing video games with Taylor. Um…definitely didn't expect this. Not that it matters. It doesn't matter. But I kinda wonder if they're hooking up.

"Hey," I say, then walk over to the couch and sit

between them.

"Hey," Taylor replies. "You okay?"

"Yep. I'm good. How about you two?" Translation: did you fuck him again? *No. Stop. I can't care if he does.*

"Dude. Remind me to never play video games with Taylor again. He's too fucking good," Dax tells me.

"Yeah, he always beats all our asses. What are you up to?"

"Playing video games?" Dax replies, raising a brow.

"I meant other than that."

He shrugs. "I'm meeting up with a guy who lives near here, so I stopped by for a bit."

I say a silent thank-you I have no right to feel. It doesn't mean Taylor and Dax aren't hooking up, just not right now.

"How was work?" Tay asks.

"Good. Mila stopped by."

"Who's Mila?" Dax asks.

"His new best friend," Taylor replies, a strange tightness to his voice.

"Not like Tay is my best friend, of course. You'll always be my number one."

"Aww. Aren't you guys cute?" Dax teases.

"I think we are." I nudge Taylor playfully with my elbow, but he gets up. "Where are you going?"

"To get a drink." He goes into the kitchen, while Dax is still taking his turn.

I get up and follow him. "Are you and Dax…"

He tilts his head, his forehead creasing. "What? No. That was a one-time thing."

I nod, again oddly thankful.

"Wait…do you want to…with Dax?" Tay asks.

"What? No," I say, which is exactly what he'd just said to me. "Besides that one night, I haven't hooked up with anyone else since last school year." Shit. Maybe I shouldn't have told him that. And why is it true? I'm still trying to figure that out.

"You haven't?"

"Nope."

"Me neither."

"Good," I reply. "I mean, not good. It's fine if you do. I don't know why I said that."

Luckily, before he can reply, Dax comes into the kitchen. "I'm gonna dip. Unless the two of you want to go again? If so, I'll bail on the other guy."

I want to say no, but I don't want to make a decision for Taylor. If he wants to explore his bisexuality more, he has the right.

"I think we're good. Thanks, though," Taylor replies, and I breathe easier for some reason.

"Damn. You two are the first not to want another shot at my ass."

"Shut up," I tell Dax. "You know you have a great hole."

"I do." He winks. "Catch ya later. I'll see myself out."

We nod and hear him go for the door. When I look at Taylor, he's looking at me again. "What?" I ask, heart beating faster than it should. What the fuck. Am I having a heart attack? I rub a hand over my chest while I wait for Taylor to answer.

15

Taylor

B RENNER CLEARLY EXPECTS me to say something, but I've been thrown ever since he got back to the apartment. He's off. In a way I'm not used to ever seeing him.

When I bumped into Dax on campus after my last class, he said he had some free time, so I didn't think twice about inviting him over. Didn't even cross our minds we might do anything else—well, maybe it crossed Dax's mind a little.

I definitely didn't think Brenner would mind.

But it's not just Brenner throwing me. Why was I relieved when he said he hadn't messed around with anyone either? I mean, I've been waiting for him to start messing around with someone, which would rip the Band-Aid off because I know it'll bother me. I'm not like him. I don't hook up with people without feeling anything, Dax excepted.

And it's been worse recently because I've enjoyed our

cuddling and watching movies together. Enjoyed feeling closer to him than ever before, and the thought of someone sliding in between us and fucking that up makes me feel…ragey.

Brenner's still looking at me in a way I can't make sense of, and I have no idea what to say, so I go with the first thing that comes to mind. "We cool?"

He flinches, like that was definitely the wrong thing. "Huh?"

"You've been weird since you got home. Did something happen at work?"

Though why would dealing with a fussy customer or a tiff with a coworker make him come home and start talking to me about hooking up with Dax and about not hooking up with anyone else since we started messing around?

Bren rests his hand on his chest and searches around the kitchen. "I think I might need to go to bed."

He darts out of the kitchen, but I tail behind him. "I'm not letting you out of this that easy."

"I just need to lie down. I'm not feeling good."

"I can tell something's up, Bren."

"Well, I'm about to be down."

I roll my eyes, still behind him as he reaches his bedroom door. I take him gently by his arm, and he turns around, his gaze shifting to where I'm touching him before locking with mine.

The fuck is happening?

I glare at him. "Talk to me, dude."

He hesitates, and my chest knots up as he has one of those rare moments when he seems to be struggling for words. It's like seeing my mom tear up—it dries my throat, makes me want to do anything to make it better.

"I hope you don't mind, but I told Mila about us, and she thinks I have a crush on you," he spits out, looking deadly serious.

I burst into a laugh, partly because I'm sure this isn't what's on his mind, but mostly because it's the most ridiculous thing he could have said.

I can't stop laughing, but I feel my cheeks warming as the idea starts to settle in.

I wouldn't mind if he did have a crush on me.

Fuck, where did that come from?

It's not a thought I allow myself to entertain for long because it's so ridiculous, and because the way Brenner's looking at me, he doesn't seem to find it nearly as amusing.

"Why did you think that was funny?" he asks, his jaw stiffening.

"Shows me that Mila isn't replacing me anytime soon because I've known you for how long? You don't crush."

"Yeah, you're right," he says, his gaze wandering.

"Why did you say it like that?"

"How did I say it?"

"Like you aren't convinced."

He shakes his head. "It's definitely not a crush because it can't be."

What a weird thing to say.

He goes on, "Because we agreed we don't want to make shit weird for our parents."

Again, I'm thrown.

"Wait," I say. "That wouldn't prevent you from having a crush. That would just prevent you from acting on it."

As the words come out of my mouth, I feel like I'm finally catching up.

Does Brenner really have a crush on me? The thought stirs a warm sensation that radiates in my chest.

As I reflect on the past few weeks especially, I recognize a lot of the sensations I've felt—the closeness, the eagerness to see him. I haven't let myself label it, maybe because I knew Brenner doesn't have those kinds of feelings, but now that he's said the word, it's like for the first time I'm letting myself admit that my own feelings have been more than just enjoying spending time with my buddy. And maybe I've been a little foolish thinking buddies hold each other as close as we've held each other until they fall asleep. A part of me can't believe it's possible, but as our gazes meet again, the realization hits me like a brick.

"Fuck," is all I can think to say.

He winces. "Was that supposed to make me feel better?"

I laugh, then fight against it.

"Oh, and now you're laughing again?" He moves closer. "Dude, not cool," he says, reaching up and pushing his fingers under my arms for a tickle.

"Fuck you." I pull away and lean back against the wall across from his door.

"You know damn well I'm a catch," he says, sounding more like his usual playful self as I resist his tickles. It takes me a moment to deflect his attempts before I reach under his shirt and give him a taste of his own medicine by playing around his abs. Now we're both bending over, twisting our bodies as we try to evade each other's hands, until we're on the floor.

I manage to grab hold of his wrists and pin them against the floor, struggling against him, though I can tell he's given up.

"So you have a crush on me?" I ask, and his cheeks flush red, a rare occurrence for Brenner.

"You're being so cringe right now."

He tries to pull away, but I grip his wrists tighter, keeping him in place.

"I'm about to be more cringe," I add, "because I might have a crush on you too."

Did I really just say that? I mean, it's kind of true. This is how I've felt before when I've dated girls in the past.

He smirks. "*Might?*"

"I've only had this new information for a few seconds, so I'm gonna need to sort through it a little more, but yeah. I've been enjoying what's been happening the past few weeks, but I haven't let myself think too much about it. It's definitely crush territory, something I'm more familiar with."

I notice a shift against my crotch, where I'm straddling his waist. "You getting hard right now?"

"You're on my crotch, pinning me to the floor, so what do you think?"

I lean close, my lips an inch from his mouth. I roll my hips, stroking against his boner. "Feels like I'm getting you back for all those times you were walking around in your briefs, with them tucked down so I could see your crack, you fucking tease."

"Whatever. Like I haven't been thinking about how it'd feel to have your cock filling me up ever since I watched you fuck Dax."

We stare into each other's eyes until I finally crush my lips against his, feeling the burst of relief as I cave to what my body's been hungry for since we started denying each other.

"You…don't think…this is a shit idea?" he fights to say between kisses.

"Probably," I manage to say before sealing our kiss

again.

I'm like a fucking animal as Bren's tongue slips into my mouth, greeting mine as they play in a frenzy, taking away all the tension that started as soon as he came home.

There's stuff we need to talk about—between these feelings and our parents—but there's a time to talk and a time to fuck.

This is definitely a time to fuck.

"We…should…get in…the bedroom," I say, wondering if he even made out the words with how determined he seemed to keep our lips together.

I would've thought it'd be awkward as fuck trying to get up from the floor and into his bedroom, but it turns into stripping down between make-out sessions, a chaotic scene of losing shirts, shoes, and pants, until we're just in our underwear. We wind up on his bed, with Bren on his back as I hook my arms around his legs, rubbing my crotch against his ass, my body acting out the fantasy that ignited the night I got a taste of ass.

Brenner snickers.

"What's so funny?" I ask now that his lips give mine a moment's peace.

"Tay went from being my straight buddy to being addicted to ass real fast."

Now I'm the one snickering. "Hearing you call me straight now that I realize I'm so not is hilarious."

"How's that all going, if you don't mind me asking? You seem cool with everything, but…is there anything you wanted to ask a bi guy?"

That's so thoughtful. So Bren.

"Honestly? I think it's easier for me since I knew your stuff first. Seeing you like guys and girls. So it might be new to me, but in some ways, I already get it, so I'm just going with it."

"Wait. You're not blaming me for suddenly being addicted to ass, are you?" he jokes.

I laugh. "Yeah, it's totally your fault. This wasn't something I probably always had in me just waiting to be activated."

"Mmmm, so I activated you? That's even hotter."

"I must admit, it helps knowing that if anything comes up that I'm worried about, I have a bi buddy I can talk to. At the moment, though, my biggest issue around the whole subject is I've only had one ass so far, which seems kind of cruel."

"That is cruel. We're gonna have to do something about that."

Fuck, he's fun.

Bren grabs a condom and lube from his nightstand while I pull off my boxers. As he settles on his back again, I snatch either side of his briefs and slide them down his legs before discarding them off the side of the bed.

"Ooh, I like aggressive Taylor," he says, making me blush. "Seriously, it's hot."

He starts to tear at the condom but stops himself. "We both said it's been six months. Was Rachelle your last partner?"

"Yeah." From the wicked glint in his eyes, I have a feeling I know where this is going.

"And we both got full panels after Dax."

"Bren, you seriously talking about me being inside you raw right now?"

"This is my first crush. Shouldn't we do something to celebrate?"

I'm laughing again. Oh, he really just has this power to get me going.

"You're right," I say, leaning down and snatching the condom away from him. "We should celebrate." I toss the condom over my shoulder, and Brenner stares me down.

It's wild to think that one minute we were debating whatever the hell we're feeling for each other, and now he's under me, looking like he wants to be drilled.

And I'm eager to give him the drilling.

"Put some lube on me," I instruct, and Bren smiles.

He pumps some into his palm before reaching down and readying my cock.

I smile as my dick throbs in his grip. "Reminds me of when you were lining me up with Dax."

Brenner releases me and leans back. As he tosses the bottle of lube on the sheets, I hook my arms under his legs, adjusting so I can see that beautiful hole…

It pulses, stirring this animalistic desire within me. "Fuck," I mutter as I line up, pressing the head against him, then watching his expression as I push in.

"You like that?" he asks. "Wanna see what I look like when you're opening me up?"

Didn't think I could get any harder, but Brenner has that skill.

His eyes roll back as his ass lets me in a few inches, but I can tell he's tight.

"You have no idea how much I've been thinking about getting my dick inside you," I confess.

"I've been wanting you to have a go at me since you did such a good job with Dax. Oh, fuck—this is what I get for not getting fucked in so long."

"I was thinking this seemed really tight."

"Yeah." He takes a few deep breaths. "Apparently getting fucked all those times before doesn't help me any now. Just take it nice and slow. Until I tell you to go fast." He winks, and as he gets a few more breaths in, I feel his ass open up for me enough to get a few more inches in.

I'm a little nervous, but seeing the way his eyes light up, it's clear he's taking me just fine.

"Stay right there and do little thrusts," he instructs.

"My pro showing me the ropes."

He grins as I move in and out subtly.

I love knowing it's just me and Bren, skin to skin like this, no barrier between us. Feeling his muscles relax and let me in just a little more each time.

When he's ready, he says, "Okay, now deeper."

I follow his instruction until I feel his hole tightening up.

When I stop, he tenses up. "Jesus, please tell me you're all the way in."

I glance down, noticing I still have a good inch left. "Close."

"How is that not all of it? Fuck. You must be harder than usual."

"That's a fact," I admit.

He smiles, like he's pleased he's the reason I'm so stiff. Taking a few more deep breaths, he tells me when to push, and as I do, the way he closes his eyes, his lip twisting into his dimple in that familiar way, assures me it's hitting right.

I enjoy the sensation of being inside him, saying, "I can't believe you've been keeping this ass from me all these years."

"Could say the same thing about that cock. Fuck, it fits just right."

A burst of pride swells in my chest.

"Okay, I'm good," he assures me.

I give him a test run, sliding back and forth. He's loosened up for me, so now I'm free to probe and explore him with my cock. He clenches his cheeks, and I can tell by his playful expression that this is just my sex expert showing what he can do.

Locking his legs in the crooks of my arms, I speed up, and he says, "That's right, Tay. Give it to me."

I obey, rocking the mattress about.

Brenner closes his eyes and reaches back, pressing his hand against the headboard as he takes me. I speed up even more, determined to give him what he wants, to be as good at fucking him as I can be. His rock-hard cock bounces on his abs as his expression tenses up, and I lean down, taking a kiss.

I want to really drill him, though, and it feels like I could do better than this position, so I lean back. Keeping his legs locked in my arms and my dick jammed up in him, I shift on the bed, walking on my knees to the edge of the bed. I carefully step off with one leg, then pull him close as I slide the other off, getting my footing before really giving it to him.

Despite my effort, he says, "Come on, Taylor. I know you got more than that in you, and I want it all."

I don't hold anything back, just throw myself into it, ramming that ass as he calls out, his expression shifting wildly, out of control as he loses himself in the pleasure I'm giving him.

"You're so good at this," he tells me, like he knows I need to hear his praise. I keep up my pace, working to impress, but between how fucking hard he's got me and how long I've been craving this, I can feel my balls tugging close as my body rushes toward release.

"You're already getting me so close," I warn.

"I feel like now that I'm opened up, I can show you just what a good bottom I can be for you. You want that?"

"Oh, fuck yeah."

"I'm gonna wear this cock out."

"Wear it out, Bren." I'm fucking begging.

"Pull out. You're gonna fuck me from behind."

I obey, pulling out and adjusting with him so he's on his knees, me standing behind and giving it to him. As I thrust, Brenner rolls his hips and moves with me, nearly as soon as I pull my cock out, pushing his ass back, taking me all the way so his cheeks clap against my hips.

"Fuck." I grip on to him and pick up my pace, reveling in the way his ass feels around my shaft, stimulating my muscles as he moans, letting me know how fucking good it feels to have me balls-deep inside him.

We work like this is our fucking job until I've got sweat beading across my forehead.

"Keep fucking me like this," he says, "and I'll make sure when you come, it's mind-blowing."

I hook my arms around him, moving close, and he

turns to kiss me as I push deep inside him. I take his cock in my hold, stroking.

"You're so fucking hard," I say as our lips part.

"I think I'm gonna blow soon. But I don't want to come before you."

"Well, I'm getting pretty close."

"Yeah?"

I nod, and he says, "Just stay still."

"Huh?"

"Keep right there."

Again, I follow his lead, and he rocks his ass, sliding me in and out of him.

"You're gonna come inside me," he says, "and then start hammering away until I shoot. Got it?"

I nod again.

I stay still as Brenner works my cock, rocking his ass. I can tell he's alternating between techniques, clenching and rolling his cheeks like a guy who's learned how to work a cock because it's got me climbing, inching toward the edge, every part of me wanting to be fucking him.

As I continue jerking him, I rest my free hand on his hip, gripping as the urgency in me mounts.

Bren's watching me as my expression twists up. "Fuck, you're so close, aren't you?"

"I'm right there."

He slows his movements, torturing me.

"Bren, fuck."

"Don't forget that after you shoot, you need to fuck me real hard, okay?"

"I will." I'm not even thinking straight. Right now, I'd tell him anything to keep him working me like this. I'm just a servant to his hole.

He leans closer, running his tongue across my bottom lip as he gives an extra squeeze of his ass around my cock, and it's like he's pulling the cum right from me. As I gasp, his lips push up against mine. I grip his hip harder as my muscles lose control and I jerk quickly, shooting up inside him.

"Fuck, yeah," he mutters as I pound away, still jerking him, determined to give him what I promised. "Taylor. Fuck me just like that."

I speed up, sweat sliding from my chin down onto his back, knowing that I'm shoving my cum deeper into him, when I feel his ass gripping me like Dax's did before he shot, encouraging me to keep up my movements until his cock throbs in my hold and I feel the warm, wet release.

He reaches back, resting his hand against the back of my head and drawing me in for a kiss.

"That's good, Taylor. Perfect," he says as he pulls away, our gazes locking, a satisfied expression on his face, assuring me I've done a good job for him. "I'll make sure to return the favor when I fuck you," he adds.

And it's like he's fucking hypnotized me with the

thought.

He looks so excited at the prospect of taking my ass, making it his, just like I made his mine. I don't have a fucking clue what that'll feel like, but if Brenner and Dax are any indication, it'll be in-fucking-credible.

He leans closer and licks up my lips.

When we first started fucking around, I might have called this a shit idea. But as much as we may have to sort out, it would have been a shit idea not to do this.

16

Brenner

"So…remember that time you told me you have a crush on me?" I tease Taylor as we lie on my bed, naked, dried cum all over me, and coming down from what was a fan-fucking-tastic orgasm.

He snickers and rolls onto his side so he's facing me. "I'm fairly certain you said you have a crush on me first."

"Lies, all lies. So…how long have you felt this way about me?"

"I'm going to smother you with a pillow, Bren."

"How can you do that to someone you have feelings for?" I bat my eyelashes playfully, hamming it up and trying to keep the mood light. We both know that having feelings for someone and talking about it is totally different for me. And then there's the added complication of our parents getting married in four months and how said feelings might cause problems with that. It's not like my dad would disown me or anything, and Nicole wouldn't do anything like that with Taylor either, but…having this happen in the beginning, before they even tie the knot…

"I know what you're doing," Taylor says, and I bite back my groan.

"Can you not know me so well? That would be really great and would make keeping my feelings to myself a whole lot easier."

"Like the fact that you have a huge crush on me?" He gives me an adorable, cocky little smirk that makes my dick twitch. We laugh together, but I can see the seriousness in Taylor's blue eyes. While having feelings for someone is newer for me than it is for Taylor, emotions have always been something he's put more thought into, and anyone who has met us for five seconds knows that Taylor is the one who will be giving all this a deeper, more thorough consideration.

"We should probably talk about what this means," Taylor says, echoing my thoughts, and I sigh.

"Maybe we shouldn't have this conversation naked."

"We're totally having this conversation naked. Then I know you won't run away."

I give him a mock scowl. "I would do no such thing."

"That's two lies in just a few minutes," Taylor jokes. "When it came up earlier, you practically sprinted for your room."

"It's very rude to call me out."

"You're right, that is rude…and actually, you *are* Mr. Feelings. You feel a lot more than you're comfortable sharing most of the time."

There's no denying that. "I share with you."

"I know you do, Bren."

I flop to my back and look at the ceiling. He's right. We should talk about this. I know we should. "I don't know what it means. I like you, and you like me. I'm not quite ready to define it further."

"I feel the same. I just wanted to ask since this is so new."

"See? We're already killing it. We're on the same page."

"Always." Taylor reaches over, setting his hand on one of my pecs and brushing his thumb over my nipple. "So…we like each other. We're best friends. Future stepbrothers. And we're having sex. We've officially decided that much."

I nod, my body slightly tingly just from being close to him and feeling the way he's touching me. "Yes."

"What about hooking up with other people?"

I growl, then frown, surprised at myself.

"That growl was kinda hot."

"Only kinda?"

"You don't like the thought of me messing around with others."

"Didn't we figure this out in the kitchen earlier?" I

grumble, pretending to be annoyed.

"You want me to be all yours, Bren?"

"Fuck yes. Are you gonna pretend you don't want the same?"

Taylor nods, affirming what I said. "You're mine."

"Perfect. We're best friends and future stepbrothers, who like each other and exclusively have sex with each other. Problem solved. How long do you think you'll take to get it up again?"

He laughs. "Not too long, but we're not done here yet."

"Damn it!" I tease, but then pull him over so he's lying on top of me, looking down at me with those bright blue eyes, his blond bangs hanging down.

He looks so hot tonight.

I love being here with Taylor like this.

"Be good, Bren, or I'll tickle you again."

That's one of his favorite threats. "Sadist!" I lean up and press a kiss to his lips. "So fucking cool that I get to do this all the time now."

"I mean…not all the time. Like, it wouldn't be smart to start making out in front of our parents. Unless you think we should tell them about us. If that's what you're saying, we need to discuss it a bit more." He quirks a brow. "Originally, we didn't think it was worth it when it seemed like it wasn't a big deal for us to stop. But now, it's clearly more than that, and I don't want to keep my hands off you. But I don't think we should tell them yet."

"One hundred percent agree. I don't want to keep my hands off you either, and this is more, but it would be a lot for them to deal with while planning a wedding. Plus, it's not like they didn't keep their relationship a secret from us."

"Yeah, but maybe we try and tell them before they walk in on me fucking your brains out."

We both laugh, before we sober, and I say, "They'd be confused and worried about what would happen if something went wrong. They don't need that stress before the wedding."

Taylor looks down at my chest, then draws circles on it. "What if something does go wrong?"

"It won't. We're us, Tay. We've been friends too long to let something come between us."

He nods. "You're right. I just needed to ask. At this point we're just seeing how things go. And we'll be honest with each other if anything changes. So if this is still going after the wedding, that's when we tell them?"

"I think so." Holy shit. What if Taylor and I are still doing this in four months? That's like a whole-ass relationship, something I've never done.

"Deal. What about our friends? The guys from the frat, I mean."

I shrug. "I don't care if they know."

"Me neither. I don't want to have to be careful around *everyone*. There's nothing wrong with us exploring this."

I grin. "We're nailing this exclusive, best-friends-who-have-sex-with-each-other thing."

"You forgot the stepbrothers part."

"Where should I add it?"

"Exclusive best friends and future stepbrothers who have sex?"

I shrug. "Works for me."

Taylor slips his hand down between our bodies, between my legs. "How's your hole?"

"Took a pounding."

He frowns. "Are you sore?"

"A little bit. Totally worth it, though. You're pretty fucking good at dicking me down."

"You're pretty fucking good at taking my cock." He ruts against me, and my dick starts to swell. "You're getting hard again."

"How can I not when a sexy, naked guy is on top of me? Don't pretend you're not getting hard too."

"Thank God for quick refractory periods." Taylor smirks.

"The joys of being young. Are we done with all the miserable talking now?"

Taylor laughs, leaning down and kissing me. It's a little awkward but also makes my heart beat faster.

"Since I went wild on your hole already…and I made you talk…how about I blow you?"

My cock throbs beneath him, my skin prickling with excitement. "I'm not going to argue with getting a shot at your mouth." I brush my thumb along his bottom lip, and Taylor playfully bites it, making me chuckle. I love that things are always so fun between us. Love that he's playful with me on levels he isn't with anyone else.

He lets my finger go, and I run my hand through his hair while he kisses his way down my body, enjoying my pecs before continuing south. "I really liked blowing you." He's only done it once, that night with Dax. "I really wanted to swallow your load."

"I wanted that too."

He rubs his cheek against my happy trail. He's got to be getting my scent, my dried cum from earlier, all over his skin. He twirls his tongue around the head of my cock, making lightning lick up my spine.

"Fuck…Tay…suck me."

He slides lower, looks up at me with hooded eyes and a smirk. "I'm getting there. Be patient."

"You know I suck at patience."

"Well, I guess we'll have to teach you how." He presses his tongue against the base of my dick, then slowly licks up to the tip.

I don't know what it is about this moment, but my body jolts upward, arching toward him and making

Taylor pull back. "Asshole."

"That's not very nice to call someone who is about to suck your dick."

"You're awfully cocky when you're in bed with me."

He quirks a brow. "Don't pretend you don't like it."

"Oh, I like it. I also like telling you to suck my cock."

He leans down, nuzzles my full balls, my fingers still in his hair. "Know why I can be so cocky with you?"

I do know, and it makes me tremble. Still, I want to hear him say it. "Tell me why."

"Because I feel comfortable with you, Bren. Because you trained me so well on how to be with a man."

I swear it feels like his words zap me with a million volts of electricity—if being electrocuted could feel good, that is.

"I love how you taste," Taylor says before taking me deep into the hot, wet suction of his mouth. He immediately begins to bob on me, doing his best to take as much of me into his mouth as he can. His gaze meets mine, a fire in his eyes, one that says how fucking hot this moment is and how well he wants to do for me. He already fucked my brains out, and now he's going to suck any sense I have left out of me, and I'm eager for it, hungry for it, want to give Taylor anything he's hungry for.

"That's it. You're so fucking hot with a mouthful of my cock. You look so sexy with your lips stretched around the first dick you've ever had."

My words seem to spur him on. Taylor goes faster, uses his tongue, lets his hand drift to my balls and play with them, before slipping a finger beneath. I spread my legs for him, feel his fingertip at my hole. He doesn't push in, but I see the way his eyes roll back and figure he feels his cum leaking out of me.

Just thinking about that sends me over the edge. Before I know it, I'm blowing my load into his mouth.

Taylor falls down beside me on the bed, his head in the crook of my arm, which I wrap around him. "I think seeing where this goes between us might be the best idea we've ever had," he says with a sleepy smile.

"Yeah, Tay. I think so too."

17

Taylor

"SO WHAT HAVE you two been up to?" Mom asks as Brenner and I settle at the kitchen table.

When Bren and I had our conversation last week, even though we discussed our parents and friends, I was a little too dickmatized to consider how weird it would feel to be around our parents.

Really, dickmatized and assmatized.

Wait, assmatized isn't a thing.

Although, it sure as fuck feels like it is now that I've had Brenner a few times since our first fuck.

"School and work," I say, my throat dry. I gulp, avoiding eye contact with Brenner, who said on the way over, *"I'm gonna enjoy watching you squirm."* Hope he's lapping it up like he laps up my cum.

"School and work?" Keith asks as he checks on the pot roast he's making for dinner. Keith has been setting up his place to rent it out, so he's staying with my mom, since this is where they plan to live after they get married.

Because of the memories they have in that house with Bren's mom, Keith plans to keep it in the family, eventually pass it on to Brenner, which I know means the world to him.

"Bren," Keith goes on, "please tell me you guys are getting out and having some fun."

"Actually, we've been having a lot of fun *inside*," Bren responds, and I shoot him a quick glare, being extra careful since Mom knows me too well for me to get away with a bluff. "Video games, movies, giving each other hell and the usu."

Nice cover, Brenner…and really close to the truth since messing around has become the usual for us.

Fortunately, Mom's too busy pulling out her iPad to notice any of my tells. When we arrived at her place, she said she had some questions about what we'd prefer for the wedding. And while she's going through things she's already texted me about, I help Keith finish prepping dinner. Once we have the meal on the table, Mom puts away her iPad and we start to eat.

"Damn, you still know how to make a good roast," I say. I've always loved Keith's roasts. "I won't mind having more of these after you guys are married. Mom, I love you, but I can't be subjected to any more of your HelloFresh experiments."

She laughs. "It'll be nice to have someone who's a natural chef around the house. I've put on ten pounds since he moved in."

"Just as beautiful as the day I first saw her," Keith says, his affectionate gaze making Mom blush. As adorable as the moment is, I feel I wouldn't be doing my job as her kid if I didn't make a gagging sound.

"Get a room," Bren adds.

"Thank you, we have one to head to," Keith teases, and we all enjoy a laugh.

"Speaking of living arrangements," Mom says, "how is the apartment working out?"

"You guys getting on each other's nerves yet?" Keith adds.

"On each other's nerves?" Brenner says. "We're best friends. It's a blast. Now we can do all the things we love."

"Please tell me it's not just the two of you," Keith says. "I could see you both playing video games and disappearing from the rest of the world."

"We have people over," Brenner insists.

Is he referring to Dax? I shoot him another look.

His eyes widen. "Like Mila," he says, and I blush, realizing he wasn't trying to sneak in a reference to our extracurricular activities.

"Oh, yeah," I say, "And Atlas, Troy, Colin, Ash, and Lance have swung by too. We have plenty of company."

"Plenty of fun company," Brenner adds, and now I know he's referring to Dax. "But we haven't seen our friends the past few days."

Because we've been too preoccupied with each other to make time for them.

"Yeah, we were gonna head to a party at Alpha Theta Mu tonight," I say. "Catch up with everyone."

And they're likely gonna find out we're a thing.

It's a strange thought.

We don't even know what the hell we are, but whatever it is, it feels good. It feels like us. Just doing our thing, and not really giving fucks about what anyone else thinks of it.

Everyone except our parents, that is.

When we finish up at Mom's, I drive us back to campus, and Brenner's got his hand on my thigh, gripping firmly.

"Making up for lost time?" I tease, since I hated not having his hands all over me while we were at our parents'.

"You fucking know it. Might need you to pull over so we can give each other BJs before this party."

"It's weird to think that we've pretty much fucked through the week and I still fucking need it."

"I don't know that *weird*'s the right word for that," Bren jokes.

"So we just gonna go to this party and let everyone figure it out on their own?"

"I think they'll suspect something when your

tongue's down my throat."

"More likely when your hand's down my pants."

"One of those will probably be a clue," Bren says. "Then maybe we can sneak off to Lance's room and beat one out real quick."

"Or let Lance know and take our time." I sneak him a quick look, and he smirks.

"Mmm…somebody's been missing these lips…this ass…this dick."

"Guilty."

I park down the street from the Alpha Theta Mu house, and when we get to the party, we run into some of the guys.

"I haven't gotten an invite to play any games this week," Lance says after we hug it out.

"We've been kind of busy," Brenner says.

"Meanwhile, why don't I ever get invited to these game nights?" asks Marty, the more anxiety-ridden part of the Alpha Theta Mu crew.

"Do you play?" I ask.

He flinches. "I mean, I didn't say I'd be any good, but I like hanging out. Being chill."

Lance cringes. "No one who's actually chill has to tell everyone they like 'being chill.'"

"It's giving desperate vibes," Payton adds.

"Anxious, desperate, uncool?" Marty says. "These are my things. Can't everyone just be glad I make them look better by comparison?"

"Is this one giving you guys trouble?" Colin comes up from behind him and drapes his arm across Marty's shoulders. "Threatening to kick you out? Trust me, it's better than him threatening your security deposit."

Marty is a notorious goodie-goodie and known for policing all the guys in the house, so I'm not surprised by Colin's assumption, considering Marty's likely given him enough hell to be more than a little annoyed.

We all catch up, the guys sharing Alpha Theta Mu gossip. I notice Lance getting close to Brenner, and though I know he's straight, Brenner was being flirty with him before the cruise. It makes my insecurity flare up.

A part of me thinks I should stuff this away, at least while all the guys are here, but hell, we said it doesn't matter if they know, so I hook my arm around Brenner, resting my hand on his hip, acknowledging it's a little fucked up that I'm claiming him in front of his straight friend.

Brenner glances my way, a warm smile spreading across his face. He rests his hand on mine, rubbing gently, which is the assurance I need—a reminder that this isn't the old Brenner who would just run around looking for the next guy or girl to mess around with. That while we're messing around, he's mine.

"What is *this*?" Colin asks, and suddenly, as if out of

thin air, his boyfriend/stepbrother, Ash, materializes at his side.

"Holy fucking shit, it's contagious," Ash says.

Not surprised that half of one of Alpha Theta Mu's boyfriend-stepbro couples would say some shit like that.

I wave toward myself, inviting the shit-giving. "Come on."

"Yeah," Brenner adds. "Get it all out of your systems while you can."

"What is everyone talking about?" Marty asks, earning a few glances.

"Brenner and Taylor are an item," Lance explains. "And they're also stepbros."

Marty winces. "But they aren't stepbrothers."

"They're going to be, though."

"Wait…but Taylor isn't queer."

"Um…" I say.

Marty blinks a few times. "Seriously? Is this a joke? Did Payton put you guys up to this?"

"Me?" Payton asks.

"Marty, you could be a little more supportive," Lance says in a tone.

"Oh fuck," Marty says. "I'm sorry. That was a dick move. I just…whatever makes you guys happy, and I don't want you to think just because I'm surprised… I don't have any judgment or anything. If you guys are boyfriends, that's—"

"We're not boyfriends," Brenner clarifies. "But we're seeing what's here. Be cool."

"Shit," Marty says. "I'm fucking it up again."

Brenner and I share a laugh. "Relax, Mart," Brenner says. "It's cute that you care."

"Your parents know?" Colin asks.

"Eh, we're gonna wait until after their wedding," I tell them. "For obvious reasons, this could make it weird."

"Weird? Really?" Ash says. "I can't imagine how that would make things weird."

That gets everyone laughing, and as it settles, I say, "Now can we just party and get over this awkward bit?"

Everyone's on the same page, and after a few more jokes, they let it go. Brenner and I grab drinks at the bar before running into Troy and Atlas, who catch Bren with his hand on my ass.

"That's so cute," Atlas tells me. "I got taken, and then you had to settle for Brenner."

I burst into a laugh. Brenner's pretty damn confident, but Atlas definitely rivals him in the cocky department.

"I'm thinking we wasted a couple of years," Brenner says. "We could have all been messing around with each other the whole time."

"What makes you think Taylor and I would have let you join in?" Atlas jokes.

"I know for a fact Taylor would have let me join in," Brenner says.

Troy growls, reminding me of the way Brenner gets all greedy for me, and then Troy pulls Atlas close. "Well, looks like you all missed the boat because this one's all mine," he says before taking a kiss from his man, like he's marking his territory in front of us.

Brenner and I exchange a look because it's kind of hot.

As they get caught up in a make-out session, Brenner leans close and says, "You think we're gonna end up with tattoos of each other?"

We share a laugh.

Atlas has one that says *Troy* under his pec, and Troy has *Atlas* on his wrist. Because these guys are ride or die for each other.

"It's hot," I admit.

"But not really us."

"I don't know. I didn't think messing around with you was really us before either."

"True," Bren says with a chuckle. He looks too adorable to resist, and I take my opportunity now that our friends are distracted, wrapping my arm around him and stealing a kiss.

I hadn't realized just how much I missed it until our lips met, our tongues teasing at each other's.

And when we pull away, someone steps up beside us,

and we turn at the same time to see Dax glancing between us.

"Mmmm-hmmmm," is all he says. "Saw this one coming from a mile away."

Brenner leans closer to him. "Pretty confident you saw the coming closer than that."

"Just so you know," Dax says, "I'm adding whatever-this-is to my CV."

"CV?" I ask.

"Oh, you guys don't have a clue. This slutty gay fairy has powers that bring guys together, apparently."

I can tell there's a story there, though knowing Dax, we'll probably never know what it is.

"Does a slutty gay fairy have a CV?" Brenner asks.

"'Scuse you," Dax says. "I am not *a* slutty gay fairy. I am *the* slutty gay fairy."

We all share a laugh.

Really, not just at Dax's joke, but at how wild and ridiculous this thing that's going on between Bren and me is.

Still, strange as it is, I know the fun's just getting started.

18

Brenner

So…I'm definitely enjoying this whole see-how-things-will-go situation with Taylor. I don't know what to call us, but we're not boyfriends. We're fuck buddies, though that doesn't seem the right qualifier either because over the past few weeks we've also started sleeping in the same bed every night, even when he doesn't fuck my brains out. And we've done so much cuddling. Like, all the cuddling. We do it when we're talking and when we watch movies. We sit close, our legs entwined, when we're playing video games. He plays with my hair sometimes while I'm doing homework, and I tickle my fingertips along his nape because I know how much he enjoys it.

Those are not fuck-buddy activities…which makes sense. Given our history, our friendship, and how close we are, of course it won't feel superficial; of course everything is going to seem a little more.

And honestly, that scares the crap out of me. Not

enough to make me stop, but I can't pretend my brain doesn't keep going to that place where I remember what it was like to lose Mom…how heartbroken Dad was, how I don't think he would have pulled out of it if he hadn't had a son to raise. And I'm frightened about anyone having that power over me. Not that Taylor would ever do anything to hurt me—I know he wouldn't—but you never know what life will throw at you.

What I'm starting to realize, though, is that Taylor already has that power over me, and always had. I've had friendships before him, obviously, but nothing like ours. He's always meant more to me than others. We have a deeper connection than I've had with anyone else, and so the more I think about it, the clearer it becomes that losing Taylor would've hurt at any point. Even before we started having sex and cuddling. And then sometimes, I just kinda look at him and don't want to stop. It's all weird as fuck. Sex with your best friend is even more awesome than sex with random people.

These are all things I should probably share with Taylor.

"What are you thinking about over there?" Taylor rolls over and wraps an arm around me. It's a Saturday, so we don't have school.

I turn so I can face him, dance my fingers down his naked chest. "About how we're naked in bed together, my ass tender, and in a little while we'll be getting fitted for tuxes for our parents' wedding."

"Oooh, kinky," he teases with a chuckle.

"You know what's funny? We're going to be staring at each other across the aisle, and all I'll be thinking about is that I know what your cum tastes like."

Taylor smirks. "Really? I'd figure you'd also be thinking about how it feels when my thick cock pushes into your tiny, little hole."

"Well, that too."

"That's what I thought." Taylor leans in and presses a kiss to my lips, almost sweetly. Who knew simple kisses could make your toes curl? Again, having sex with your best friend is *awesome*.

All too soon, Taylor rolls over and climbs out of bed. "Come on. We have stuff to do."

"Can't we just stay in bed all day?" I bat my lashes.

"That doesn't work with me."

"Sometimes it does."

He snickers. "Not this time. I'll make us some breakfast."

My stomach growls. "It's not like I'm going to argue about food."

We tug on clothes, make omelets together for breakfast, then play some video games before forcing ourselves to do homework.

Eventually it's time to get ready, and after our shower, I try my hardest not to, but I can't resist blowing him. Afterward, Taylor drives us to the tuxedo store where our parents made an appointment for us. They picked out what they want ahead of time, so we just have to go in for the fitting.

"I hate tuxes," I complain.

"You look hot in them, though. Remember when we took those twins to prom? I didn't realize it at the time, but I was noticing how hot you looked in your tux more than paying attention to my date."

I rub my hands together playfully. "Oooh, tell me more. Was I your bi-awakening even back then?"

"No, it was Josh Anderson from the basketball team."

"What the fuck." I whip my head in his direction. "Him? He was an asshole. I hated that guy."

Taylor laughs. "I'm giving you shit. I didn't have my bi-awakening in high school with Josh Anderson."

"I'm way hotter." I cross my arms, pouting a bit.

"Wait. Are you seriously jealous? I'm joking about a fake crush. And we literally fucked someone together since then."

"I'm not jealous. I just thought you had better taste."

"Hey, I like *you*, don't I?"

"Good point," I agree.

"I didn't want Josh in high school. This is all newer to me. I didn't make that up. I mean, were there likely signs earlier that I ignored or didn't understand? Sure. Like how I remember thinking you looked hot in your tux. I didn't think it meant I wanted to fuck you, though. But I can assure you you're what made me ready to take this step, Bren."

I turn his way and grin. "You basically just said you're in love with me."

"I did not say that." He pulls into the parking lot and finds a space.

"Whatever you say, Mister I'm-in-love-with-Brenner."

I get out of the car, and Taylor follows right behind me. "You sound like you wish that was the case." He opens the door to the building for me.

I clutch my stomach and pretend puke. "Ew. Love is gross."

"Can I help you?" a blond man with green eyes asks. He's wearing a suit and has a tape measure around his neck.

"We have an appointment. Brenner Dean and Taylor Falkner."

"Oh yes. Your parents are getting married, right? You're part of the wedding party."

"We are the wedding party," I reply. Our tailor doesn't look impressed with me. "Hey, Taylor and tailor," I tease.

"It's his first time in public," my Taylor jokes.

"Well…yes. Let's get started. Taylor, come with me. My coworker will help you, Brandon."

"Brenner." Other Tailor is a dick.

A woman approaches, and I follow her toward the back where they went. There are a few rooms, and Taylor is in one of them already, while Asshole Tailor waits outside.

"I'm Heidi. Your suit is inside. Go ahead and put it on, and then we'll get started."

I nod and go into the room. Taylor and I could have gone into one together, but I'm pretty sure that's frowned upon. I hurry into all the clothes, then open the door to only see Heidi waiting for me. Asshole Tailor must already be inside.

"One of your parents is getting married, right?" Heidi asks.

"My dad is marrying Taylor's mom."

Heidi makes small talk while telling me how to move and stand, taking measurements and sticking pins in places, but I can't stop focusing on what's going on in the other room. Asshole Tailor is really chatty in there. I can't make out what they're saying, but twice he makes my Taylor laugh, and what the fuck? Asshole Tailor didn't seem that funny to me. I'm also pretty fucking sure Asshole Tailor is queer, and if he thinks he's going to hit on my…whatever it is we are, he has another thing coming.

"Can you lift your arms?" Heidi asks, and I really wish I could tell her no and go to the next booth and see what's so funny. But I do what she says while she pulls things in a really weird way.

More mumbling from the other room.

Taylor laughing.

"Psst!" I say loudly.

Heidi frowns. "Yes?"

"Not you. I was talking to Taylor…not the tailor, my Taylor, I mean."

She chuckles. Thankfully, Heidi's chill, but Taylor doesn't seem to hear me. "Is he your…" she asks.

Well, shit. "Best friend," I finish for her.

"Nice. Bet it's cool that your parents are getting married."

I doubt she would be saying that if she knew we're sleeping with each other. Or that I'm standing here jealous. This situation is messing with my head.

Luckily, no more laughing comes from the booth next door, and a little while later, we're walking out of the store together. "Asshole Tailor wants to fuck you."

Taylor laughs. "What? No way. Wait. You're serious? He's queer?"

"You haven't gotten the homing beacon installed yet?" I tease. Clearly, it's not something every queer person immediately recognizes in another.

He rolls his eyes. "Second time *jealous* has come up

in one day. That's so cute."

"Like you weren't jealous at the party last month."

"I'm not denying it."

We should maybe talk about what that means, but luckily, he doesn't press me to open up and share my feelings right now. It would be hard to share something I don't yet understand. "Good. I'm not either. Oh hey, you know what? I heard there's a new arcade over here. We should go."

"Are you taking me out, Bren?"

"I mean, I figured you would pay, but I'm willing to negotiate."

He reaches out and laces our fingers together. It surprises me for a moment, and Taylor tugs me closer, giving me another of those sweet kisses I never saw the draw of before him. "The arcade sounds fun, and no worries, I get the jealousy. Like I said, I felt the same about you. That must be normal for best friends who are future stepbros and having sex with each other."

I laugh.

Yeah. Normal. I sure as hell hope so.

We detangle our hands and get into the car. Taylor looks up the new arcade, then drives there. This is actually perfect. We haven't done something like this together in a long time.

"You know I'll kick your ass at everything we play, right?" Taylor teases.

"Yes. I'm used to it by now."

"You want me to let you win?"

I gasp. "Hell no."

"Good. Because I wouldn't anyway."

We get to the arcade and find a parking spot. It's loud inside from all the games and people.

"Race you!" As soon as the words are out of my mouth, we start running toward one of the machines for coins like we're twelve years old.

Taylor gets there before me, and I pretend to be annoyed, but of course I'm not. We get a prepaid game card, then head straight for the games. We play old-school fighting games, newer shooter games, and the zombie game Taylor loves. He beats me at everything, like we knew he would, but I hold my own pretty well.

Eventually we end up at the air-hockey table. "Your winning streak is about to end," I say gleefully. If there's one thing I always win at, it's air hockey.

"Maybe." He shrugs. "I can't win everything."

I laugh. "You asshole." Then wrap my arm around him and kiss him, before we each go to our end of the table. Taylor puts the coins in, and the puck pops out on my side. "Well, lookie here," I tease.

"You're gonna need all the good luck you can find."

"That's what you think." I set the puck down, up-nod him and say, "I wanted to sneak into the room with you and Asshole Tailor and blow you."

"What?" he asks just as I shoot the puck, and it goes right into his goal.

"You fucking cheater."

"I play to win, baby." I throw in a cheesy wink for good measure.

"Whoever wins gets to top tonight," Taylor says, making me fumble the paddle. It's the distraction he needs to shoot at my goal and score.

"One–one. I play to win, baby," he throws back at me.

Game. Fucking. On.

19

Taylor

I LOVE TOPPING Brenner. It's probably my favorite thing in the world right now, rivaling that time I was hooked on *Remnant*.

But my head's in a weird place as we continue playing air hockey, both of us fighting for the chance to claim the other's ass. I really want to win, but fuck, I wanna lose too.

Brenner must realize his advantage because as we hit the puck back and forth, he says, "Thinking about how good it's gonna feel when I stomp your ass?"

"We're five–six," I say, "so I just have to land one more and you're finished."

"We both know you don't want to win, though," he says with a distracting smirk as I block my goal and send the puck back to him.

"Trust me, you and Dax have already sold me on the idea."

I've been curious what it'd feel like to bottom for

Brenner…in no small part because of our threesome. The expressions on their faces. The way their eyes rolled back when it felt just right. Evidently, the prostate is a mind-blowing level waiting to be unlocked in me.

"You should have said something sooner," Brenner says, his bangs bobbing against his forehead as he hits the puck back. "I didn't want to push you before you were ready, but of course, I was selfishly enjoying everything I could too."

"I would never want you to deprive yourself of anything you really wanted," I say, blocking him again, then sending the puck back, bouncing it off the side of the wall.

Brenner's sharper than usual—he's not the carefree, no-shits-given guy I'm used to. This is a man who wants my fucking hole.

And for a guy who hadn't really thought about that kind of stuff before, it's hot as sin.

Brenner prevents me from entering his goal, though, and sends his own quick attack back, the puck landing in my goal.

"Fuck," I mutter.

"Tied up. Whoever lands this one wins."

"Don't think I don't notice you're playing better than usual. Someone's really after this hole."

He wipes the back of his hand across his forehead, beading with sweat, evidence of just how badly he wants me.

"You have no idea," he says.

I grin before serving the puck, pushing past the con-flict between the part of me that loves to win and the part of me that desperately wants to explore this new thing with Bren. I want him to get it, but neither of us would be happy with an undeserved victory. Just not in our blood.

As he sends the puck back, he says, "Come on. Let me in. You know you're gonna like it."

"I know I will," I say, sending the puck right back.

"All you have to do is slip up, and we both can have exactly what we want."

I know what he's trying to do—get inside my head, and if anyone has that power, it's him. But two can play that game.

I say, "Don't act like you haven't been thinking about it when we've been messing around. What I'll feel like, as a guy who's never done anything back there."

The puck clicks between us, our reflexes today better than they've ever been in our entire lives.

"Like I've saved it just for you," I go on. "Just beg-ging you to give me more, thinking how no one's ever given me pleasure like that before."

He flinches, and I take my opportunity, ricocheting the puck off the side, but he blocks again and says, "Right before I make my come face while ripping one loose in you."

The image is so vivid—his expression locked up, his body stiff and tense as he fills me up the way I've filled him up so many times—that I'm frozen in place as the puck clicks off the back of my goal.

I'm expecting him to rub the victory in, the way he usually would, but we're just standing on either side of the table, staring at each other.

All that talk we both intended to distract the other with has done so much more, and if he thinks we're going to a gaming machine after this, he's lost his damn mind.

Brenner smirks. "We should probably head back to our place now," he says, echoing my thoughts.

For guys who can usually talk to each other about nothing nonstop, we're sure awfully quiet on the trip back to our place.

Feels like it would have been better if I could have just dropped my pants right after and let Brenner have me on the air-hockey table.

But life's never that fucking convenient, is it?

Brenner says, "I just want you to know, since you lost, I'll be extra gentle."

I laugh because I know that's how he'd be anyway. "Oh, that's thoughtful of you."

"Obviously only until you tell me not to be gentle anymore." He sneaks a glance at me, and I roll my eyes, though the anticipation of what we're about to do is setting off sensations in my chest, swirls of nerves broadcasting to the rest of my body the news of what's about to go down. It intensifies the closer we get to the apartment.

It's not a long trip, but sure feels like it. And we haven't even gotten in the door before he jumps me, shoving me against the wall, his lips locking against mine.

Taking what's his.

All his tonight.

Despite how excited I am, there are some nerves too. But I know Brenner has the experience, that he'll do what he needs to make sure it's comfortable for me.

We're a fumbling mess as we make our way to my bedroom. What would usually take a minute takes about five since neither of us can keep our greedy hands off each other.

When we get into my room, I pry him off me, pushing him back so he sits on my bed.

"Feisty tonight, aren't you?" He rests his palms on the mattress behind him. "But just so you know, if you don't feel up to it, we don't have to do anything."

"A bet's a bet."

His eyes narrow in that sexy way they do sometimes, and he wears a mischievous smirk, clearly reveling in his well-deserved victory.

I step back from him, and he glances me over, like he's trying to make sense of what I'm up to, which I love because it's amazing, given how well we know each other, that I can still surprise him.

I stand in place, waiting, until he asks, "What are you doing?"

"I'm your prize. So this means you get to tell me what you want me to do."

His eyes flare with excitement, and my cheeks warm.

"You should have told me this is how it was going to go down before air hockey. I would have kicked your ass a lot faster."

"Please. I don't think I've ever seen you break a sweat for anything other than my hole."

His smirk expands into a grin. "Well, I'd never lie and say that wasn't the case."

He leans back, studying me like he's thinking real hard about how to take advantage of this moment.

"Okay," he says. "Strip for me."

This is how I know Brenner is the one to share this with.

He's fun, playful.

He pulls me out of my comfort zone, but in the best way, like when we messed around with Dax.

I grab the hem of my shirt, but he raises his hand. "Hold up." He hurries to the nightstand, fetching the lube and returning to the edge of the bed. "Got that out of the way so I can just fuck you once I've got you ready. Proceed."

I can't help chuckling at how serious he's acting about me doing this stupid thing, but I pull my shirt off, and as soon as it's over my head, he says, "Freeze. Right there."

I obey, staying in the strange position as he pushes to his feet and approaches me.

His hands gravitate to my hips before probing around, his gaze taking in my body. "Mmmm," he says. He kneels, and as his hands knead into my flesh, he kisses my abdomen, trailing his way down.

I keep in place, like a statue, and he licks under my navel, stirring a wild sensation within me that pulses back to my ass. Then he pushes back to his feet and takes my shirt the rest of the way off, discarding it behind him.

"Now lose the rest of it."

I start to kick off my shoes, and Brenner says, "No. Make it sexy."

"Sexy?"

"You know what I mean. Make. It. Sexy."

It's not a request. It's an order.

And given that he won the game, I'm committed to doing whatever the fuck he wants. Not really just because he won, but because I know it's more fun when I give in to Brenner.

I finish removing my shoes, slowing down my

movements.

Brenner's eyes are fixed on me, drinking me in as I unfasten my belt, slipping it off. I unbutton my pants and pull them down, exposing my thighs for him, then my shins before stepping out of them, so that now I'm just in boxers and socks.

I turn to face away from him, sliding my boxers down slowly. Bren releases that familiar low growl, and in it, I can feel his desire for me.

Fuck, why does it feel so good to be wanted by him?

It makes me less self-conscious as I lower my boxers, exposing my ass inch by inch, hoping to torture him so that he's stiff as a rock when he takes me.

Reminds me of what we talked about earlier, how I'd never considered this side of myself—not only being attracted to a man, but wanting him inside me, needing him to shoot his load deep in my ass the way I need Brenner to do tonight.

As I keep lowering my boxers, I glance over my shoulder and notice him licking his lips, staring at my ass cheeks.

"Keep going," he presses, and I hear the impatience in his tone.

I obey, and when my boxers are at my thighs, he cups my ass cheeks in his hands, burying his face against them. It stirs something within me, something deep and wild…this animal that just wants to be fucked by him.

Brenner kisses and bites at my ass cheeks, worshipping them with his mouth.

"I'm gonna take such good care of this ass, Taylor. When I'm through with it, you're gonna know why I was the right person to open it up."

"That's what I want," I confess, as though this isn't even me, but just this deep hunger within me that I need him to sate.

He slides his hands up my boxers, curling his fingers into the sides and dragging them the rest of the way down my legs until they're on the floor. He gives my ass cheek another kiss, then a lick, before rising to his feet behind me. He guides me forward, pushing me against the wall beside my mounted big-screen TV, and I feel his thick erection as he slides it between my ass cheeks, rubbing against me. His arms hook under my arms as he pulls close and kisses behind my ear.

Between the nerves he excites and my anticipation, a thrill surges through me, and I roll my head back, enjoying the sensations radiating through me.

"All this time," he whispers, "you've been wondering what it'd feel like to have a man inside you. No. *Me* inside you."

"Yes."

He licks behind my ear as he strokes his cock against me some more, each stroke nagging at something in me that makes my ass feel fucking empty as long as he's not in it.

"Please," I beg. "I need it inside me."

"I need it too. Fuck, I hate myself for leaving this hole untouched all this time. You deserve to know how good it can feel, Taylor. You deserve to know what it feels like when my shaft's shoving up against your prostate; when it feels so good, you can't stand it."

My cock's so fucking hard, and I feel it pulse when he reaches around and grips it. "That got you precoming, didn't it?" He checks before snickering again. "Oh, there it is, Tay. Fuck, if this gets you going, just wait until I'm fucking you."

"Stop teasing me. This is torture."

"How did you think you were gonna survive if you'd won that air-hockey game?"

Really, he must know I would have probably given it to him either way.

He kisses me gently, in that tender way that's become more familiar since we've gotten closer. In a way I know is reserved just for me.

"Keep this sexy ass right here," he says. "This is where I want you. To start, I mean."

As my cheeks warm again, a smile tugs at my lips.

When he pulls away from my body, it's like he leaves me feeling empty inside, my nerves disappointed. I hear him pump some lube, and then he moves up behind me, wet fingers pushing between my ass cheeks, then rubbing against my hole. I close my eyes, appreciating the sensation, my body relaxing at his touch as he slides his fingers inside gently.

He kisses my shoulder, warm breath pushing against my flesh, making the back of my neck prick with sensation. "You ready to take me, Taylor?"

"Fuck me, Bren."

He pumps some more lube, and then I feel his cock push up against my ass.

Damn, he's hard tonight.

And I love knowing it's for me.

Love knowing he's about to satisfy this wild curiosity he's elicited since all this started.

Just as I expected, Brenner is slow and patient. Doesn't rush anything.

I feel the pressure as the head pushes in, the stimulation as he inches into me.

"*Fuuuck*," drags out of my mouth.

"That feel good?"

"You have no idea."

"You don't really either…yet," he assures me, and it's hard to understand what he means when the pressure is hitting just right, but then he pushes farther in and…

"Holy hell."

He chuckles. "Right?" He leans close, wrapping his arms around my torso, whispering in my ear, "Taylor, meet your prostate."

My head rears back, like it's beyond my control as bursts of energy surge through my nerves, making me arch my back, forcing more of him into me. A wave of heat moves through me, mixing with the nerves swirling with excitement. I can barely see straight, like my body is too focused on what he's doing to me to take in my surroundings, so I close my eyes, simply absorbing the pleasure he's giving me as he continues guiding his way into me until I feel his hips press against my ass.

His lips return to my neck, kissing and nibbling, stimulating me with his tongue as his cock hits against that sweet spot, making me feel as though every centimeter of my flesh has come to life.

"You're taking me so well, Taylor. I'm impressed."

He steadily pulls out and then pushes back in, taking me even higher as my body vibrates with pleasure. I moan, making sounds I've never made before, and when I turn back and his gaze meets mine, I see the determination in his expression before he leans forward and takes my mouth.

He keeps fucking me, and even as I call out, his mouth is relentless with kisses.

I can feel how much easier it is for him to thrust now that he's primed me for that cock, his strokes becoming broader and more forceful in a way that feels so fucking good, I can feel my cock getting wet as more and more precum pushes right out of me.

"Fuck, Taylor, you could make me shoot up in you like this. But you wanna see my face as I'm coming for you, right?"

"Yes," I whisper, and he slips out of me and guides me to the bed. I lie back, and he pushes into me. I love that he's looking down at me while he fucks me because I can see the desire in his eyes. How he's fucking wild about having me like this.

Just seeing the hunger in his eyes makes it even more arousing as he fucks me, which explains why so many people have wanted that cock before me.

My body's a fit of sensation as he hooks his arms around my thighs and gives me a good pounding, drilling against that spot.

"Finally getting what all the buzz is about, aren't you?"

"Fuck yeah. Give it to me, Brenner."

He's a fucking machine with my hole in a way only a sex god like him could give me.

He's got me so worked up, my body trembling, pre-cum dripping into my navel.

As I lose myself in the bliss, he grabs my wrists. He pulls them out to my sides and keeps fucking me hard.

"Fuck, Taylor, you keep making that face, and I'm gonna shoot inside you."

His words hit something within me, some psychological prostate that gets me so aroused so fast, I can't help moaning. "Brenner, I don't think I'm gonna last much longer," I warn.

"Give it to me," he says, not letting up his pace, hitting me just right to the point where it feels so intensely good, I wonder if I could die from feeling too good.

"I don't want to come until you come inside me."

"I can go anytime right now. Just say the word."

"The word."

Brenner picks up his pace even more, panting, striking that spot, and I force myself to keep my eyes open to see his face twist up, locking in that familiar way as his body jerks about.

There's something so satisfying about knowing he's emptying inside me, and it allows me to let loose. A burst of pressure releases, and I'm practically screaming as my climax tears through me, warm rushes streaking across my abs.

As we moan together, he glances down at my mess. "Christ, you weren't kidding about being close."

He continues pushing into me, shoving his cum back farther for a few lingering moments before crushing his weight down against me.

He's still got my wrists pinned down, so I say, "Trying to keep me as some kind of sex prisoner?"

"I mean, if you want me to let you go…"

"Don't you dare."

He grins, clearly satisfied with this power he has over me, then takes my bottom lip between his teeth, nibbling gently before pulling back. "Guess that'll teach you to lose to me more often."

"Eh, I think I just tricked you into making me win."

He laughs. "Oh, I think we both won tonight."

Can't say he's wrong there.

20

Brenner

"CAN YOU HAND me that other strand of lights?" Dad asks, the two of us sitting on the roof of Nicole's house. He's always loved decorating for Christmas. Mom loved it too. Our house was the brightest on the block, and now Nicole's house is getting the Dean treatment—Dad's words, not mine.

Even when I was younger, I would help him decorate. Back then, I wasn't climbing the ladders and sitting on the roof, but he always found jobs for me to do, always wanted me to be involved so then we could unveil together whatever light-filled extravagance he came up with.

With his work in construction, Dad is good at these things, and he had me working with my hands for as long as I can remember. I enjoy doing it with him, and while it started out as something we did for Mom, and then for ourselves after she passed, it's cool to be doing it for Nicole and Taylor. We both know that seeing all the colors and decorations will put a smile on their faces. And while I've always enjoyed this time with Dad, this year it feels like a new way of moving forward.

I hand him the strand, help him stretch it out, and we begin stapling them down.

"You doing okay, Bren?" Dad asks as we work.

"Yeah, why wouldn't I be?" But I know what he means, and honestly, I'm feeling some kind of something.

"Christmas has always been an important time of year for us. God, your mom loved it. Do you remember how often she would play holiday music? Every year I would swear I never wanted to hear it again, but by the next year, I was ready to see her smile when she would sing along."

The memory of her blooms in my mind, seeing her smile, hearing her singing. "Remember when you would dance with her in the kitchen?"

"You pretended you hated it."

"I didn't," I admit. Of course, at the time, I thought it was gross seeing how much my parents loved each other, but deep down I knew it wasn't. It made me happy, made me want what they had one day, and when we lost her, made me want to do anything in my power not to care about someone so much.

But you failed at that, didn't you?

"I know." Dad reaches over and places a hand on my

shoulder. "But this…you're okay? Us doing this on Nicole's house? You were feeling some conflicting emotions, and that's valid. I can imagine heading into the holidays, us decorating Nic's house… It's okay if you're having a hard time."

"I know," I tell him, and I do. He's so fucking great. The best dad a guy could ask for—and even more proof that Taylor and I are doing the right thing by waiting to tell them about us until after the wedding. Until we know what this is. But strangely, part of me wants to talk to Dad about him. I've never told him about anyone I was sleeping with before, but those people weren't Taylor. "I'm good. I promise. I can't pretend I don't miss her or that this isn't new territory for us, but I love seeing you happy, and I like doing this for Nicole and Taylor too. They deserve someone good in their lives, and now they have you."

"They have us," Dad amends. "You're pretty awesome."

"The awesomest," I tease, and we laugh.

"You get it from me," Dad tosses back, and we share another chuckle. "Taylor is good with it all too? Nic and I…you're both the most important things, and we worry."

"He's all right. He really just wants his mom happy the way I want you happy."

"Nic and I really are lucky. We have the best sons."

I smirk. "Clearly."

We work in silence for a few minutes before I say, "She's going to love this—Nicole. When she and Tay get home. It'll make her happy. You're doing good, Dad."

"Oh, thank God. I feel like I've been a mess most of the time."

I'm not sure he's a mess at anything. "What, um…what was it like? When you realized you were starting to have feelings for her?"

I have no idea why I'm asking…or maybe I do. Maybe it's because of how much things are changing between me and Taylor and what I'm afraid that means.

"Scary, really. I never imagined loving anyone but your mother. But I noticed small things at first…like thinking about her a lot when she wasn't around. And when she was, I just wanted to look at her all the time. I'd find myself watching her…in the least creepy way possible."

"Stalker," I joke.

"She just…she made me feel good. Everything was better when I was with her. And then one time—"

"If this is a sex story, stop right there."

He rolls his eyes. "It's not a sex story, you weirdo. But one day, we were at the house, and she was looking at a photo of your mom…and she asked me to tell her about Gil. I never really talked about her except with you, but I wanted to share her with Nic.

"We sat on the couch for hours, talking about her. I pulled out photo albums and told her stories about your mom and you, and she listened and asked questions. You could tell there was no jealousy or discomfort hearing me talk about someone I used to be in love with. It was evident she knew what I'd felt for your mom, and that it didn't mean I didn't care about her. I don't know how I would feel hearing the person I'm in a relationship with talk about someone else who clearly had a place in their heart, but Nic understood. She wanted to know about your mom because she was a part of me, and I think that's when I realized I was in love with her."

I nod, looking down at the work we're doing, unsure what to say. That was really cool of Nicole, but I'm not surprised. That's how she is. Taylor is kind like that too. The situation is different, but how many times has he listened to me talk about my mom? How many times has he gotten me to share things with him I wouldn't typically share with anyone else? And when I do, I always feel better, even though I assume the worst in the beginning. I can chalk that up to our friendship, but as I sit here, on the roof of his mom's house, hanging her Christmas lights and thinking about the past few months with him, about all the laughter and games and cuddling, the homework sessions and how he pushes his thigh against mine to steady me when I'm bouncing around…about how fucking incredible it is now that he lets me inside him and I know I'm the only man who's ever been there…maybe it's time I acknowledge that it's about more than just our friendship, amazing sex, and a silly crush.

"Why do you ask? Have you met someone?" Dad's voice is soft, questioning.

Have I met someone? Years ago. I just didn't see all the possibilities open to us…and now I'm falling…fallen? Hell, I don't even know. What I do know is he's the son of the woman my father is about to marry, and I can't spring that on Dad now.

"Ew. Gross." I act like a kid, while also not lying to him. I didn't say no, and though I do have feelings, they are kinda gross.

Dad laughs. "You will one day, and there's nothing like it, kiddo. You won't think it's so gross then."

"You clearly don't understand my maturity level…or lack thereof."

Dad nudges me with his arm. "Come on. Let's get this finished. We're going to make the whole neighborhood jealous," he says playfully.

Yes, yes we are.

It takes us a few more hours to get everything done. Taylor and Nicole are out for the day, shopping and spending time together. They pull up just as we're finished getting everything cleaned up.

She parks her car in the driveway, the two of them

getting out.

"Oh my God! It looks great!" Nicole exclaims.

"Wait until it gets dark." Dad pumps his brows, then wraps his arms around her. They hug, him whispering something in her ear, and I can't stop my gaze from shooting to Taylor.

He gives me a small smile in return, then steps closer to me, throwing his arm around me in a way that will look playful to our parents but that I really need right now.

"Get a room, you two," he jokes.

Dad pulls back from Nicole. "Did you guys have fun?" he asks Taylor.

"Yeah. It was nice. We brought dinner," Taylor tells him, then squeezes my arm before going back to the car to grab the takeout.

The four of us go inside and eat the chicken and potatoes they brought, laughing and talking, and when we're done eating, it's dark outside, so we go out to look at the house. It's gorgeous, with tons of lights and yard decorations. A light-up snow globe and outdoor Christmas trees.

I feel the heat of Taylor's arm against mine, the way his fingertips brush my hand, caressing and sweet.

"It's incredible," he says.

"I did it all myself," I say, making everyone laugh.

We stand there for a while, in awe of it, before Taylor and I head back to Peachtree Springs. We have a week left of school before break, and both of us are working through our time off, but we will come home for Christmas Day.

"You okay?" Taylor asks as we're driving back.

"Yep. Still reveling in my kickass light-decorating skills."

He reaches over and rests a hand on my thigh. "I know how much your mom loved Christmas, Bren. It's okay if you want to talk about her."

And just like what Nicole did for my dad, Taylor is giving me understanding and love about my mom. It means more to me than I could ever say.

We spend the whole drive home talking about her and all her wild Christmas adventures. It's exactly what I need…and maybe he is too.

21

Taylor

As my eyes flit open, Brenner's curled up against my chest, his arm locked around my waist. I relax, enjoying his body heat, a sharp contrast to the apartment, which is cold as fuck.

There've been a lot of mornings when either I've woken up with Brenner on me, or I've been curled up against him. One of the perks of seeing each other.

It was nice spending the holidays with him. Not like we haven't hung out over Christmas and New Year's in the past, but this time it's been as more than friends. Even though we had to be discreet around our parents, the little grazes and glances meant everything to me.

And that light shit he and Keith put together for us…damn, as if I needed a reason to like these guys more than I already do.

As I gaze down at Brenner clinging tight to me, his head is tilted just enough for me to get a glimpse of that pretty mug. I always knew he was attractive. I love my charming, playful Brenner, but there's something vulnerable about him now, without the walls he puts up.

The walls I understand because I have mine too, even if they're for different reasons.

He shifts before planting a kiss just under my pec.

I'm wondering if he's even awake yet or if kissing me gently has become so instinctual, his body's going through the motions.

Whatever it was, it sends a wave of goose bumps pricking across my flesh.

I embrace the sensation before he stirs and glances up at me. As if he didn't look hot enough without the help of those hypnotic brown eyes.

He groans.

"Morning," I say.

He shakes his head, clinging tighter. "Let's stay in bed today."

I chuckle. "We can't. We're helping Atlas today."

Last week, our friend asked if we'd swing by with some of the guys from Alpha Theta Mu to help with the winter social he's managing through a local nonprofit. Atlas does a lot of volunteer work, something he kept hidden from us, his best friends, for years. But after he and Troy got together, he became more open about this side of himself, even letting us know whenever he needs help.

"Oh," Brenner says. "That today?"

"You know damn well it is. We talked about it before we went to bed."

"Yeah, I'm just tired. Baby wore this ass out last night."

"You topped last night."

"Still exercises those glutes with all that thrusting, and I feel like I have to fuck ten times harder than you to make up for all that time you missed out on."

My hole twitches at the thought of how we've made up for lost time the past few weeks.

"At least we have a little more time to cuddle," he says, and it's like he summoned my alarm because it goes off on the nightstand, and we share a groan.

No time for cuddles after all.

We drag our asses out of bed, eat some cereal, then get ready. When we arrive at the middle school where the event is being held, I see Atlas and the Alpha Theta Mu guys hanging out by the gymnasium. While we wait for someone to unlock the gym, Atlas recaps the event.

It's a social through Activate Kindness, serving kids with special needs. As Atlas is explaining everything we need to get done before eleven, when the event starts, I can't help thinking again about how in all the time we've known him, he hid this side of himself. Didn't want anyone to see that big-ass fucking heart of his. Although, I always knew it was there.

I figure because of the Piece of Shit, I have this radar

that picks up on who's a real asshole and who isn't, and the moment I met Atlas, despite all the walls he put up, I knew he was a good guy.

Once a custodian arrives and unlocks the door, we head inside, taking on responsibilities in groups. Lance, Ash, Marty, and I set up the DJ booth, while the others tackle decorations and the refreshment table.

"Technically, we shouldn't have taken any of this equipment from the house," Marty says as he pulls a speaker off a cart he brought.

"As the president of Alpha Theta Mu," Lance says, "I order you to shut the hell up."

"You're a president, not a dictator," Marty tells him.

"Ash, you think I could convince the other guys to exile him from the house?"

"Don't even joke about that," Marty says. "Last time you joked, you wound up president."

"Yeah, so I wouldn't fuck with me if I were you," Lance teases, and Ash and I can't help but laugh.

As Lance sets up his laptop on the table, he practically sings, "So how are the lovebirds?"

I'm waiting for Ash to respond when I notice all three are looking at me.

"Huh?"

Ash winces.

"How is that directed at me? You're in a relationship too."

"We see *those* lovebirds all the time," Lance says.

"Too much," Marty jokes.

"Can you stop calling us lovebirds?" I ask. "That's weird."

"Do you want him to use the B-word instead?" Ash raises a brow. "Are we there?"

The B-word.

Boyfriend.

Even though Ash didn't say it, a warm sensation stirs in my chest.

I glance over to Brenner, who's putting streamers up with Troy. As he catches my gaze, he makes an overdramatic move like he's about to tumble off the ladder, making me laugh.

"What the fuck was that?" Lance asks, pulling my attention back to them.

"Um…nothing."

"Is it time for the B-word?" Ash presses, seemingly serious this time.

"It's not a curse word," Lance tells him, then to me, "Are you guys boyfriends?"

I quickly shut it down. "No, no, no, no. And if I find out anyone is conspiring to do some kind of weird-ass boyfriendposal for us, I'm gonna lose my shit."

Last year, Alpha Theta Mu had a whole event for Ash and Colin becoming boyfriends, including a party in the living room. Brenner and I were invited, and fun as it was, fuck if I'd ever want all that attention on us, even if we were getting together.

Ash laughs. "Don't worry. We'll wait until you're actually boyfriends before we throw you a boyfriend-posal."

"Yeah," Lance says, "that's like Boyfriendposal 101 shit."

I roll my eyes. "I'm adding that to the list of reasons why I'm glad I never joined a frat."

"You're a little late," Lance says. "You and Brenner are basically Alpha Theta Mus by association."

"Yeah," Ash says. "We adopted you like Frat Cat."

"I'm just giving you hell, man," Lance assures me with a laugh. "I'll reword it to get less shit: how is whatever-the-hell-you're-doing-with-Brenner?"

"That's great," I say. "Not much to report. We're the same guys we were before. We just do other stuff now."

Wake up in each other's arms most days.

Share gentle kisses before heading off to work or school.

Get more excited than ever before to see each other again.

The more I think about it…lots of boyfriend shit.

"I really miss a relationship," Lance says as he starts connecting USB plugs into his laptop. "It's nice having someone to wake up next to. Someone to watch a movie with at night. Someone to go on dates with. And I mean, morning BJs are always nice."

"Yes, they are," Ash and I say nearly at the same time before glancing at each other and smiling.

"No need to boast, assholes," Marty says.

"If I'm being honest, Lance," I say, "when you were originally coming with us on that cruise and were gonna stay in the same room as Brenner, I was a little worried you guys might be doing stuff like that. Kind of jealous, actually, since I know he thinks you're hot."

"Brenner was into me?" Lance asks.

"Oh my God," Ash says. "How could anyone miss that?"

Lance shrugs. "Went over my head."

"Straight guys," Ash says, shaking his head.

Lance stares off, like he's considering what that might mean, which seems strange for a straight guy. Makes me wonder if there might've been more of a chance of that happening than I'd considered.

And though I know there's no threat there, that jealousy I felt before resurfaces. "Okay, Lance, no need to think about it now."

"Oooh," Marty says, "someone's real defensive about their non-boyfriend."

And something about putting *non* before boyfriend really grates on my nerves.

Feels like I'm broken.

I push through it, finish setting up the DJ stand with

the guys before parents and kids start arriving. Lance starts up the music, and the rest of us help out with touching up the decorations.

Once we finish up, Atlas encourages us to engage in the party, get the ball rolling. Brenner was basically born to be a hype man for something like this, and he, Troy, and Atlas take the lead. Doesn't take long for things to get going, and we're able to let loose and have some fun too, alongside clusters of parents and kids dancing and enjoying the music together.

We're maybe half an hour into the event when Atlas asks me if I can grab some extra utensils from his car. En route back to the gymnasium, I'm about to head inside when I hear—

"Come on, Sadie. Just give it a try."

"No, Mom. I want to go home."

I pass the door and step around the corner of the gym, where I find the arguing duo—a blonde girl about fourteen or fifteen in a tee with a graphic that looks like Charli XCX riding a unicorn, and next to the girl, a woman I assume is her mother. The girl is holding an iPad.

A part of me thinks I should stay out of this, that it's none of my business. But another part encourages me to approach. "Hey, how's it going?"

Sadie turns to me and points to her ear, suggesting she can't hear me. But I just heard her talking to her mom.

She must see the confusion in my expression because she says, "I can't hear you. I'm deaf. I use this…" She turns her iPad toward me. The words I just said are on the screen. Must be a speech-to-text app. "And I read lips, which isn't easy, so enunciate and don't talk too fast."

"Oh, okay. That's cool."

"But we're actually about to go."

"Sorry," her mom says. "She's in a mood right now." Her mom gets her attention, signing as she says, "Sadie, you came here to meet people." Her mom turns to me, still signing. "We just moved here a few months ago, and she had to leave all her friends behind in New York. It's been an adjustment. She's been kind of lonely…"

"Mom, stop," Sadie says. "I want to meet people my age. Those are all kids in there. Or this guy who works here."

"Volunteering," I say, "but fair enough."

Again, I consider why I approached. It's her life, but something keeps me in place.

"Well, there are older people here too," I say. "I could be your friend."

She's glaring at the iPad before she directs it at me. "You're a volunteer, so you have to say that."

"Actually, because I'm a volunteer, I can just walk away or go home, or do anything else other than this, so

I'm standing here because I want to."

Her expression relaxes.

"I mean, me and my friends are older than a lot of the people in there," I say, "but we're all having a good time."

"Yeah, I don't just want to meet people. I want to date."

"Well, some hot guy could be coming later—"

"Because you just assume I'm straight?"

"Oh, I—"

"I'm queer as hell. I'm a lesbian."

"I'm sorry she's being like this," her mom says.

"It's fine. I'm queer too. And, Sadie, I think you could have fun if you go in. I'm actually more of an introvert myself, and it's not as easy for me to meet new people. But my best friend ever is outgoing and can chat up anybody, and he's basically shown me that you can meet pretty cool people anywhere if you're open to it."

She looks at her iPad, frowns, and shows her mom the screen. Her mom smiles before signing to her, and they both burst into a laugh. I'm guessing the app made some error transcribing what I said.

Sadie studies my face for a few moments, then says, "You seem like a cool guy, but I'd rather spend the day at home."

Yeah, maybe I shouldn't have approached. I'm about to head back into the gym, when an idea springs to mind. "How about I make you a deal: you come in and have the best time you can with my friends and the guests, and if a girl around your age comes in, I'll introduce you. You could at least make a new friend that way."

She reads the text, her eyes narrowing. I'm sure she's gonna refuse, but she says, "I'll give it a try. But you gotta dance with me and Mom so we don't look like losers on our own. And I'll blame you if it sucks."

She starts toward the gym, and I tell her mom, "Well, she's definitely gonna be a handful for any girl she does date," just as Sadie opens the door and turns to us.

"I saw that!" Sadie says. "And I told you I can lip-read too."

"I know. I waited until you were looking to say it."

She and her mom get a kick out of that as I lead them inside, noticing Brenner at the door, his eyes wide. Clearly, he heard at least part of our conversation.

Sadie leads her mom to the dance floor as Brenner walks alongside me. "I was coming to see if I could get a quick make-out session. Wasn't expecting to see that side of Taylor."

"Is this your boyfriend?" Sadie asks him.

Jesus Christ, what's with the B-word today?

I'm waiting for Brenner to correct her, and when he doesn't, I figure I should, but by then, Sadie's already dancing with her mom.

22

Brenner

"How'd that happen?" I ask Taylor. "Sadie?"

"Is there more than one random girl you were talking with tonight?"

"Look who brought jokes," he teases, and for some reason, I can't stop myself from pulling him close. Taylor comes easily, my arms around his shoulders while he faces me. "I heard them talk. She didn't want to come in, and…" He shrugs. "I guess I understood her because I was the type who was standing on the sidelines when I was her age too—though probably not as sassily," he jokes, and I laugh.

"So Taylor to the rescue?"

"I wouldn't go that far."

I grin. "I would."

"Are you flirting with me?"

"Are you just noticing?" I reply playfully, and Taylor smiles, then leans in and kisses me. "It was cute, seeing you with her. That was a nice thing you did."

"Kinda like how you befriended me when I was quiet and kept to myself?"

I roll my eyes. "You're giving me too much credit. I just thought you were a cute boy I could play video games with. I didn't anticipate that meant signing up to losing to you for the rest of my life."

"You win once in a while." He smirks.

My heart is beating stupid-fast for some annoying reason. Hearing how Taylor was with Sadie has me all shmoopy, which is totally not my jam. But then, everything with Taylor seems to have me feeling that way lately.

"If you'd said you *let me* win every once in a while, we would be having our first fight as…whatever we are." *And by the way, Taylor, if you could tell me what this is, that would be fucking awesome.* Sadie asking if he was my boyfriend made my stomach feel like a butterfly habitat throwing a party in there.

If this happened with anyone else, I would talk to Taylor about it, but now it's Taylor who has me feeling this way. And I know I can talk to him, I *will* talk to him, but talking is always a whole lot easier when he prods me along.

"I know you better than that. Even if it was true, I wouldn't tell you…"

"Wait…so how do I know if you're letting me win or

not? I will kick your ass if you do that, Taylor Martin Falkner."

"That's not my middle name."

"That's beside the point," I reply, and he laughs, then drops his forehead against mine.

Tell me. Tell me what this is. Tell me you're feeling more too.

Or I could just ask him. Look at me. That's growth. Yay. "So…about what—"

"Taylor! Can you come help me for a minute?" Marty asks, and Jesus, why is it always him? There is a good chance one of us might murder him one day.

"Hold that thought. I'll be right back."

I nod as Taylor slips away with Marty, who basically just ruined my life. Or, you know, maybe not, but still.

"How come you're not dancing?" Colin asks me. Why couldn't Marty have asked for his help instead of Taylor's?

"I don't know," I reply, but he's right. That's my kind of thing.

"You look confused."

"Um…thanks?" I'm not sure how else I'm supposed to respond to that, but Colin just laughs.

"I used to be confused too."

"No offense, buddy, but I think you still are." What the hell is he getting at?

"That's what you think, but you'll see." He pats my

shoulder in a way that says, *aw, poor Brenner,* before slipping away, I assume to find his boyfriend.

As I push away from the wall to go do…who knows what, I see Taylor heading toward me, only to be intercepted by Sadie.

She takes his wrist and drags him to the dance floor. Her mom is smiling but looks pretty tired. Taylor turns my direction, a look on his face that says, *help!* but also, it's clear he wouldn't deny this kid because he's seen a kindred spirit in her. Taylor does everything in his power not to let people down.

Unless he's had a drink or two in him, Taylor isn't much of a dancer, which is proven by how awkwardly Sober Taylor is moving to the fast beat of the song Lance is playing from the DJ table.

His gaze finds mine again, and even from a distance, I'm pretty sure he's blushing, while trying to dance because a girl he doesn't know asked it of him.

And there go the butterflies again.

All it takes is one quirk of his finger and I'm heading his way, while also laughing, because I wouldn't be me if I didn't laugh at him.

"Nice moves, Tay."

"Shut up and dance with me."

"Guys, you have to look my direction when you speak," Sadie tells us.

Shit. I'll have to be better about that. It strikes me

then that that might be why they're so close to the speaker. Sadie is using the vibrations to dance. That also explains the iPad she's carrying.

I glance up to see her mom lingering close, and the knowing look tells me she sees I'm putting it all together in my head.

I make sure to face Sadie as I say, "He's a terrible dancer!" He's not, really, but it's fine to give him shit.

"Let's see *your* moves," she replies, and I can tell she'll be a force to be reckoned with when she's older.

No way I'm not taking my moment to shine, though, so I start dancing. I take Taylor's hands, trying to get him to move with me.

"I'm not dancing with you. You just said I'm terrible. You didn't think that at Crave."

No, no I didn't. But I ignore that. With my hands on his hips, I say, "Loosen up. Pretend…" I throw a glance at Sadie and switch direction. "Just don't be so stiff."

He laughs, and there's not a doubt in my mind that he knows I was going to make a joke about fucking.

Sadie is in her own world. It's clear she loves dancing, and as unsure as she was about coming inside, she's living it up now, throwing her arms up in this carefree way that is contagious. When I let go of Taylor, Sadie grabs his hands, twisting the two of them and getting him to move faster, to get into what we're doing. She does a circle around him, Taylor spinning to follow, but she ducks under his arm and he drops his head back and laughs, just getting lost in the moment while I can't help but get lost in him.

We stay out there for a good twenty minutes, dancing and laughing until my stomach hurts.

When I take Taylor's hand again and lift it, Sadie winks at me, walks under our arms like a bridge, and then just…keeps going.

"Where is she heading?" I ask.

Sadie turns around and tosses a playful grin our direction, then signs something to her mom, who waves at us and follows her.

Taylor shrugs. He doesn't let go, doesn't pull away, so I don't either. We keep dancing, our bodies moving in unison.

But then Lance cuts in and announces, "We're going to slow it down for a few minutes," and Taylor and I just stand there like a couple of idiots.

"You want to dance with me, Bren?" Taylor asks, and okay, why do I have goose bumps from such a simple question?

"Since you asked so nicely." I pull him closer, and we squeeze each other tightly, no space between us as we sway to the music.

"We should have tried this at prom," Taylor says close to my ear.

"Our dates might have been a little upset. I don't think they would've been as understanding as the teenage matchmaker who just left us."

We chuckle, Taylor's chest vibrating against mine. I inhale his scent, a heady mix of cologne and sweat, and damned if I don't immediately feel drunk off it.

A picture of my parents dancing together in the kitchen fills my head, making my hand fist in Taylor's shirt.

"You tensed up," he says.

"Just thinking," I reply, then shake my head. It wasn't that long ago I was going to just ask him what's going on with us, see if he's feeling more too, but then Marty happened, and now I'm dancing all close to him and stalling. "My parents used to dance a lot like this. Dad and I were talking about it the other day."

He pulls back a little so he can look at me. "Yeah? Then I'm glad I asked you."

And somehow, it's the most perfect thing in the world he could have said and prompts me to open my mouth and blurt out, "What are we?"

"What do you mean?"

"I mean, *what are we*? Are we still just best friends and future stepbrothers who have sex? Because lately—and it's okay if you don't feel the same—but lately, I feel like we're…"

"More," we say in unison, and share a laugh.

Taylor says, "I wanted to say yes when Sadie asked if we're boyfriends. The guys mentioned it earlier, and it just felt right."

"Oh fuck yes. I was freaking out. Now that I know that the first time I want to be boyfriends with someone isn't going to turn into me being rejected, I can breathe."

Taylor's brows pull together. "You thought I would reject you?"

"Well, not if you have good taste."

"I have the best taste."

"Just so I know I'm getting this right, we're talking about me, correct?"

Taylor smiles. "Yes, you idiot."

"I can't believe you just asked me to be your boyfriend while calling me an idiot," I tease.

"Pretty sure you're the one who asked me."

"I think we asked each other." I let my hands travel up and down his back, savoring the feel of him. "Our parents…"

"We'll tell them after the wedding. It's in a little over a month. They'll understand, right? They have to."

"They have to," I agree, though my stomach is in knots. Our concerns are still the same. Our parents are happy and in love, and we don't want to do anything to mess that up…but we deserve to be happy too. "I'm scared," I admit softly—and only because this is Taylor and I can tell him anything.

"That they won't understand?"

"Yeah, that too, but also…"

My words hang in the air, but I don't have to finish them. Taylor squeezes me tighter, and I know he knows what I mean. "I'm not going anywhere, Bren."

"You can't promise that. My mom didn't expect to die so soon, but she did, and it broke my dad."

"I'm sorry. I can't imagine how much that must've hurt both of you. I don't know how I'd even make it if anything happened to Mom. And you know I'd never want you to do something that scared you, but if something did happen to either of us, I'd rather know I took advantage of every moment I got to have with you while I could."

I nod, knowing he's right. I won't walk away from this because of fear. I want every moment I can have with him. I don't want to waste any of them.

"So…we're boyfriends now?" The title makes my heart feel like the stupid thing could float away. And I like it. Too much. So of course I have to act like it's no big deal. "This will be fun."

"Be my boyfriend," Taylor says. "Dare you."

"Goddamn it! Why didn't I think to say that?"

"Guess you're not as good as me."

"You have your moments," I reply, feeling happier than I ever have. Now we just have to keep our relationship a secret until after the wedding, and hope all this doesn't blow up in our faces.

23

Taylor

WHEN THE SOCIAL wraps up, we help the guys pack up, and it's a little after eight by the time we're heading back to our place.

But this time, something's different.

This time, we're boyfriends.

Brenner Dean is my boyfriend.

And I'm his boyfriend.

That's fucking wild.

It's the best feeling, and even better seeing how excited he seemed about it throughout the rest of the social.

On the way to our place, Brenner says, "Glad some girls Sadie's age ended up showing."

"I am too. Although, she was having plenty of fun before they got there, which I was happy about. Not sure she'll go on any of these dates she was bound and determined to get, but if one of them clicks, I imagine her mom will be driving them out to the nearest Applebee's for a nice Friday evening get-together."

Bren laughs. "That's the tragedy of trying to date when you're that young. Needing your parents to drop you off on dates."

"You think when we tell our parents, we're not going to have to go on dates with them?"

He cringes. "Fuck. Don't spoil all the sexiness of today."

I laugh. "Just being realistic."

"Well, stop."

"Or you'll do what?"

"Give you another dance lesson."

"Asshole."

Bren rests his hand on my thigh. "Is that what you're gonna give me tonight?"

"Is that what you want tonight? Some ass?" I sneak a glance as he considers it.

"I'm trying to decide if I want to fuck my boyfriend or get fucked by my boyfriend. What does my boyfriend want?"

Between him touching my leg and saying the word, my cheeks flush with heat as desire pulses through me.

"Yeah, that's right," he goes on as he slides his hand toward my crotch. "I know what my *boyfriend* likes when I say it."

There it is again, and he's emphasizing it in a way that's really getting me going. Brenner and this word shouldn't have this kind of power over me, but it's so hot, I don't really give a fuck.

"Oh, you like that *a lot*." He grips the stiff erection crimping in my jeans.

Fortunately, we're around the corner from our place.

He offers another stroke before pulling his hand away, and it's fucking torture.

"You can just enjoy that feeling until we get in the bedroom."

I gulp and focus on the road. Feels like an eternity before we get through the main gate of the complex. And as I slide into my parking space, something primal and determined rises within me.

Brenner sports this cocky grin as we get out of the car, clearly loving the way he got me all wound up.

"Maybe we should watch a movie first?" he says as we head through the breezeway and up the stairwell. I shake my head, but he doesn't let up. "We could order pizza and finish it before the movie."

I roll my eyes. "How about we bake some brownies? What's that? Another thirty minutes?"

"Not a bad idea," he says, and I search around before spinning toward him. I don't even know what's come over me, but before I know it, I have him pinned against the wall by our neighbor's door, my lips smashing against his as I rub this crimping erection against him.

As I pull away, he gasps, and I whisper, "Kissing you now shouldn't feel any different than all the other times we've kissed."

"No, it shouldn't," he says before my mouth is back on his again.

I don't know what it is—the way he got me all worked up, or because we're not just fucking around. That he's my boyfriend.

Brenner Dean is all mine.

I pry my lips from his, searching around the breeze-way. "Obviously not gonna fuck you out here."

He shrugs. "Wouldn't be the worst thing we could do."

"No, we're not doing that," I say through my teeth. I take his hand and scramble for my keys. When I get him inside, we hurry into my room, and I push him against the wall beside the door, locking lips.

"Someone's awfully feisty tonight."

"Someone made me feisty." I nibble at his bottom lip, tugging before pulling away, our gazes locked.

"Yeah, so what are you gonna do about it?"

I move quickly for another kiss, and we make out as we clumsily make our way to the bed. I strip down, then remove his shirt and pants, so he's just in his briefs. I hurry to the nightstand to get lube, which Brenner eyes with a strange expression on his face.

"What is it?" I ask.

"Just had the wildest thought. You remember before I came out to Dad, when we had sleepovers in my room?"

I nod.

"Those nights when we were sleeping in the same bed, never even messed around once."

"We weren't attracted to each other back then," I remind him.

"I mean, not like I *never* thought about it."

"Perv."

"You know it," he says. "We'd sit on the edge of the bed, playing video games with the volume as low as we could so Dad wouldn't think we were staying up all night."

"I remember." I could never forget all the fun we had.

"It's just wild to think about all those nights we spent together, and that if someone had told me this is where we'd wind up, I woulda told them they were full of shit."

"Same."

I reflect on those days when we were just friends having a good time. Laughing a lot. Wanting to hang out as much as possible.

But tonight I want him more than I've ever wanted him before.

I want everything he'll give me, but this time as my boyfriend.

"Have you decided what you want from me to-night?" I tease, and his gaze narrows.

"Working on it. Here, get in."

He scoots over to make room for me. I slide in beside him, and he moves close, draping his leg and arm over me. His hand gravitates right to my ass.

"That what you want?" I ask.

"Feeling it out." He gives it a firm squeeze and growls, poking at that fire he's stirred in me. Then he leans back and slides his hand around to the front, grabbing my shaft and giving a few gentle strokes. "Hard to decide when my boyfriend has the best cock and ass I've ever had."

I roll my eyes. "We both know that's not true."

His forehead creases. "Are you kidding me right now? You think you could dick me down into a relationship if that wasn't true?"

"I think you like me for more reasons than my ass and my dick."

He shrugs. "Well, two things can be true at the same time. I can like you for those things *and* because you're an awesome guy." He winks, practically glowing after delivering the compliment.

"Someone's really nailing this boyfriend thing."

"I know, right? I haven't even done this shit, and I'm already winning."

As I laugh, I notice a shift in Brenner's expression, the broad smile fading quickly as something familiar takes over. Something that reminds me of moments when we were hanging out as kids, something I could see even back then.

"What is it?" I ask.

He starts to say something but stops himself. "Nothing."

I angle my head, glaring. "It's clearly not nothing, Bren. Out with it."

His gaze wanders.

We talked about his mom earlier, so I get why that would flare up from even recalling a time closer to when he lost her. And I just want to be here for him through it.

I wait patiently for him to share before he says, "I was thinking about what it was really like when you would come over, especially if you'd just had to spend time with the Piece of Shit."

Oh…

A ball of tension constricts in my chest as his words bring back the reality of those nights—both of us struggling with our shit, using video games and jokes to escape the pain.

"Yeah," I say, reflecting on the bottled-up rage I'd still have in me on those nights.

And now that he's brought it up, it really feels like we're back in his bedroom, and I'm carrying the bullshit from having spent the day with my father.

"I remember being so glad when he would let me

have sleepovers at your place," I say. "Like God forbid I spend any more time with Mom, but that was like my sanctuary. *You* were my sanctuary, Bren."

"You were mine too. Even before we started discussing it, it was nice being around someone who had his own problems to deal with. It somehow made what I had to carry feel a little more manageable."

"I know what you mean." I reach up to him, stroking my knuckles along his cheek. "I don't know how I would have survived all that if you hadn't been there."

"I don't know that I would have even wanted to survive it if you hadn't been there."

I roll toward him and prop myself on my elbow.

"Even before all this," he says, "feels like it's always been just you and me against this fucked-up world."

As his gaze locks with mine, I see all the vulnerability Brenner normally hides from everyone else behind his charm and playfulness. The part of him that's just a kid still crying for his mom. The part of him he's scared as fuck is gonna get hurt again.

"It has always been you and me," I say as I lean into him, taking a kiss.

I grab the back of his head, drawing him closer as I slide my tongue into his mouth, then guide him onto his back, straddling his leg as he hooks his arms around me.

"Taylor," he whispers as he pulls away from another kiss. "I know what I want."

24

Brenner

I STILL CAN'T believe how much has changed in the last few months. Our parents are getting married. We'll be a family together. And now us—being together, being his. I've never wanted to be anyone's before, but I want that with Taylor. Want to feel…possessed by him, connected to him, just another way to show that we belong to each other.

"What, Bren? Tell me. I'll give you anything."

I smirk. *"Anything?"*

Taylor brushes his lips against mine so fucking sweetly. It's wild to me that he can be so fucking hot, so sexy, but it's also entwined with a sweetness I've never wanted from anyone else before.

"I want everything," I say.

"Me too," he replies, the fire in his eyes telling me he knows exactly what I'm saying. It's not the first time we've flip-fucked, but I always love it when we do, when we both get a shot at each other's asses, while also losing ourselves in being fucked. "I'm gonna take you first. Gonna fuck you so good, and then I want to come with this cock deep inside me." He wraps his hand around my straining erection, stroking it through my cotton underwear.

"I think that can be arranged." I smile against his lips, then chuckle when Taylor rips my briefs off like he's dying to feel me beneath him. Reaching back, I grab the lube from the nightstand and toss it to the mattress beside us.

He's on his hands and knees, looming over me, his face a mixture of concentration and hunger. "It's so hot seeing my boyfriend naked beneath me."

"Your boyfriend that's waiting for you to claim his ass."

"My boyfriend who has never been very good at being patient." Taylor leans down and flicks his tongue over one of my nipples. I arch my body toward him, while he bites and sucks at my pec, one of his hands traveling south and finding a home around my cock. He strokes, my precum making the slide easier.

I wrap my arm around him, tug him closer, hand tangled in his hair. We've done a lot of fucking over the last few months, but this already feels different. There's an added intensity to being with your boyfriend that's a high I never expected.

"Fuck yes, Tay. Tug on it with your teeth a little," I

tell him when he switches from one pec to the other.

He does as I say, making fireworks go off in my bloodstream while I wrap a hand around his swollen shaft and stroke him too.

"You're hungry for my cock."

"I mean, I'm not going to complain," I joke, and he gives me a smile that I feel in my chest.

Taylor grabs the lube, pumping some into his hand before he falls to the bed beside me, pulls me so I turn to face him and hitches my leg over his thigh. Our mouths pull together with a force too strong to deny, while his hand sneaks around my body, fingers slipping into my crease before he's pushing the tip of one inside me.

A whole-body shudder rocks through me at the simple feel of being penetrated by a single digit. I bite at his lip, starving for him. Taylor hisses in reply, but all it does is make him kiss me harder, work a second finger inside me.

My cock aches, everything on me throbbing. I pinch at his nipples, let one of my hands slide down his back and cup his ass, finger dancing up and down his crease and wishing like hell I had self-lubing fingers.

I laugh into the kiss, which makes Taylor pull back slightly. "Something funny?"

"Just wishing I could squirt lube into your ass with my fingertips."

"Or you could always grab the bottle of lube."

"Then I'd have to let go of your ass."

He shakes his head. "You're an idiot."

"A sexy idiot you're about to fuck."

Taylor growls in response, and I have to say, as much as I love all Taylors, this sex god Taylor is one of my favorites.

He rolls me onto my back, fingers still inside me, then kisses his way down my chest. Just as his mouth wraps around my cock, sucking me deep, he pushes three fingers into me. I thrust forward, fucking into his mouth and making him gag.

"Shit. Sorry. Felt good," I say breathlessly, but Taylor responds by taking me deep again, swallowing around my dick while he fucks me with his fingers and nearly makes my whole world come apart.

"Damn it. I'm gonna come. If you don't stop, I'm gonna fucking shoot."

That's all the encouragement he needs. Taylor pulls back, immediately making me feel empty without him. He pumps lube into his hand, slicking up his cock. "No coming. You can't come until you're inside me, Bren. You have to be good while I fuck you, and then we'll come together when you're inside me."

My dick twitches in response, and I really hope my stamina doesn't fail me.

"Get on your back. I want to ride you," I tell him.

Taylor lies on his back, and I straddle him, holding

the base of his cock and slowly lowering myself on top of him. He's so fucking big, and this angle always takes me a minute to adjust to the pressure and the fullness of Taylor's dick stretching me out.

"That's it. Take me. Take your boyfriend inside you."

I tremble. "Can you stop being so fucking sexy?"

Taylor laughs, but then sucks in a deep breath when I lower myself on him completely. "Oh fuck. You feel so good."

"You fucking love my ass, don't you, love how I take you in, how I squeeze your cock." My dick bobs while I move on him, Taylor's hands on my hips, fingers digging in. "You can't even speak, can you? Too lost in your boyfriend's ass." Turnabout is fair play. He made it hard for me not to come; I can do the same to him.

"My ass," Taylor says, and my dick twitches again.

"Stop being so good at this." I push down on him again. Taylor strokes his hands up and down my torso. His eyes roll back, muscles tight, and I can see how good this feels, see that he's closer to his nut than he wants me to believe.

"Fuck...*fuck*," Taylor says, and I pull off him, my body complaining just as much as his is when he arches for me, reaching out to try and grab me.

I slick my fingers with lube, then slam my mouth down on his while I push two fingers inside him.

Taylor's teeth dig into my lip the way I'd done to him just a little while ago, and it makes tendrils of pleasure twist and turn inside me.

I work him open as quickly as possible, feasting on his mouth, only pulling back to tell him how good his ass feels and that I can't wait to come inside him.

"Do it. Fuck me, Bren. I want your cock so much."

I swear I'm nearly blind with lust as I pull back, slick up my dick, then roll him so he's slightly on his stomach and side. Taylor bends one leg upward, and I straddle the bottom leg, using my hand to spread his ass cheeks, then push inside his tight, pink hole.

"God yes," he says, just before I rail into him with hard, fast, deep thrusts. He's so damn hot inside, his ass squeezing my cock just right.

Taylor turns his head and looks up at me, this person who has been such an integral part of my life for so long and who's now *more*. All the moments we've shared, every game and dance and night out, every talk and joke and laugh have been leading to this moment.

I pull out of him, and Taylor rolls onto his back. I push his legs up, then slam into him again.

"Jerk your cock, Tay. I want you to come all over that pretty chest of yours while I fill your ass with my load."

"Do it. I'm so close. Come in me. I want it."

The room around us disappears as I lose myself to

the pleasure. My orgasm hits me, cock twitching inside him, balls emptying in spurt after spurt into Taylor's eager body.

He tenses beneath me, muscles straining as the first jet of his release hits his chest, then again and again, his ass tightening around me, squeezing all I have to give.

"Holy fuck. That was the hottest moment of my life," spills from my lips. I'm on the verge of collapsing beside him, but instead I lean down, licking his abs clean of all his cum. "Don't want this to go to waste."

Taylor threads his fingers through my hair. "That's it. Lick it all up, Bren."

I do as we both want, then lie down beside him, turning his head toward me and kissing him, letting Taylor taste himself on my tongue.

"Being boyfriends is the best," he says, and I nuzzle his neck and smile into it.

"We should have done this a long time ago."

"For sure…but you know, we decided to wait to get into a relationship until right before our parents get married."

We share a laugh because…how can we not? It's wild that we had all this time together and didn't start dating until now. "Yeah, but if we'd have done that, our parents might not have gotten together."

"Good point." He draws circles on my skin with the tip of his finger. "I can't believe it's almost time for the wedding."

"Same. It'll be interesting." To say the least. "Not much longer, and we'll be watching our parents say I do. And then we'll tell them we're boyfriends." Totally my new favorite word.

Taylor doesn't reply right away, and I ask, "Are you okay?"

"Yeah. Perfect."

"Me too."

<h1 style="text-align:center">25</h1>

<h1 style="text-align:center">Taylor</h1>

T HE NEXT FEW weeks, aside from work, school, and get-togethers with our parents, Brenner and I are inseparable.

If anyone had asked me before last summer if I thought we could be any closer, I wouldn't have believed that was possible.

But I would have been wrong.

So fucking wrong.

I never really considered that a stupid word could change so much, but *boyfriend* is more than a word. Knowing Brenner's mine and I'm his makes me feel like everything's right in the world.

When the weekend of the wedding finally arrives, Brenner and I check into the hotel on the lake, abutting the venue property.

"The whole stepbrother crew is here," Troy says as he helps me decorate the arbor by the dock near the lake.

My mom and Troy's mom know each other through

our friendship with Atlas. They became close after Troy's mom divorced Atlas's asshole dad, something Mom could help her navigate, considering her own past with the Piece of Shit. Ash and Colin are here too. Their parents have gotten close with ours since Atlas's pool party the summer before last.

"We should start a club," Troy adds.

I glance around. Mom and Keith are busy running around, dealing with one drama or another, so I'm not worried about them overhearing. But there's a lot of mutual friends of our parents and family here, some of whom relish gossip, so I want to make sure no one's in earshot.

Fortunately, it's just us.

"Don't worry," Troy says. "I'm good at keeping secrets. Not gonna out you and your stepbro."

"My *almost* stepbro."

"For like a day. You must be so relieved to finally get through this so you can be open."

"You have no idea."

"I get it. It changes things. I'm so proud of being the guy Atlas wants to be with, and I want everyone to know, especially the people most important to me."

"It's been hard keeping it from my mom. It's for the best, but before I met Brenner, she was the one I confided in, especially about important shit. It's weird having to keep this bottled in. Like, if they came out with a special edition of *Remnant*, I'd want to tell her all about it because I'd be so excited." As Troy pulls a face, I say, "Shit. That doesn't sound very romantic."

"Trust me, coming from you, that sounds strangely sweet."

I blush. "Brenner gets me thinking about a lot of strangely sweet things."

"You don't have to tell the guy who has his boyfriend's name tattooed on him," he says, displaying the *Atlas* inscribed across his wrist.

It's not really my thing or Brenner's, but the fact that he can display it so prominently and proudly for everyone to see is something I envy right now.

Troy says, "Good luck keeping your hands off him for the next twenty-four hours. I think we both know, the more you have to keep from touching each other, the more tempting it becomes."

The only saving grace is that there's so much wedding prep, I haven't had to encounter him too much. Although, that's also one of the things that's annoying me.

After Troy and I finish up with the arbor, I join Atlas and Brenner, setting up tables where we'll have the rehearsal dinner tonight and reception dinner tomorrow. Mila sets up at the bar nearby. I'm glad Brenner asked her to come along. On top of being really cool, she's done way more than even some of my family to help get everything set up for Mom and Keith's big day. It means a lot to me.

Once I finish up with the guys, I tackle a few more tasks before heading into the guesthouse for the rehearsal. I hurry upstairs to the bridal suite, where Mom's been sorting things out with her *bridesmates*—a term she found more fitting since she wanted to include one of her guy besties. But when I head in, I'm surprised to find her on her own.

"Where your friends at?"

She's standing by the closet where she's hung her wedding dress. "Jane attempted an at-home perm yesterday. Thought it'd go great with the dress. Spoiler alert: it doesn't, and she's freaking out. So Todd and Beth are trying to figure out what to do with it. I asked if they could manage it here because I don't need any more stress right now. So I'm admiring my dress to remind myself of the fun bits before I get back to work."

With how much there's been to do since we arrived at the venue, I imagine she could use a breather. Unfortunately for her, I have a few things I need to get out of the way: "Sherrie has questions about the guestbook, and the catering's running thirty minutes late, which shouldn't be an issue. Oh, and Dakota's really excited to be your flower girl. She wanted me to tell you that. I would jump up and down as much as she did when she said it, but I think you get the idea."

Mom laughs. "That's sweet." But I can tell she's still tense, so I take her hand.

"Breathe, Mom. And keep admiring that dress because you're gonna have to get used to wearing it to make it worth how much it cost."

Her gaze narrows. "It didn't cost that much. And I stayed within the budget you drew up."

"Still a lot for a bunch of fabric."

"But it's such pretty fabric." She strokes it, her gaze settling on the dress as she runs her fingers along the train. Even though she's looking at the dress, I can tell her mind is elsewhere. Maybe appreciating the life she'll share with Keith.

"I'm just teasing, Mom. Tomorrow is your big day. And you get to have a fancy dress to celebrate finding such a great guy."

For the first time since I entered the room, she takes a deep breath, her shoulders relaxing as she takes my hand. "Thank you, Taylor."

"It's kind of my job to make sure you're chill for the big day."

She chuckles. "I didn't mean for relaxing me. Thank you for that too, but I meant being so cool about Keith. Even though we were trying to protect you and Brenner in case things didn't work out, it was more than that. I was nervous too. Given what a terrible experience you had with your..."

"Piece of Shit."

"I'm not calling him that," she says, though her smile suggests she wishes she could.

"Why not? Not like the courts can come in and use it against us anymore."

Her expression shifts to concern. "It shouldn't have been like that. I should have left him sooner. Maybe if I had…" I can hear the regret I know she carried all through my youth.

"Mom, you're not responsible for what that asshole did to our family. He made his choices, and given how much he'd beaten on your self-esteem by the time you left, I'm honestly shocked you were able to. Today, I see this strong, confident woman who can do anything she sets her mind to. That's not the woman I knew when I was a kid. She was always walking on eggshells and trying to say the right thing."

She bites her lip. "You know I wasn't like that when I met Chris? He was charming and kind and warm. I thought I'd found the one. Looking back, it's easy to see little signs. Things I thought of as teasing or him being playful. Chipping away little by little, and once I had you, it really started to come out. This other side of him that was just…nasty. It wasn't directed toward you, so I think I told myself that as long as he was good to you, it was fine."

"Sure, I remember plenty of times where Dad was

nice or kind to me, but when he was unkind to you in front of me, that wasn't kind to me either."

"I see that now. Wish I could have seen it back then. That it hadn't had to be after losing Aria that I woke up. And it wasn't even me. It was when you snapped at him, and I saw that you, this kid, knew what he was saying was wrong. I saw Chris through your eyes, and that's what did the trick. You know you saved me, right?"

In a moment, I recall the most I've ever seen her struggle. The pain. The sadness. And those vicious words from his mouth that made me finally let him know I'd had enough.

"Hey, Mom. You're not the only person who's gotten with the wrong guy. And you got out. You got me out."

Her eyes water. "But I didn't."

If only it were so easy, but life never is. There was the difficult custody battle, and I had to stay with him for too many years before I was free.

"You didn't do that to me," I assure her. "He and the courts did."

"Doesn't make it any better."

Now I'm tearing up thinking about how fucking painful that time was, how many years I went just wishing that the Piece of Shit would leave us the hell alone.

"No, it doesn't make it better," I tell her. "But all we

can do is keep moving forward. You're getting married tomorrow. To an amazing guy who will treat you the way you deserve to be treated."

Tears burst free from Mom's eyes, and she raises her hand to her face.

"That was supposed to cheer you up," I say, running back through what I said to see where I fucked it up.

"Oh, Taylor." She fans her face. "These are happy tears." She sniffles as she pulls her hand away from her face. "I just never thought I could feel like this again. After Chris, I accepted that I'd never get to have the happily ever after I imagined. And I thought that was fine. I had you and made friends, and I didn't think it could get better until Keith came along and changed everything."

There's a sparkle in her eyes. I catch glimpses of it when I see her with him, the sort that maybe can't make up for all the pain, but at least makes it all somehow worth it.

Reminds me of what I have.

When I'm with Bren.

"I know the feeling," I say.

This catches her attention, and she tilts her head. "What?"

Fuck.

"I meant, I understand what you mean."

She winces, like she's not quite sure she buys it. How

could she? She knows me too well for that.

I open my mouth, like some part of me just wants to spit it out: *Brenner does that for me, and I want you to know he makes me as happy as Keith makes you happy.* I'd love to share this with her, but it's not just my news to share. And this definitely isn't the time. So I press my lips back together. I must stifle it for a little while longer.

There's a knock at the door, saving my ass.

"Come in," Mom says, and Brenner pokes his head in.

"Sherrie is really stressed about the guestbook," he says.

Mom and I burst into a laugh. Really, of all our concerns, that has to be at the bottom of the list.

"Okay," Mom says, "we both have enough to do before the rehearsal starts. So let's get to it." She squeezes my hand. "Just know, Taylor, you were the one who saved me. And I'm glad you're the one giving me away to Keith."

When Mom discussed it with Grandpa, even he said, *"I wasn't even considering it'd be anyone other than Taylor."*

I get the answers to Sherrie's questions, and Mom promises to text Jane to make sure she doesn't come back with anything dramatic like self-cut bangs. I give her another hug, then head out with Brenner.

We're not far down the hall before he grabs my wrist

and pulls me through a door. In no time, he's pushing up against me, his lips against mine.

"Fuck," I moan as he pulls away, those dark eyes set on me as he licks his lips. "Been missing that all day."

"You and me both."

"And if I didn't think your cousin Sherrie would lose her mind, I'd jerk you off right here."

Bren grabs at my crotch. "I'm already making you hard," he says as he feels along my stiffening cock.

"You can't tease me like this."

"We get through today, and I somehow survive being Dad's best man, I'll do whatever the hell you want tonight when we get back to the room. Now shut up and make out with me for a few more minutes so I can deal with the rest of my family for the next few hours."

We enjoy a quick make-out before prying away from each other and resuming our tasks.

Brenner helps with decorations while I deliver the word to Sherrie about the guestbook. Then we keep busy until it's time for the rehearsal.

The wedding planner explains the order of everything, and we do a walk-through of the ceremony. He shows me how to walk Mom down the aisle, and when the rest of the groomsmen and bridesmates join us, it's apparent Todd and Beth's efforts haven't done much for Jane's perm. Unless the nest on her head is somehow better than what it was before.

Shortly after, Sherrie heads down the aisle with Dakota, and despite her earlier enthusiasm, our five-year-old flower girl looks a little shaky, but she manages to reach Mom and Keith before bursting into tears.

"Oh, baby," Mom says as she, Keith, and Sherrie hurry to comfort her.

When Dakota's sobbing subsides, Mom and Keith exchange a look, Mom's lips twisting into a smile, the sunlight sparkling in her eyes like they did when we were discussing Keith earlier.

Keith's grinning too, like even with this little hiccup, he knows he's the luckiest man in the world to be here with my mom.

And fuck, now I'm tearing up, and this isn't even the actual wedding.

I turn and catch Brenner's gaze, and it's clear by the glint in his eye that he caught the moment too. It's nice sharing this with him, both of us getting to see just how right our parents are for each other.

It's the sort of thing that reminds me, as much bullshit as a person can go through, even when things seem bleak, you never know what life has in store for you.

Just like I sure as hell didn't know what it had in store for me and Bren.

THE FOLLOWING MORNING, I wake with Brenner in my arms.

After the rehearsal dinner, we hurried back to our room, and Brenner gave me a generous blowjob before jerking off on my abs. It was the most we could muster after running around all day.

Now I'm happy to have him in my arms, clinging to me.

"Don't wake me up," he whispers.

I laugh. "You're clearly already awake."

He buries his face in my chest. "Uh-uh," he says like a kid.

"Come on. It's a good day. It's the day we officially become stepbrothers."

He peeks up at me. "Mmm. That's more what I'm interested in. Now you're really stuck with me." He offers a quick kiss. "But seriously, I need a few more minutes of sleep."

"That's fine. You mind if I run down and grab some breakfast? I'm starving."

He releases me, and I slip out of bed, hurrying into my sweats, tee, and Crocs. "Want me to bring you anything?"

"Nah. If you do, I can't pretend I have to eat to delay having to do shit through breakfast."

I chuckle and grab my key card. "Sounds good."

As I start for the door, Brenner says, "Hey, your

phone! It's on the nightstand."

I roll my eyes. "Bren, I'm just heading downstairs to grab a few muffins and coffee, and I can do without another fake crisis from Sherrie for like five minutes."

He laughs. "Fair enough."

I head out the door, and by the time I reach the first floor, I'm starting to feel a little more energy, even pre-coffee, which is promising. As I start through the lobby, a familiar face catches my attention, and I freeze in place.

A man stands at the front desk, chatting with the receptionist, who throws her head back, laughing at something he said. And as a smile plays across his lips, goose bumps prick across my flesh.

Because it's not just any man.

It's the Piece of Shit.

26

Brenner

I MUST'VE CRASHED hard for a little while after Taylor left because I feel groggy as hell when I open my eyes. I'm surprised our parents let us sleep in, but since they're having an afternoon wedding, we have some time. I'm also super glad they haven't seen that the second bed in Taylor's and my room is untouched. I can't imagine not having him in my bed every fucking night for the rest of my life, which should be a total mindfuck, but it's not. It's my favorite thing ever.

Damn it. Now I can't go back to sleep. Groaning, I roll over and see Taylor's phone on the nightstand. I stumble out of bed and look at the time. Hmm. He said he'd be five minutes, but I'm pretty sure it's been more like twenty. I assumed he'd go to the buffet, but maybe he got snagged by family or someone in the wedding party and is eating with them.

I take a quick piss, wash my hands, brush my teeth, and get dressed, before grabbing both our phones and heading down to find my man.

When I get to the restaurant, I scan the tables to find him. The hotel and venue are both oversized cabins, with a lot of dark-brown logs and a rustic feel that's perfect for Dad and Nicole.

I spot my dad first, at a table with Nicole, both sets of grandparents, and my uncle and his wife.

"Good morning, sleepyhead," Dad says with a wide grin. I swear I've never seen him happier than he is right now, and that fills me with more joy than I know what to do with.

"I can't help it. I worked my fingers to the bone yesterday." Everyone at the table laughs, but I keep looking around for Taylor. Where the fuck is he? "You two kids ready to tie the knot?" I tease.

Dad takes Nicole's hand and kisses it. "I can't wait."

"Me neither."

"Damn, Dad…smooth. You got moves." I wink, but my chest feels tight, and I can't put my finger on why. It has nothing to do with Dad and Nicole. There's not a doubt in my mind that if it's possible, my mom is looking down at us right now and is so damn happy for him.

"He gets it from me," my grandpa says, and we share another round of laughter, while my gaze roams the room, searching for Taylor.

"We have a few hours before we all need to get ready,

right?" I ask, though I know the answer.

"Yep." Dad tells me what time we're meeting in the groom's suite, where we'll all be getting ready together.

"Have you guys seen Tay?" I nervously wring my hands together, the tightness inside me growing. I'm likely overreacting. Maybe I missed Taylor and he went up in another elevator, or maybe he's with the guys, or went for a walk, or a million other possibilities.

"No, I haven't. Did you text him?" Nicole asks.

"He left his phone in the room." She cocks her head slightly, and before worry can set in, I say, "I'm sure he's with the guys since my lazy ass didn't want to get out of bed with him this morning."

I feel Dad's gaze on me, and it takes me a moment to realize what I said. If I try to cover it, it will just look worse, so I play it off like it's nothing. "I'll go wrangle him up."

"Okay. Tell him to text me," Nicole says, and I let out a relieved breath that she doesn't sound worried. If she's not worried, I shouldn't be either.

"Will do." I slip away before they can ask me anything else.

I wait until I'm out of view and heading toward the elevators before I call Atlas.

"This better be good, Brenner." His voice is groggy with sleep, which makes my hope sink.

"Is Taylor with you?"

"No…is he supposed to be?"

"What's wrong?" I hear Troy ask and figure he's in bed beside Atlas…which is where Taylor and I should be.

"Nothing's wrong. I'm sure he's fine. He just went to breakfast and never came back. He left his phone in the room. And he's not in the restaurant, and our parents haven't seen him."

"You probably missed him and he's back in your room," Atlas assures me.

"Yeah, you're right. I'm heading there now."

"I'll have Troy message Colin to check with him too." Atlas is trying to help, and I appreciate it, but the fact that he's asking around also makes me more concerned. Maybe I'm not freaking out for no reason.

"Thanks, man. I'm getting into the elevator and might lose my signal. Hit me back if he's there."

I end the call, my hands shaking, my heart beating too fast. Logically, I know I'm jumping the gun here, that I don't need to be this worried, but I can't help it. What if something happened to him? What if I lose him like we lost Mom?

I pace the elevator, grateful it's empty and wishing I had a fidget spinner or something to keep my restless hands busy. As soon as the doors open on our floor, I rush out, jogging down the hallway to our room. The red light flashes when I slide the card over the lock.

"Fuck." I do it again, and when I see green, I push the door open. "Tay?" But I know I won't get a response. The room looks just like it did when I left, and I don't feel him in here, don't smell that Taylor scent or sense him the way I do.

My phone rings, and I fumble it, dropping the stupid thing to the floor. Atlas's name shows up on the screen, so I quickly bend to pick it up. "He with them?"

"No. He's not in the room?"

"Fuck. No. I…"

"Hey. He's fine, Bren. He probably went for a walk around the lake. He's good. I promise. We're on our way, and then we'll go find him, and he'll tell you you were being an idiot for worrying."

I want nothing more than for him to tell me I'm being an idiot for worrying. "I'll meet you guys out front," is all I can manage to say.

I scribble a quick note, telling him to keep his ass in the room and call me if he comes back, then hurry downstairs. On the way, I shoot Mila a text to see if she's seen him, but sometimes she's terrible about checking her phone.

Blood rushes through my heart, making it feel like it's going to break a hole in my chest. I push open the doors to go outside, the whole time hoping I don't see our parents. Nicole is expecting Taylor to message her. It's their wedding day. The last thing I want is for them to worry. *Please don't let them have a reason to worry.*

My gaze snags on Atlas, Troy, Colin, and Ash, and I nearly stumble as I hurry to them. "No one has seen or heard from him yet?" I hear the panic in my voice, not having the strength to hide it.

"No, I haven't seen him all morning," Colin says.

"Me neither," Ash confirms.

I run a hand through my hair, tug on the strands until I feel a burn in my scalp. I'm losing my fucking shit, and I don't know how to stop it.

"What about Mila? Has she seen him?" Troy asks.

"I texted her, but she hasn't messaged back." I tug my phone out and call her, but it goes straight to voice mail. "She might've gone for a jog."

"Then Taylor's probably with her," Colin tries to soothe me.

"When the fuck have you ever known Taylor to go for a jog?" I snap, then immediately get buried in guilt. "Shit. I'm sorry. I'm freaking the fuck out."

"No worries. We get it." Atlas squeezes my shoulder. "He's fine, Bren. It's a big day. I'm sure he just needs some time to himself. Come on. We'll go find him. You come with me," he says, and sends Troy a look.

"I'll go with Colin and Ash," Troy confirms, and we go separate directions.

There's the lake, docks, numerous gazebos, and trails all around the property. There are a million places he can be, all of them making a lot more sense than something bad happening to him, but I can't help remembering my mom just getting a cold, and then going into the hospital and dying.

"You good?" Atlas asks.

"No," I answer honestly. "I just…need him." I've never needed anyone or anything, not for a long time, and not the way I do with him.

"And you have him. You've always had him. From the second I met you both, I knew it was only a matter of time before you ended up together."

"Yeah?" I ask, trying to focus on what Atlas is saying while we make our way around the lake.

"For sure. And this is coming from a guy who didn't think anything positive about relationships until I fell in love with Troy…but I knew you and Taylor would be good for each other."

We are good for each other. The best. And I think I've always known it too. "Tell me again that he's going to be okay, Atlas."

My friend puts his arm around me, the guy with a heart of gold, even if he rarely shows it. "He's going to be okay."

As we hurry on our way, I hope like hell he's right.

We make it as far as we can around the lake before heading for the trails. Each second that goes by, my pulse slams faster, my worry intensifying. If the others found him, they would message us. I haven't heard from Mila either, and all I can do is hope they're together.

There's not much time left before I have to tell our folks I can't find him, that Taylor is missing on their wedding day. How can I break Nicole's heart like that? How can the universe be breaking mine too?

We're heading toward the trees when Mila jogs down one of the trails toward us.

And she's alone.

She smiles when she sees me, but then a concerned look washes over her face. "What's wrong?"

"Have you seen Taylor? He left our room for breakfast this morning and no one has seen him since."

"I saw him earlier with an older guy, maybe in his forties…they were walking out of the hotel. He didn't see me, though, and I didn't speak to him. Things looked intense. I figured it was a wedding issue."

An older guy? My heart drops. Who in the hell would he be with? "What did he look like?"

"Um…tall. Clean cut. Short, sandy hair. Similar to Taylor's hair, so I thought he might be related…an uncle or something."

My heart stops. The Piece of Shit. Taylor is with the Piece of Shit. "I gotta go," I say, then run back for the hotel. I hear Atlas and Mila behind me but don't stop, can't, not until I get to Dad.

The whole time, I tell myself he won't hurt Taylor.

He never had in the past, but why is he here? Why is Taylor with him? And just because he didn't physically hurt Taylor in the past doesn't mean he won't now.

My head is pounding, my chest hurting from the cool weather and running as I hurry into the elevator, hitting the button over and over as if that will make it move faster.

As soon as I get to Dad and Nicole's room, I'm banging on the door, feel like I'm outside my body, like none of this is real.

The door pulls open.

"Bren? Is everything okay?"

"I can't find Taylor." I shove into the room, and it takes me a moment to realize our friends are right behind me, that along the way Colin, Ash, and Troy showed up and must have been in one of the other elevators. "We were in bed, and he said he was going for breakfast. I wasn't ready to get up, so I stayed and fell back asleep. I haven't been able to find him since. We looked everywhere. Mila said she saw him with a man this morning, and…and it sounds like Chris." My hands fist. "Fuck! This is all my fault. Why didn't I go with him?"

"Chris?" Nicole asks, voice shaking with panic.

My gaze meets hers. "I'm so sorry. I fucked up. I should have taken care of him." I turn to my father, his body a blob through my tears. "Dad. Please…we have to find him. I can't handle it if anything happens to him. I love him."

I love him so fucking much, I ache with it. I can't imagine my life without him. I think I've always loved Taylor, and I always will.

I swipe at my tears.

"Bren?" he says, clearly feeling stuck between me and Nicole, both of us losing it.

"I'm sorry. I know the timing is terrible. We were going to wait until after the wedding to say anything, but…" I step closer to Nicole. "I'm sorry," I say again. "I didn't mean to mess anything up."

"Oh, Brenner. You have nothing to apologize for, do you hear me? Nothing at all. You have always been so good to my son. You're the best friend he's ever had. He's thought the sun rises and sets with you every day since the moment he met you." She holds my face in her hands, the same way my mom used to do. "It'll be okay, do you hear me? We're going to find Taylor, and everything is going to be okay."

It doesn't matter how many times I've heard that today, I don't know how to believe it, but still I say, "Okay."

When she pulls away, Dad wraps an arm around her and leans in, kissing her forehead. I see all the emotion behind it, the *thank-you* because of how she's being with me, the *I'm sorry* and *it'll be okay* for Tay, and the *I love you too.*

"Do you have his phone number?" Dad asks Nicole.

"Not anymore," she replies.

"Okay, you call the police. I don't know if they can do anything. Taylor's an adult, and he hasn't been gone long, but let's see what they say. Can you stay here in case the police come and so someone is here when Taylor gets back?" he asks, and I love that he's not telling her what to do, but asking her since Taylor is her son.

"Yes. I…"

"I know," Dad says. "We're going to find him. I promise."

"I'll stay with Nicole," Mila says.

God, she's fucking great.

"Perfect. Now let's go get Taylor," Dad tells us, and somehow, I know he'll make sure everything will be okay.

27

Taylor

"I T'S GOOD SEEING you again," the Piece of Shit says.

Things have been a blur since I saw him in the hotel lobby.

I vaguely recall grabbing him and dragging his spinner luggage out into the parking lot, insisting he take me to his car. Once we reached it, I directed him to take me on a drive. *"I'll tell you when to stop,"* I told him, like I was taking him hostage.

"Taylor, I just wanted to see your mom on the big day."

"I'm only here to support her. You know I love you both."

"I saw the invitation on Instagram and thought it would be a pleasant surprise."

Once he made it through some bullshit story about how this all came about, he kept trying to get me to talk, but I've been too determined to get him as far away from the venue to pay attention to much of it. Only thing I know is I'll let him fuck this day up for Mom over my dead body.

At some point, he said, *"Let's grab some breakfast and chat,"* so now we're sitting at a booth in a diner. I'm mostly trying to calm my anger because if I lose it, I don't know what I'll fucking do to this bastard.

I haven't craved vaping since Brenner found new ways of keeping my mouth busy, but damn, I could sure use a hit to take the edge off right about now.

As I'm about to say something, the waitress comes over with the coffee he ordered.

"Do you have oat milk?" he asks.

"I can check."

"No," I say through gritted teeth. "He's fine with this."

The way he eyes me, it reminds me of other times when I was younger and called him out on what he said about Mom, the thing about Aria that finally made me snap. He knows he fucked up by showing here today.

"Yes, I'll be fine with this," he says, echoing my wording.

The waitress has barely turned around before I say, "What the hell are you doing here?"

"I told you—"

"And I don't believe any of that bullshit about coming to patch things up."

He winces. "Does your mother let you talk like

that?"

I glare at him. "You wouldn't know either way."

"That's not by choice, and you know that."

As I find myself able to think straight, I notice the changes in him—more grays, a few more lines along his eyes. Evidence of the time that has passed since I last saw him.

"I just don't know why *this* has to be the choice, Taylor. I care about you and your mother. I've tried to contact you, but you changed your number. You've blocked me on all social media accounts."

Occasionally he's tried to hit me up on socials, and I've promptly blocked him.

"So you do know I don't want to see you, but you came anyway. On the day Mom's getting married, I should add. You don't think I know what you're doing?" I scoff. "You haven't changed a damn bit."

Now I'm cursing intentionally to piss him off, really giving this my full-blown teenage-asshole tantrum, the way I would when I was forced to stay with him.

"You're still trying to do it," I add.

"Do what? Be in your lives?"

"Convince me you're not the monster I know you are."

He cringes. "A monster? You know I'm not that."

"Yes you are. A monster who's terrified of being seen for what he is."

"I can understand how your mother's convinced you of that with all the years she's had to get in your head."

"You may have managed to convince the courts and a few of my family counselors, but you've always known I never bought it. And it just drives you crazy, doesn't it?"

"Taylor, you were too young to understand the dynamic between Nicole and me—"

Heat flares in my chest. "Don't even say her name." Given how chill I normally am, I'm shocked at the hostility in my tone and all this pent-up rage.

He takes a breath, raising his hands in surrender. "There were obviously things happening behind the scenes that you never knew about. And I never would have said anything disparaging about your mother. It wouldn't have been appropriate."

"You tried to convince me she was turning me against you plenty of times. Was that appropriate? Was it appropriate to make that comment about Aria?"

His gaze sinks to the table. "We all make mistakes, and that is one I regret every day. But you're an adult now, and surely you realize you can't define a relationship by one incident."

The fury he stirred mentioning Mom's name intensifies, burning like he fucking ignited something behind my rib cage.

"*One* incident?"

"That is what it's always been about. I remember how you snapped. And I remember how Nicole jumped on the chance to turn you against me."

The heat in my chest spikes so quickly, I can hardly think straight. "What are you talking about? You think I don't remember all the incidents before that? You think I didn't hear the little digs? Telling her she'd made dinner wrong? Or the bad example she was setting for me? Or the way you'd happen to mention how nice some of the women you knew looked because they were taking care of themselves. How she was letting herself go. Calling her stupid. Those were just the things you said in front of me, so I can't even begin to imagine what you were saying when it was just the two of you."

The way he's glancing around the diner, I can tell he's more concerned about people noticing the spectacle I'm making than about the things he said to Mom.

When he refocuses on me, he says, "How is this all coming up just now? Where has this been when you were younger?"

"I didn't have to say anything back then because you knew what it was all about. Just like you know why you really came here. And it has nothing to do with making amends with me or Mom. It's the same game. You want to control her like you did back then. And me."

I hate myself for how I'm tearing up. I wish I didn't have any emotion, wish I could hate him so much that I wouldn't feel or show this, but I can't help what I've pushed down for so long.

"I'm just an object to you," I say. "I was always someone you could use to control her more. It's the only reason you wanted custody. It's the only reason you dragged us through hell to get it."

"I wanted to know my son."

"Then why didn't you try to know him when you won?"

He remains silent, his gaze shifting about like he's trying to come up with an answer.

"You had years to convince me you were a decent guy, but you never did because you knew I saw the real you. And you can sit here playing this same character I saw you play before the judge and to every social worker we dealt with, but I'm not buying it."

He's quiet, once again, like back then, knowing the jig is up. There's no hiding behind the bullshit anymore.

Another burst of rage pulses through me.

This one surprises me, though. Because it's not the anger I'm used to when I think about him for what he did to our family. It's something deeper. Something that stings at a wound I haven't even let myself acknowledge.

"Do you even care?" I ask, my voice softer, and as he opens his mouth to reply, I say, "Don't answer that. But when this conversation is over, I want you to remember that the first words out of your mouth when you saw me were explanations about why you were here. And about how happy you were to see me, but you didn't ask about me or my life. Did you know I'm seeing someone right now?"

He shakes his head. "Obviously, we haven't had time to discuss anything that's going on in your life, but that doesn't mean I don't want to."

"It's a guy too," I spit out, "and I don't even think you'd be queerphobic about it because you had plenty of queer friends, but even if you were, I wouldn't give a fuck. I feel nothing about your opinion of what I do. And you actually know him too. It's Bren. From high school. And he…fuck, he's one of the parts of my life that lets me know that I don't have to live in the hell I did back then. The reason I look forward to waking up in the morning. Because I know I'm gonna get to see him again. And we're gonna laugh, and watch movies, play games, and go hang places and just enjoy our lives together. Because as far as I can tell, that's all life is about. And I feel sorry for you. Because you could have been a part of all that. You could have been around for Thanksgivings and Christmases and birthdays. Mom will get to be a part of our lives because she gives a damn. But you only care about being a part of a family if it means squashing someone else's happiness. Because I guess that's how miserable you are."

He stares at me, clearly in shock, then says, "I didn't

come here to mess anything up for your mother."

There it is again.

"And just like that, you show your hand yet again," I say, which earns a narrowed gaze. "Because after everything I just shared, a dad who gave a fuck wouldn't have jumped in to save his own ass. He would have asked about Bren. He would have been hurt that he couldn't be a part of my life. But you don't care any more than you did back then."

Again, I see that shift in his expression. Like he's been caught.

"You know how much you hurt Mom, but I don't think you realize how much you hurt me. You robbed me of a dad who could have been good to me and her. You robbed me of a dad who I could have jumped on the phone to tell about a project or a test I'd done well on. When I got the job I wanted or even just beat a level on a game. You could've been one of the first people I told about Bren. To tell you how he makes me feel, and how I can't imagine a life without him. And to have that feeling of sharing my happiness with a dad who maybe even would have teared up knowing I found someone who can be as good to me as he was."

The emotions coming up about Bren are surprising even me, but also speak to just how close we've become since we started seeing each other as more than friends.

I battle back tears. I don't want the Piece of Shit to

see me lose it, though I can feel them trying to break loose.

"You weren't there for me as a kid," I force out, "and you sure as hell can't be here for me now."

I sniffle, managing to keep in the tears before finding the anger within me once again, harnessing it to get to what must be done.

"And since I know you better than anyone, I know that even after everything I've said, you're still thinking you could find a way to smooth this over and get me to make nice so you can attend the wedding. I want you to know that if you try to so much as show your face near the hotel, I will tell every single guest what you did to us. Every comment you made to Mom, particularly the one about Aria when Mom was grieving the loss of a child. I didn't talk back when I was a kid because it was clear you and everyone from the courts didn't give a damn about what I had to say, but today, I will not be satisfied until I have convinced each and every person there what a piece of shit you really are. And if you think this is a bluff, I dare you to try me."

I don't think I've ever said so much or been more serious than I am in this moment.

Honestly, it's hard to be sure if it's a bluff or if I just know the Piece of Shit well enough to anticipate his response, because I can see it all over his face now.

I've won.

Finally, after all these years, he's the one who can't say anything to get himself out of this.

"So," I say, catching my breath. "Let me tell you how this is gonna go down…"

28

Brenner

MY CELL RINGS, and I tug it out of my pocket, exhaling a sigh of relief when I see Taylor's name on the screen. He must be back in the room. "It's him," I call out to Dad, with whom I'm making a second trip around the property. My fingers are trembling when I answer the call.

"Are you okay? Did that motherfucker do something to you? I swear to God, I'll kill him if he hurt you."

"He didn't hurt me, Bren. I'm fine. How did you know I was with him?"

"Mila saw you with a man, and when she described him, I knew who he was." Dad rushes over, watching me as I talk to Taylor. "Are you okay?" I ask again.

"Yeah, I just…need you."

My heart stumbles at hearing him say that. I don't want Taylor to ever be hurt, but I want to be the person he knows will always have his back, the one who soothes the aches of the world for him. "I'm coming. We'll be right there." We're already heading back toward the resort. Luckily, it will only take us a couple of minutes to get there. "Your mom. She knows too, and she's worried. Do you want Dad to message her and let her know you're okay?"

"Shit," he replies. "No, I'll do it."

"Okay. See you in a minute." There's a slight sting in my thighs from how fast I'm walking. I know how much everything with the Piece of Shit hurts him, and the last thing I want is for him to have had to deal with that today of all days.

"Is he all right?" Dad asks.

"I think so," I answer as I shoot a group text to everyone else, letting them know Taylor is back. "I just need to see him."

"You're really in love with him, aren't you?" Dad smiles.

"Yes…and it's scary as hell."

"Love is always scary. I was scared when I fell in love with your mom, and felt the same with Nicole, but it's also the best thing that's ever happened to me—both times."

I chuckle, wanting to ask him a million questions, wanting to make sure everything will be okay. But the truth is, he can't promise that. None of us can. We just have to enjoy the time we have when we have it. "Come on. Let's hurry."

I pick up to a jog, Dad right beside me as we hurry back to the hotel. Just as we're getting on the elevator, I get a text from Taylor to meet him in our parents' room. "He's with Nicole," I tell Dad, who hits the button for their floor.

I'm practically bouncing on my toes, unable to stay still, heart racing. I need to see Taylor so bad, need to make sure he's okay.

Dad uses his key card, and as soon as I step in, I see Nicole and Taylor hugging, his mom crying as he tells her it's okay and that he's sorry for scaring her.

"I was worried sick." She pulls away, and Taylor's gaze catches mine.

"I know. I shouldn't have left with him. I just needed to get him out of here. I didn't want to do anything to ruin your day, but it looks like I might have done that anyway. I thought I could get back before you realized I was gone."

"You did *not* ruin my day, Taylor. You didn't do anything wrong. You were just being you…trying to take care of the people you care about."

He sniffs and wipes his eyes with the back of his hands. It's killing me not to go to him, not to take him in my arms, but he deserves this time with his mom. Also, I'm not sure how to react around our parents, and I forgot to tell Taylor they know about us.

"Thanks, Mom."

Nicole takes his hand, and the two of them sit on the edge of the bed. "What happened?" she asks.

"When I went to get breakfast, I saw him. I tried to think of any way I could to get him to leave. We ended up at a diner not far from here, and he started in with his typical lies, making himself seem like the one who was mistreated. And I just…I don't know. Today isn't the day to talk about him. It's supposed to be your and Keith's day."

I shuffle on my feet, trying to keep myself steady.

"Would you like me to leave?" Dad asks. "If you'd like a moment with your mom, I can do that, Taylor, but if you're really just concerned about us, your mother and I agree that you won't ruin this day. You and Brenner are the most important thing to both of us."

My boyfriend's gaze snags on my dad's and doesn't let go. I can see the emotion in his stare, see a story in his eyes I can't read, but I think he's coming to a realization.

"You don't have to go," Taylor tells him, then glances at me. "We're family. And thank you for that. Chris…we were never the most important thing to him."

Dad walks over and kneels in front of Taylor. "That's his loss. I know I'm not your father, and I would never try to be something you don't want me to be, but you *are* family to me. You're the son of the woman I love. You've always been there when Brenner needs you. You've been his best friend, and now you're the man my son is in love with. He couldn't have chosen a better partner, and Nicole couldn't have had a better son. You'll always be important to me, and I'll always be here for you."

I'm caught between wanting to hug my dad for saying exactly what I know Taylor needs to hear and wanting to kill him. Taylor's eyes go wide, shooting back and forth from Dad to Nicole to me.

"Sorry. They know about us. I was losing it a little, and it just came out."

"In love with?" Taylor asks, his thoughts clearly snagging on that part.

"Surprise." I give him a large grin. "Thanks for that, by the way, Dad. I haven't told him yet."

My dad pushes to his feet and joins me again. "Oops. Sorry." He gives an honest bashful look.

"I feel like a million things are going on that I need to address, but first..." Taylor turns to his mom. "You're okay with it? Me and Bren? We didn't mean for it to happen. We were going to tell you, but we didn't want to risk causing problems before the wedding. But I..." His voice goes softer, probably because the first time we're saying or hearing this from each other is in a room with our parents. "I love him too. It took seeing the Piece of Shit again to realize just how much."

My body feels all hyped up, like there is too much pleasure pinging around inside me and I might combust from it. Taylor loves me too. My first and forever boyfriend is my best friend, and we're totally in love with each other.

"Oh, Taylor," Nic says. "Of course I'm okay with it. When you found out about me and Keith, you said you wanted me happy, and that's all I want for you too. Brenner is perfect for you, and honestly, I wonder how I never saw it before, and maybe started wondering about the two of you recently."

He chuckles. "We wonder how we never saw it before either."

"I guess everything happens when it's supposed to." Dad puts an arm around me, just as Nicole pulls Taylor into a hug. She says something quietly in his ear, he nods, and a moment later, she's signaling for us to walk over to them.

And then we're suddenly one huge four-person hug that would be cheesy if I saw it happening to anyone else. But for us, in this moment, it's perfect. We've built a family together, and while it might not be a traditional family, for us, everything is right.

We sit down and spend some time talking. Taylor tells us the rest of what happened with Chris. I feel so much pride in Taylor for standing up for himself, for telling his dad how he feels, for truly seeing his dad for who he is and knowing that he deserves better.

A few minutes later, Dad says, "Why don't you boys

take some time together before we meet in the groom suite to get ready."

"Oh shit. There's a wedding today," spills from my lips. I got so sidetracked, I forgot.

"Yes, there is." Nicole beams at my dad, and he gives her the same look in return.

"Okay." Taylor stands. "Thank you both for today." He gives my dad his attention. "Thanks for everything and for loving my mom the way she deserves."

"Always." Dad hugs him. "And I meant what I said earlier. I know I'm not your father. I don't want to overstep, but I can be that for you, if you ever want."

"I already do," Taylor replies.

Dad gives him a nod, and then I take my boyfriend's hand, lacing our fingers together, and lead him to the door. We're quiet on the way to our room, but the second we're inside, we're in each other's arms. "I was so fucking worried about you."

"I'm sorry. I wish I had my phone on me. I just didn't know what to do. I wanted to protect Mom and Keith's day."

"I know…and I guess we were worried about nothing when it comes to our parents. They definitely seem okay with the fact that you're in love with me," I tease.

"Wait a minute. You're the one who said it first. You told your dad you're in love with me," he plays around right back, and then we pull slightly away so we can look each other in the eye.

"I love you," we say in unison. "Damn it!" we both add, then fall to the bed, laughing together.

"I was going to say it first." I brush his hair off his forehead. "I mean, without my dad telling you for me."

"I think it's kinda cool that we said it at the same time."

And he's right, it is. "That tracks."

Taylor's hand travels down my back to my ass. "I wish I had time to fuck you."

"Tonight. For now, we have to make sure our parents have the best wedding." I press my lips to his, then reluctantly pull away. If I don't, we'll very much end up naked and all over each other.

"Hey, where are you going?" Taylor says when I roll out of the bed.

"To start us a shower."

"Do we have time for a quick BJ?" he asks.

I turn and wink at him. "Only if you're lucky."

29

Taylor

TODAY'S BEEN A whirlwind.

I thought the Piece of Shit would be the biggest shock of the day, but then to come back and discover that not only had Brenner told Mom and Keith about us, but he's in love with me.

That was a lot.

And also…just what I needed.

I do love Brenner, something I felt in my soul as I told the Piece of Shit how important Brenner is to me.

And as if finding out about Brenner's feelings wasn't enough, it touched me how understanding and caring Keith was, being there for me the way a father is supposed to be there for family. Being the sort of dad for me that I never knew.

It was like the Piece of Shit's master plan to mess today up backfired and wound up bringing us all closer together.

The only thing that sucks is that Bren and I barely

have time for a quick blowjob—because apparently, I was lucky—before we rush to get changed into our suits, then get to work to pull this wedding off, since we have to make up for the lost time when everyone was searching for me.

Fortunately, despite the Piece of Shit's attempt to foil Mom and Keith's wedding, the ceremony goes off without a hitch and the reception is a blast.

By that evening, when Brenner and I finally manage to slip away to our room, I'm looking forward to some private time, since the whole day has been about navigating our families and the gossip that came up when they found out who showed up to ruin the big day.

"You look too fucking hot in this damn suit," Brenner says, undoing the buttons of my jacket as our hotel room door closes behind us. "Could barely focus on the vows because this thing was getting me all stiff."

"You think I didn't notice?"

"Please." He grabs at my crotch. "I saw you getting a semi too."

I mean, can't deny that. "I like you in a suit. Aside from the rare dance or school function, the most dressed up you get is your work apron."

"It's true. This isn't really our thing, which is why we need to get out of these clothes like five minutes ago."

We tear at each other's clothes, struggling more than usual because there are so many fucking buttons that we're not used to managing. And suspenders, and what the fuck kind of murder weapon is the buckle on this belt supposed to be?

When I manage to get his shirt pulled off his shoulders, I realize… "Wait, we gotta unbutton the cuffs."

"Jesus Christ, there's more to this thing? Fuck it."

Bren moves forward, taking my mouth, his breath fresh with mint and vodka as his tongue teases mine. I forget about our desperate attempt to get out of our clothes and just enjoy the way he tastes and being close to his body again. It hasn't even been that long since we've messed around, but it feels like for-fucking-ever.

As his mouth travels to my throat, his expert tongue stimulating my nerves, I roll my head back, savoring the sensation.

"Fuck, Bren," I say as his lips trail down my body, along the open placket of my shirt, as he makes his way down my torso in broad, wide, tongue-filled kisses.

When he's on his knees, his face at my crotch, Bren repositions to manage with his shirt. His cuffs are restricting his movements, but he's able to unfasten my fly and pull down my pants with my boxers.

"Let's make up for lost time," he says before taking me into his mouth.

I moan, keeping it down since we have so much family staying in the hotel, and they don't need to hear me calling out their newest relative's name while we're messing around.

Brenner worships my cock with those skills he's perfected over the years, before rising to his feet. He searches behind him before saying, "Where the fuck are these damn buttons?"

While he's looking for them, a burst of inspiration moves through me. I hook my arm around his waist and legs and scoop him off the floor.

"The hell, Tay?"

"I honestly didn't think this through," I admit since I can only take short steps with my pants still around my ankles. But I really play it up, make like I'm carrying a fucking boulder. "I knew you should have only had one slice of cake."

He bursts into a laugh as I lay him on the bed, his hands still bound by his cuffs.

He had his chance to pleasure me, so it's my turn now.

I crawl onto the bed, sucking and licking at his happy trail, moving up with one sweeping lick until I reach his chin, which I nibble at.

"Mmm," he says.

"I kind of like you being all twisted up under me like this," I confess as my dick gets stiffer than usual.

"Now here's something new," he says, desire in his eyes.

I crawl down, unfastening his fly and dragging his

briefs and pants down, exposing his stiff cock. I lick along the shaft, letting my lips graze his flesh.

"Fuck, Taylor," he mutters.

I work his cock the way he's taught me to tease and play with him, until he says, "Get the lube, Tay. I want you to fuck me."

"Don't have to ask me twice," I say, practically leaping off the bed.

But apparently, in my excitement, like a real dummy, I forgot that my pants are still around my ankles, so my move to get off the bed leads to me just rolling right off.

As I hit the ground with a *thud*, Brenner says, "Tay?"

Now I'm laughing my ass off, and as I roll and look up at him, I see the worry in his expression shift into a relieved smile.

"Damn, guess you wanted to fuck me that bad," he jokes. "This ass must be as incredible as I always knew it was."

I kick my shoes off, pull off my pants and boxers, then remove my shirt. Brenner kicks off his shoes and pants and briefs, but I say, "Don't you mess with those cuffs."

I grab the lube from my bag and rejoin him in bed, though I'm still blushing and chuckling from my epic fail.

"It's okay," Bren says as I lie alongside him. "I'll still let you fuck me."

"Out of pity?"

"Eh, I think that's what you do for the guy you're in love with."

My cheeks warm again as I gaze into his eyes.

Like when we agreed to be boyfriends, something's shifted since we shared those words. Something subtle, but I see it in the way he looks at me. There's a confidence in me about what we share, how deep it is.

"I love you, Bren."

His adorable smirk perks up. "We said that already."

"Yeah, but...I really like saying it."

His smirk stretches into a grin. "Well, in that case, I love you."

I feel the truth of his words in my fucking bones, vibrating through my being.

He offers a tender kiss, adding to the sensation.

I roll on top of him, and he fans out his arms as much as the cuffs will permit so I can rest my arms on either side of him. Our cocks stroke alongside each other as we take each other's mouths. When we finally manage to pull away, I gaze into his eyes and say, "You think fucking is any different when you're in love?"

"Only one way to find out."

I lube up, and Brenner lifts his legs so that his ass is on full display for me. I crawl between his legs, lining up my cock with his hole. "You're the one who showed me how to do this."

I see the pride in his smile as I push the head in, and he moans as his body opens up for me, letting me in inch after inch. I lean close, placing my arms at his sides as I manage to get the last of my shaft fully inside him.

"I taught you well, didn't I?" Bren reaches up, clearly having to fight against the fabric binding his wrists as he rests his hand on my cheek.

"I hope you plan on teaching me more."

"I think it's time for the student to become the master. Maybe we learn some things together."

I lean back, grabbing his wrists and guiding them toward the headboard. He shifts to allow the back of the shirt up, and pulls his other arm up, clearly knowing where this is going. I bunch the shirt up so the cuffs are over his head, making sure he's locked in place as I thrust gently. His body vibrates under me as I watch him reveling in the experience.

As I build into a steady pace, I lean down, and he eagerly welcomes my kiss.

Wild to think we went from what felt like exciting but silly blowjobs, when I thought it was just for fun, to having a threesome where he showed me how to work a man's body, to being here with him, feeling physically and emotionally like I'm giving him my all.

The shirt is a fun treat, but after we really get going, I unbutton the cuffs, and we work our way through different positions, Brenner getting his turn to top.

Feels like this isn't just a fuck—this is what it means to make love, to celebrate being in love with each other.

We wind up with me on my knees at the headboard. Brenner pushes in from behind me as sweat drips down my body. It's stunning what we've been able to do, working off what adrenaline remains from the day.

As his cock gets in deep, heat flares in my cheeks.

We share a kiss, my head turned toward him, my mouth refusing to part from his as he speeds up, and before I can even say it, he says, "You're getting close."

Because he knows me that fucking well.

But he's not the only one.

The way he's moving, the fullness of his cock inside me, I can confidently say, "You are too. Do it. Give it to me, Bren."

His thrusts are broad and powerful as he grips my cock and strokes me.

Our rhythm is so in sync. Just right, and I swear I can feel him swell just before his body works through the familiar pattern that assures me he's coming inside me. And it's enough to build that final swell in me before I break free, calling out, surely louder than I should, as he pumps the cum right out of my shaft.

We exhale into each other's mouths before catching our breath.

I chuckle, surprising even myself.

"What?" he asks.

"Who would have thought Quiet Taylor and Chatterbox Brenner would fall for each other?"

"Quiet Taylor? I'd say that was pretty loud. I wouldn't be surprised if there are complaints." He licks at my lips, then nestles his face against mine. I can feel his sweat mixing with mine as he kisses my neck. "You have no idea what you're in for."

"What do you mean?"

Still balls-deep in me, filling me with that cock, he whispers against my flesh, "I am going to love you so good, you're gonna have to always up your game to even get close to what I give you."

I snicker, though I can't deny the emotion that moves through me at the suggestion.

And I can't help myself. "Consider it a dare."

EPILOGUE

Brenner

May

As soon as our caps fly into the air, Taylor pulls me into a hug. We're both jumping up and down, grips tight on each other's gowns, happy as hell because we're both college graduates. Everyone is cheering and shouting, my heart beating like crazy as I pull back and look at my sexy boyfriend, my best friend. "We fucking did it!" I tell him.

"Hell yes!"

The past three months have been fucking awesome. Having a boyfriend is hands down the best thing that's ever happened to me. Scratch that. Having Taylor for my boyfriend is the best thing that's ever happened to me. I have more fun with him than I do with anyone else. He not only always makes me laugh, but he makes me feel *good*, and I'm so lucky to have him.

"Congrats, man!" Atlas says from beside me, and I can see the pride in his eyes. Knowing that on some level, as happy as he is today, that we both have one thing in common—we're wishing our moms could be here to celebrate with us. He was close to his mom too, something I didn't learn until later in our friendship, and she passed away as well.

"Congrats, bro." I pull him into a hug as Taylor and Troy do the same to each other before we switch so I can give Troy his props too.

"I can't believe we did it!" Colin says. Ash is younger than him, so he isn't graduating with the five of us.

"I can't believe *you* did it," I tease Col, who nudges me with his arm. "I'm giving you shit." Colin might not have a lot of common sense, but he's incredibly smart and a hard worker.

"Party tonight at Alpha Theta Mu?" Colin asks.

"Fuck yes," I reply.

"Do we have to?" Atlas jokes, making us laugh.

"Yes. We're being social tonight…but I'll have a treat for you afterward." Troy wraps an arm around him.

"Do I get a treat afterward too?" I pump my brows at Taylor.

"You love parties, so why do I have to treat you?"

"Well, I love sex too, so I figure that's a good enough reason."

"Works for me." My boyfriend grins, then kisses me. "Come on, guys. We should find our parents."

We head the direction where they were sitting.

Troy's mom is there for Atlas and Troy, along with Colin's mom, who drove in from North Carolina, his dad and stepmom, Ash, of course, and my dad and Nicole.

I take Taylor's hand as we make our way toward them, and then we're immediately hugged to death by a whole lot of parents giving us a shit ton of congrats. It's fucking awesome. The stepbrothers thing hasn't been a problem with any of our family or extended family, but even if it had been, Taylor and I know we have two caring parents in our corner.

"I'm proud of you," Dad tells me. "Your mom would be so happy today."

I swipe at a stray tear that leaks from my eye. "I know she would be." We give each other a nod before I give my attention to Nic. "Hey, Mama Two." It's something I've started calling her for fun, and some-where along the way, it stuck.

"Oh, Bren. Congratulations." She hugs me while Taylor shares a moment with Dad. The two of them have gotten closer the past few months, and I know that will continue to grow. Taylor will always know what it's like to have a good father now. "You boys ready to go out to dinner?"

We plan to eat with them before they head back home and we go to the frat house for the party. We end up at our favorite Korean BBQ restaurant, sharing good food and lots of laughter, and then they drop us off at our apartment.

"Shower?" Taylor asks, then chuckles when he realizes I'm already ripping off my clothes.

"What's taking you so long?"

"I'm right behind you."

"Yeah, but you're not nearly naked enough yet."

He playfully throws his shirt at the back of my head.

I turn around and walk backward. "Much better. I'm enjoying the view."

"You're such a dork," he jokes.

"Your dork."

A spark ignites in Taylor's gaze. "All mine. Always."

"You know it."

We end up on the bed, jerking each other off first, then get into the shower, washing away the fat load drying on our skin and getting ready for the party tonight.

I hear the music the second we pull up, Lance likely doing his thing at the DJ table. There's a jump in my pulse. I really do love parties, and this one is for an incredible fucking reason.

"You're excited," Taylor says.

"How can you tell?"

"The way you're practically bouncing in the seat was a good clue, but mostly, just because I know you." He tosses a quick look my way, smiling.

"You do." And he chose me. Fucking wild.

"It's why I like you so much," Taylor says, as if reading my mind.

"Damn. You got game. You already have me. You don't have to sweet-talk me."

Taylor turns off his car. "I like to sweet-talk you."

"I love us."

He grins. "I love us too."

We get out of the car and head toward the Alpha Theta Mu house. Music has the area bumping. We go through the house, and it's already packed with people.

"Atlas said they're in the backyard!" Taylor shouts over the music, just as my phone buzzes against my hip.

I peek at the screen. "Mila is back there too!" I shout back.

We work our way through the sea of people, and I suck in a deep breath of fresh air when we're out back. There are tables and a keg and the scent of weed makes my nose tingle. The Alpha Theta Mu house is definitely on point tonight.

"There they are," Taylor says, and we walk over to where Atlas, Troy, Colin, Ash, Marty, Mila, and her girlfriend, Alexis, are. They've only been dating for about six weeks, but my friend is already head over heels for Alexis.

"Hey, you two." Mila grins.

"What's up?"

"Happy graduation."

"Unfortunately, it's not all my schooling." I still have grad school to complete my architecture degree.

"It's not going to be the same without Troy in the frat anymore," Marty says.

"One less person to bug you," I reply.

"Or is it one less person for Marty to bug?" Taylor asks, earning the finger from Marty.

"Remind me again why I agreed to DJ?" Lance steps up to us. "What am I missing?"

"Being the DJ?" I tease, since he can't really do that from here.

"Ha-ha. Payton is taking over for a bit."

"We were just talking about how different the frat will be without Troy," Taylor catches him up.

Lance shrugs. "Well, at least we still have our Task Frat Challenge Master."

"He didn't seem to help you win this year," I remind him.

Sigma Alpha was the official winner of the Task Frat Challenge for the year—whatever the hell that means—which I know has grated on Lance's nerves.

He glares at me playfully. "Well, Ty Lancaster better enjoy the victory while he can because Alpha Theta Mu is gonna bring it."

Ty's the president of Sigma Alpha, whom Lance might describe as his archnemesis. All in good fun...at least I think it is.

We fill our cups with beer and sit around talking for a while. Eventually Dax shows up, making his rounds to talk to all the good-looking guys here tonight. I can't stop thinking about what Marty said, though. While some of us will still be around Peachtree Springs and some will still be going to Peach State, it's going to be different now.

"What's wrong?" Taylor wraps his arms around my shoulders, running his fingers along my nape.

I playfully start bouncing my leg like a dog, and he laughs.

"What's wrong?" he asks again.

"Nothing really. Just thinking about the fact that we're all growing up." We've all gotten so close over the last four years. It's weird when life moves forward.

"It'll be different for sure, but there's other exciting things in all our futures. Plus, I can't imagine all of us not being friends for the rest of our lives. We'll visit Atlas and Troy, and Old-Ass Atlas will yell at us to get off his lawn."

"Hey, fuck off. Who said I will still want to be your friend when I'm old?" Atlas interrupts.

"Because you *love* them," Troy tells him.

Atlas shrugs. "I guess." But he's smiling, then gives me an up-nod.

I hate to get a little emotional, but the beer is getting to me, so I raise my Solo cup and say, "To friendship. May we all annoy Atlas and frustrate Marty for the rest of our lives."

"To friendship," they all say, and we clink the cheap plastic together in a promise.

"Now, unless you want me and Tay to pull an Ash and Colin and start getting busy in front of everyone, I need to take my man home."

"I'll call a car," Taylor says. "I can come back for my ride tomorrow."

We say our goodbyes and go out front to wait for the car.

"You okay?" Taylor asks.

I look at him and feel so much love, so much happiness, I could burst. I'm thankful every day that I not only have Taylor for my best friend, but that I'll have him as my partner for the rest of my life. "I'm perfect. I have the best boyfriend ever."

Taylor smirks. "You do. Lucky guy."

I chuckle. "Aren't you supposed to say you have the best boyfriend too?"

"But how can I have that if you already do?"

"You're a brat."

Taylor wraps an arm around me and pulls me close. "I love you, Brenner. We're gonna be so happy."

"We are. Always." I can't wait to see what our future holds, and whatever it is, I know we'll be together. "I love you too."

THE END

BONUS CONTENT

This scene takes place between the prologue (the first time Brenner and Taylor mess around) and Chapter 1 (when the guys go on a summer cruise with their parents).

Taylor

"YOU GUYS SERIOUSLY gonna just let me die like this?" Marty asks.

"I'm coming to get you," Lance says. "Give me five minutes."

"You've been saying that for the past fifteen minutes." Marty groans as he fidgets with his controller, his character dodging a few more bullets in the game.

"Bren and I are almost there too," I assure him. "Just stay alive."

"That's fucking easier said than done," Marty says through his teeth as he dramatically messes with his controller in a way I'd expect from someone who's not used to multiplayer games.

It's a Saturday night, a rare occasion when we're able to get a bunch of our friends together. Clustered in the living area of Brenner's dorm room, Lance, Marty, Brenner, and I are spread across the sofa. Ash is playing too, practically sitting on his boyfriend on the love seat, and judging by how many times he glances back at his man, he doesn't give a fuck if he dies in the game—unlike Marty.

Since Atlas and Troy got together, we've had several opportunities to hang with the Alpha Theta Mus. Despite my preconceptions about frats, the guys are actually pretty cool, and even Marty's starting to grow on me a little.

Only a little, though.

"What time is it?" Brenner asks, then checks his phone. "Troy and Atlas should've been here by now."

Usually Atlas hosts our gaming nights, but he and Troy had some event for the nonprofit Atlas helps out with, and Brenner's roommate is out for the night, so we decided to have it over here.

"The hell, Brenner?" Marty says. "You have time to check your phone, and I can't take my fingers off my controller for a second."

"Yeah, it's like that sometimes," I tell him.

"Story of my life," Marty grumbles.

Brenner and I exchange an amused look.

When we messed around that first time, I figured it wouldn't change much about us, and I was right. We're still Bren and Tay—partying, playing games, cracking jokes with one another. Only difference is now some-times after a party or game night, Brenner gets me off. And then we'll still crack jokes after.

"Are those five minutes finally up?" Marty asks.

"There's, like, two bridges and then I'll be there," Lance tells him, but I notice an ambush surrounding Marty on all sides, and it doesn't look good.

"Dammit!" Marty calls out as his screen starts flash-ing red.

"What happened?" Lance asks.

"I got shot."

"Well, we told you to stay alive."

Marty glares at him, and Lance is in stitches.

"On that note," Ash says, "can we pause so I can check on the calzones?"

When we agreed to meet up, Ash and Colin volun-teered to make calzones, something they learned on one of their date nights because apparently, on top of all the PDA, they're also into being adorably datey, which would annoy the hell out of me if I didn't think they were kind of cool.

"About time," I mutter, since I was starting to think it would have been better to order pizzas.

As we pause, Ash pushes to his feet.

"Right behind you," Colin says, and there's barely an inch between them as he rises and they head toward the kitchen.

"We're gonna send a chaperone in after you two," Marty calls out.

Brenner chuckles. "From what I understand, that wouldn't really be an issue for them."

"You two behave," Lance calls after them, "or we *won't* send a chaperone in."

"Nice one," Brenner says, giving him a fist bump.

Lance repositions on the sofa, winding up a little closer to Brenner, and a knot forms in my chest.

Weird…

I'm totally fine with Lance. Hell, Brenner and I have hung out with him when he's come over for games and at frat parties and Crave. But Lance and Bren have connected more, maybe because Bren's the talkative one between us.

"These suite-style dorm rooms are really nice," Lance observes. "Decent, roomy living area. Separate kitchen area. Two bathrooms."

"Definitely better than the traditional dorms," I say, which earns a look from Brenner.

"Yeah," he says. "Like you're not basically our third roommate."

True story.

"I'm just glad my actual roommate isn't an asshole," Bren says. "With the lottery system, you never know. Still, it'll be even better when Taylor and I have our own place and can hang whenever we want." We exchange another look, both of us surely thinking about the fun we'll get up to when it's just the two of us.

"Speaking of the summer," Lance says, directing his attention to me, "I was meaning to ask you about that cruise you and your mom are going on. I was looking at cruises and trying to find good ones."

"Hey, I want to go on a cruise too," Brenner says. "But I can't afford to get a room for myself since most places I looked, you either pay per person or a much bigger fee for a single. We should team up to cover it and go with Taylor and his mom."

"That sounds fun," Lance says. "Those things cost a lot?"

"It's a chunk up front, but manageable," I say. "And sometimes they have deals through the place we book."

"Send me the info. Maybe I'll do it," Lance says with a shrug.

As much as I love my mom, I know it'd be a better time with friends there, especially since I'm not likely to venture out and do stuff on my own.

I pull out my phone and send Lance the details so I don't forget.

Colin and Ash return from the kitchen, and given how red Colin's cheeks are, I don't imagine they were just checking on the calzones.

There's a knock at the door, and Ash heads over, letting Troy and Atlas in.

"We're here," Troy says, "so you can start the party now."

Brenner and I hop up from the couch to greet them, and we're all catching up until the timer on Ash's phone goes off.

"We're up," Colin says, squatting down and scooping Ash off the floor.

"You're gonna knock something down!" Marty frets as Colin whirls a laughing Ash around, neither seeming to have heard Marty.

Troy gives Atlas a mischievous look, and Atlas says, "Yeah, fuck around and find out," which gets them laughing too.

Colin carries Ash to the kitchen, and they pull the calzones out of the oven. We grab plates, and I notice that with Atlas and Troy sitting between Lance and Bren on the sofa, that knot in my chest has eased up.

Which again…*weird.*

"I think the last time we hung out was after that party at Sigma Alpha," Atlas says, then takes a bite of his calzone. "You guys went out after?"

"No," I reply. "We came back here and played some games."

Brenner makes eye contact—we both know damn well that's not all we played.

"Bren, you broken?" Atlas asks.

"What?"

"You used to get more action, but feels like the last few times we've chatted, you guys have just wound up crashing at each other's places. You lost your touch?"

Atlas quirks a brow, and Brenner turns to me. "What do you think? I lost my touch?"

I purse my lips together to keep from laughing.

But as I think about how his lips feel around my cock, I gulp. "Nah, he's still got his touch." And I must admit, I like that we share this secret.

Atlas winces, his gaze shifting between us. He knows us well enough to know when we're hiding something, and we're being a little too obvious right now.

Bren says, "We've actually just come back from a private funeral for what used to be your sex life. You know, back when you were smashing it all the time instead of being locked down by this jock."

And just as quickly as Atlas was catching on to something because of how well he knows us, Bren's beating him at his own game, knows how to get a rise out of him.

"Sounds like someone's jealous I'm in a relationship and get to smash it whenever I want."

"Like I'm jealous that you get to be tossed around like a sack of potatoes by this hunk of muscle," Bren says before his expression twists up. "On second thought, you guys have been going at this for a while. What are your thoughts on playing with a third?"

Atlas must know Bren's only kidding, but he and Troy are both possessive, jealous fucks, and they both tense up at the suggestion. "Over our dead bodies."

Brenner and I burst into a laugh as they both glance around, their reaction having given away just how many feels they have for each other.

"Hey, where did Ash and Colin slip off to?" Marty asks.

I vaguely recall them sneaking into the kitchen again, and I imagine we'll be hearing some sex sounds soon, so I can't help myself. "The rumor is, if we're real quiet, you can hear the ghosts of all the guys who died in this dorm."

The room erupts with laughter, and Brenner sneaks a look my way, clearly impressed with how I played that.

And I must admit, as much as I'm enjoying a night with the guys, I'm ready for them to get out of our hair so we can have another moment to ourselves.

Brenner

"I THOUGHT THEY'D never leave," I tell Taylor the second we close the door behind them. It was a blast hanging out, it always is, but all the talk about sex and me not getting any got my cock all boned up.

I could use an app, but lately, whenever I feel like

having some fun, I get on my knees for Taylor.

"Why? Is there something you wanted to do?" he asks, mischief in his tone.

"You."

Taylor chuckles. "How about we clean up first?"

"How about I clean cum off your abs instead?" I pump my brows.

"Nah. Well, not *yet*. We need to take care of this mess."

I groan. I can tell by the sound of his voice that he wants to enjoy torturing me. That's not usually Taylor's MO, but he gets feisty sometimes and likes to be playful or tease me.

"Fine. You're so boring," I joke, but when I look around, I can see why blowing him while surrounded by empty soda cans and dirty plates would be gross.

"I hope you know we're not living like this when we get our apartment."

Taylor and I are getting a place together next school year, hopefully in the same complex Atlas lives in.

"I'm not making any promises." Taylor cocks a brow, but I ignore him. "Our friends are slobs."

"You're the one who just said you won't make promises that our apartment won't look like this. Plus, they offered to help, but you rushed them out."

He has a point. "That's because I thought I was going to get your dick out of it."

"Patience." He reaches down and cups himself. "You can have it after you clean up."

Well, hello. That's fucking hot. I never would have expected Taylor to be so vocal when it comes to sex, but maybe he is because it's with me. He knows he can let loose and doesn't ever have to censor himself.

"Hm…but you have to be naked."

"What?" His pupils widen, and I grin.

"If I have to wait to blow you until after we clean, you can at least be naked while we do it. Call it motivation." When he doesn't reply right away, I add, "Dare you," and heat flares in his expression.

We've always enjoyed a good dare. It's how I ended up blowing him the first time. What's a little BJ dare between best friends?

"You have to take your clothes off too," Taylor says.

I rip my shirt off and toss it to the floor. My jeans and underwear quickly follow. "Done." My cock is already half-hard just from this playful challenge.

Taylor takes off his shirt, then folds the thing and puts it on the end table. Damn it. I didn't consider I'd have to clean up my clothes too.

Still, I watch as he takes off the rest of his clothes, his dick thick and growing by the second under my gaze. "You're so fucking hot," I say as he folds his jeans and puts them with his shirt.

"You need to pick up your clothes, Bren."

I groan again, pretending I'm annoyed. I give myself a slow stroke before folding my clothes and putting them with his.

As I pass by Taylor, I make sure to brush my body against his, my fingers dancing down the length of his dick before I reach for the plates on the coffee table. He hisses in response.

"What…is someone horny? This whole make-me-wait thing might backfire, huh?"

"No. I expect it to be fun," Taylor counters.

"Why? Because I might drop something? Oops! I just did."

I kneel in front of Taylor, pretend I'm picking something up off the floor, then swipe his cock from tip to root with my tongue.

"Got it," I say.

"I don't think you did."

Oh, *now* he wants my mouth.

"You must have missed it," I tease before grabbing the plates and taking them into the kitchen.

I hear Taylor playfully grumble, followed by the sound of aluminum crumpling as he picks up the cans.

When we both reach the counter where I put the dishes, Taylor says, "Here, let me throw away the leftovers," but the trash can is on the other side of me, so he has to lean over and press his dick against my thigh to toss them.

My cock twitches.

"Two can play this game, Bren."

"You're not supposed to be good at this too," I tell him, earning myself a smile.

We keep that up, Taylor brushing against me here, my hand stroking his dick there, my mouth finding a way for a quick suck before getting back to the task at hand.

It doesn't take us long to get the small space cleaned up, and once we do, I walk straight over to Taylor. He grins, his back against the wall. His tongue sneaks out and licks his lips, and I almost lean in and kiss him. Luckily, I stop myself because he would probably wonder what in the fuck I'm doing. We don't kiss each other. I suck him off.

"What are you waiting for?" Taylor asks, stroking himself.

"You want my mouth, Tay?"

"You know I do. It feels so fucking good on my cock. I love to see you take it."

Heat blooms in my gut, and I immediately go down to my knees. He's got such a gorgeous cock, flushed, pink head, thick and veiny.

Taylor holds it at the base, then uses the tip to trace my lips. "Lick it."

"Make me," I answer, aching and throbbing already.

"Fuck yes." Taylor pushes his erection past my lips,

and I let him, sucking him, bobbing on him, savoring the musky scent of his arousal and the feel of his heavy cock on my tongue.

I love sucking dick. I get just as much out of this as Taylor does—even more so with him, I think—because I like the idea of getting my best friend so hot for me. I love the idea of driving him wild and being the one to make him come. It's an incredible rush.

"Fuck…so good." Taylor's fingers tighten in my hair as he gives me small thrusts of his hips. I take them, love them. One of my favorite things is to have a guy fuck into my mouth. Every time he hits the back of my throat, I swallow around him, give a *hum* of pleasure, and the greedy sounds it elicits from Taylor go straight to my balls.

I pull off him.

"Hey, where did you go?"

"Nowhere," I reply, then spit in my hand before jerking myself off. I'm already slick with precum, and the saliva helps make it an even easier ride.

And then my mouth is stuffed full of his cock again, Taylor telling me how good I feel, to get going. "Suck it, Bren. So good. So sexy seeing you swallow my cock." And I continue to pleasure us.

I can feel my balls tightening. They're heavy with my load, and it won't be long before I'm painting the carpet with it. I don't even care. I'm too turned on, but I also need Taylor to let go first. I need to earn his cum before I shoot.

I use my free hand on his balls, playing with them, alternating between licking them and blowing him. They feel so fucking tight and full of his release. I can't wait to swallow it down.

"I'm so close. Are you going to swallow it for me?" he asks, as if there's another option.

"You know I will. Push in deep and come down my throat."

"Damn, that's hot."

He fucks into my mouth, pushing in as deep as he can go, balls against my chin, my nose buried in his pubes. We both pull back and then come together again, over and over, working in sync for our nut.

I'm still jerking myself, my body feeling tingly, and then Taylor thrusts in again, pulling my hair and burying himself in me. He calls out my name as he lets loose, spurt after spurt of his load on my tongue and sliding down my throat.

I take it all, savor it, and then I'm coming apart too, color exploding in my vision, balls drawing up while I surrender to my orgasm.

I pull off and drop my forehead against his stomach, both of us breathing heavily.

"Goddamn, Bren, that was fun."

"Lucky I'm so good." I look up at him, Taylor's gaze

tilted down at me, and I can't help smiling.

"Maybe it's just because I have such a great cock."

"Nah, it's all my mouth. And since I did most of the cleaning before…"

"I'm not cleaning up your jizz, Bren."

"One, two, three, not it!"

"That's not how this works."

We both laugh, and again, I'm so thankful we have this, that we're best friends who now come together sometimes, and I know nothing will ever change between us.

ABOUT THE AUTHORS

Riley Hart

Riley Hart's love of all things romance shines brightly in everything she writes. Her primary focus is Male/Male romance but under various pen names, her prose has touched practically every part of the spectrum of love and relationships. The common theme that ties them all together is stories told from the heart.

A hopeless romantic herself, Riley is a lover of character-driven plots, many with flawed and relatable characters. She strives to create stories that readers can not only fall in love with, but also see themselves in. Real characters and real love blended together equal the ultimate Riley Hart experience.

When Riley isn't creating her next story, you can find her reading, traveling, or dreaming about reading or traveling, spending time with her two snarky kids, and swoony husband.

Riley Hart is represented by Jane Dystel at Dystel, Goderich & Bourret Literary Management. She's a 2019

Lambda Literary Award Finalist for *Of Sunlight and Stardust*.

Find Riley:

www.rileyhartwrites.com

Devon McCormack

Devon McCormack grew up in the Georgia suburbs with his two younger brothers and an older sister. At a very young age, he spun tales the old-fashioned way, lying to anyone and everyone he encountered. He claimed he was an orphan. He claimed to be a king from another planet. He claimed to have supernatural powers. He has since harnessed this penchant for tall tales by crafting worlds and characters that allow him to live out whatever fantasy he chooses. Devon is an out and proud queer man living in Atlanta, Georgia.

Find Devon:

www.devonmccormack.com